GRIZZLY MOUNTAIN

ARCADIAN BEARS, BOOK ONE

BECCA JAMESON

ACKNOWLEDGMENTS

Many thanks to Heather, who helped me with both the plot and the setting. Can't thank you enough for being such a loyal fan!

CHAPTER 1

Isaiah Arthur leaned against the side of the brand new, dark blue Honda Accord, holding a woman's jacket to his nose. He didn't need the proximity to her clothing to catch and memorize her scent. The open car door was sufficient.

He breathed in deeply again, letting his eyes close briefly as he inhaled her essence. Clean. Feminine. A hint of vanilla, probably from her shampoo. "When did she go missing?" He tried unsuccessfully to shake the lure of her pheromones from his head.

The woman was lost. He had a job to do. Find her. She might not even be alive, and his cock was stiff from leaning into her car to grab her jacket in the first place. One whiff of Heather Simmons and his knees buckled.

"The last time anyone heard from her was yesterday morning. I think she has a room at Bear Lodge in Silvertip. She emailed her hiking route to her mother but never checked back in last night. Mrs. Simmons called us about an hour ago." Glen Montrose, of the Parks Canada Warden Service, ran a hand through his thick dark hair, his face grim.

Isaiah lowered the jacket, tossing it back into the car reluctantly. "At least we're dealing with a smart hiker this time." It was a good sign that she'd informed someone of her intentions and arranged a check-in time. From that little information, he had hope she also had hiked away from her car prepared for the elements.

He glanced at his watch. Eight o'clock. Heather spent the entire night in the mountains somewhere. He had no doubt he would find her, but had she brought enough clothes with her to survive a night in the cold? The temperatures had dipped below freezing last night.

Isaiah closed his eyes and breathed in. The only scents in the area, besides Heather's and Glen's, were wild animals and pine. The only noise was the rustling of the trees and the scamper of small animals.

He glanced around the small gravel parking lot. No other cars had been left overnight in this secluded area where hikers sometimes parked before trekking up the mountain. The gravel area was surrounded by a thick grove of trees, and when Isaiah lifted his head, he had the most glorious view of the mountains to the north. Alberta, Canada, was one of the most beautiful places on earth.

Heather Simmons was up this mountain somewhere.

Isaiah was restless to get moving. The sooner he found the missing hiker, the better her chances of survival. And he prayed she was indeed alive.

This was the thirteenth rescue he'd done for Banff National Park, and it never got any easier. Nine of the hikers he was asked to locate had been found alive, either lost or injured. Three had not been as fortunate. He said a silent prayer that today would turn his saved tally to a double digit.

Shoving off the side of the car, he rubbed his hands together and faced Glen. "I better get going. It's cold out here." He stated the obvious, but he didn't need any further details. He had what he needed—her scent and the last known time of contact. Nothing else mattered.

It wouldn't take him long to track her. As a bear shifter, his sense of smell was superior to nearly every other shifter known to exist. He could shift quickly, run fast, and track in minutes.

Montrose knew that. It was the reason he'd called Isaiah an hour ago to request his help. They had an arrangement. It worked. Although only a select few people working for the National Parks Service were shifters, they managed to connect with Isaiah's extended family whenever their assistance was needed. It wasn't feasible for a park warden to shift and take off looking for a hiker in the middle of the workday. Eyebrows would rise.

Isaiah's only concern was the location of Heather's intended hike—way too close to the divide between his family, the Arthurs, and the neighboring pack of bear shifters, the Tarbens. The feud between the two packs went back more than a century, and crossing into the other pack's territory was forbidden.

Isaiah personally thought the entire feud was shit, but he wasn't a member of the ruling body, and frankly, he didn't want any part of it. If the two packs wanted to battle over a fucking imaginary line in the mountains, let them duke it out for all he cared, as long as no one asked him to get involved.

The truth was, he had friends in the Tarben family. He knew for a fact several others in his generation did, too. They kept their relationships private to avoid pissing off the elders from either pack, but secret meetings had occurred between members of the two families for decades.

Isaiah had known one of his best friends, Austin

Tarben, for half his life. The two of them had met up secretly for fifteen years. They bitched often about the absurdity of their families' feuds.

Shaking the errant thoughts from his head, Isaiah stepped away from the car, closed his eyes to settle his mind, and shifted. In moments he shook off his human form and allowed the transformation to take place. He leaned forward as his hands became paws and his body took on all the qualities of his other half—the grizzly bear. Fur replaced skin, bones lengthened and shortened, his face elongated.

The few humans aware of the existence of the bear species often referred to the process as magic, but Isaiah didn't see it that way. Shifting was simply a trait he possessed, no different from being able to roll his tongue, wiggle his ears, or lift one eyebrow while lowering the other. The members of his pack could transform into bears.

Isaiah glanced back at Glen before bounding away. He could have spoken to the other shifter telepathically, but there was no need. He already knew which direction to head. His ability to scent was as fine-tuned in human form as it was in his grizzly, but he could cover more ground faster with a more direct route as a bear. And he was instantly warmer.

His temperature ran high even in human form, but racing through the trees and climbing over rocks and foliage was far easier and more expedient in his bear form.

How far had Heather managed to get before she got lost or injured yesterday?

Please, God, let me find her alive.

Finding a victim no longer living was never pleasant, but something about this particular woman had his fur standing up. Her scent called to him. Lured him.

He hadn't even seen a picture of her. It wasn't necessary. He would know her by her scent the moment he got close.

Heather Simmons was furious with herself. Her self-recrimination was unreasonable because she hadn't done anything to warrant the feeling, but it consumed her nonetheless. She had followed her usual strict protocol for hiking—carrying a backpack filled with everything an experienced hiker needed, informing someone of her plans, and educating herself on the lay of the land.

None of that made her less frustrated that she'd stepped wrong about two hours into her hike and twisted her ankle badly. Now she was cold, tired, hungry, and pissed. She wasn't overly concerned about being rescued. Her mother was diligent about her checking in. When Heather hadn't made the call last night to assure her parents she'd made it back to civilization, they would have informed the cavalry.

She was on the path, wrapped in her Mylar blanket, eating a protein bar, and waiting.

She had studied the map of the area thoroughly. It was three miles back to her car. That distance was too far for her to hike with her left ankle swollen and painful. About two miles off the path to the east she would encounter a ranger station, but that would require her to break a cardinal rule—never leave the path.

It was still early in the morning. She wouldn't make a decision like that until midafternoon. If she had to, she could go another night. But damn, it was cold.

With a deep breath, she glanced at her surroundings. It was truly breathtaking. If she wasn't cold, frustrated, and a bit nervous, she would be enjoying the scenery. It was late in the hiking season. Fall in the Banff National Park could be unforgiving. When the weather changed, the path she was on would no longer be hikable.

But today it was gorgeous. The path itself wasn't wide where she had twisted her ankle. It was extremely unobtrusive, surrounded by dark green pine and fir trees. The ground cover was still lush. And every time she lifted her gaze, she was treated to snow-capped mountains.

Closing her eyes with a sigh, she tucked her face toward the ground and huddled under the Mylar to warm her cheeks.

Water was going to be a problem before anything else. She had carried enough to last more than a day, but when she'd left for a ten-mile hike, she had not anticipated being gone over twenty-four hours. As soon as she'd realized she was in trouble, she'd begun to ration her water supply.

"Fuck," she muttered under her breath. This trail was popular. Another hiker would probably come upon her before long, even if no one had been sent to rescue her. The trouble was, it was late in the season for hiking, which cut down on the number of people willing to endure the lower temperatures. She had also left a bit later in the day than most hikers, which meant no one passed her on their return last night.

A noise caught her attention, and she lifted her face to find her worst nightmare. A grizzly bear. A big one, too. It was simply meandering around, paying her no attention, but her heart rate soared.

The snap of a twig to her other side caused her to jerk her gaze in that direction to find a man approaching. A giant of a man wearing jeans, hiking boots, and a flannel shirt. He didn't have a coat. He held up a hand, palm out, fingers spread. With his other hand, he touched his lips with his index finger.

She jerked her gaze back to the primary threat, the huge bear. Hopefully the human was there to help her or she'd gotten lucky, but the bear was another story. It hadn't come to help.

Suddenly, the bear turned toward the man and rose onto its hind legs.

Heather sucked in a sharp breath and held it. The animal was even larger than she'd thought, and it looked like it was about to charge the man still approaching in her peripheral vision.

"You do not want to do this, dude. Back off," he stated, as though English were a language the wild grizzly would obey.

She twisted to lift her gaze toward the man, stunned to find him two feet from her side. He was equally impressive in his stature. At least six five. Huge. His brown hair was thick and recently cut and styled, and he had a few days' growth on his face.

Even though she was injured and her life should have been flashing before her eyes, she found herself unable to take her gaze off the burly mountain man. Damn.

"Heather Simmons?" he asked, glancing down at her as though now was a good time for introductions.

"Yes." Her mouth was dry, and it had nothing to do with a lack of water. She tried to swallow and spoke again with a bit more *umph*. "That's me."

"Isaiah Arthur. Your mom called the park warden."

Heather smiled. Of course she did. And then a roar filled the air, causing her to yank her attention back to the bear as it clambered onto its front paws and padded forward, stalking them. "Shit," she muttered.

"Listen, asshole. Back the fuck off," Isaiah shouted as he stepped past Heather and got between her and the bear.

Is he insane?

The giant grizzly kept creeping closer, lowering its head. If she wasn't mistaken, it narrowed its eyes in defiance and bared its teeth in anger.

Every piece of literature Heather had read about how to deal with bears in the area suggested she not engage them. If she sat perfectly still, it would probably wander away and ignore her. But this crazy mountain man seemed to have a different idea.

Isaiah straightened to his full height and pumped out his chest. His hands were fisted at his sides as though preparing for a fight. Yep. He was certifiable. Was he the only person the local police could come up with to rescue her?

"Shouldn't you maybe not taunt it?" she proposed.

Isaiah ignored her, continuing to advance.

She had to lean to one side in order to see the bear's face with Isaiah in her line of sight. What good would it do for him to get himself killed after coming to rescue her?

"Back off. She's injured."

How the hell did Isaiah know that for sure? And again, why did it seem he was trying to reason with a motherfucking bear?

Okay, so yes, he probably assumed she was injured. Otherwise she would have hiked out of the mountain yesterday and never met him *or* the enormous brown mammal, who could and probably would snap her in half and eat her.

Although she hadn't been able to hike out of the mountains on her injured ankle before now, faced with this angry grizzly, with her adrenaline racing through her blood, there was a decent chance she would find the strength to ignore her ankle and run down the mountain while the bear enjoyed his first meal—Isaiah Arthur.

She had no intention of being dessert.

The bear growled again, a menacing sound that came out like a warning. If she didn't know better, she would think the two males were communicating. Isaiah lowered his head, his feet spread wide. She couldn't see his face, but she truly believed he was staring the bear down in a contest of wills.

Yep. He was indeed certifiable.

The Mylar blanket slid from her shoulders to pool on the ground. Her backpack lay next to her. It seemed prudent at this point to back up, so she dug her good foot into the dirt on the path and scooted backward, wincing as she dragged her other leg along.

Perhaps she could at least haul herself into the trees and hide. *Is that a thing? Hiding from a bear? Don't they have an amazing sense of smell?*

As if her situation weren't beyond dire, a noise behind her alerted her to the approach of someone or something else. She jerked her head around to find another huge grizzly prowling forward.

All the blood rushed from her face, leaving her faint. She thought she might pass out, and then she noticed something that didn't make a damn bit of sense. The newcomer didn't even glance at her. Its focus was on the idiotic man and the first bear in their ridiculous standoff. In fact, giant furry guy number two padded right past her to stand next to Isaiah, increasing the intensity of the standoff.

Isaiah didn't glance at the newcomer either.

The world had gone completely mad.

Obviously, Heather was asleep. This was a dream. A nightmare. A strange coma caused by hypothermia or something. She didn't think it had been that cold during the night, but maybe she'd fallen asleep and not woken up.

Suddenly, the first bear rose onto its hind legs again

and rushed forward, knocking Isaiah to the side while shoving past the second bear. It happened so fast, as if the first bear caught Isaiah off guard. Hell, it caught the second bear off guard, too.

Heather stopped breathing when she realized this was it. Her life was over. She was going to die on this mountain on her third day in Canada. She would never show up for her first day of work. She would never be able to tell her parents she loved them. She would never see her sister again.

She continued to scramble backward, to no avail. There was no chance of escaping this enormous grizzly. It loped toward her rapidly. As soon as it hovered over her, it lifted a paw and batted at her, hitting her arm. Its claws ripped through her thick jacket and her thermal shirt to score her biceps.

She saw the wetness of her blood oozing into her clothing, but felt nothing. In a flash of fur and a roar of noise, the attacking bear tumbled to the ground beside her. The second bear to arrive on the scene pounced on the first, and the two of them rolled to the side, away from her, in a gruesome battle.

Isaiah raced to her side, scooped her off the ground, cradled her to his chest, and ran from the two bears.

Heather couldn't stop the whimper that escaped her lips. She also couldn't catch her breath. She squeezed her eyes closed and pressed her face against her strange savior. Her injured arm was smashed against Isaiah's body. She still felt no pain, but she felt the wetness of her blood.

He held her tighter as he slowed his run to a jog and continued away from the fighting grizzlies.

She couldn't hear them anymore, but she wasn't sure if she mentally blocked out their battle, if they'd gotten far enough away, or if her ears were simply ringing from stress.

Finally Isaiah slowed. He lifted one hand to brush a lock of her hair off her face and then tucked a finger under her chin to tip her head back. "You okay?"

She opened her eyes to find him staring at her with a furrowed brow. Concern was etched into his stiff facial features.

"Heather?"

"Yeah," she murmured.

He winced as he leaned her a few inches away from his body to eye her arm. "Fuck." There was a line of blood on his shirt.

"Sorry. I'm getting blood on you."

He jerked his gaze back to her face. "Woman, I don't care about my stupid shirt."

"Oh." *Then why did he cuss?* She wasn't injured badly enough to die, for heaven's sake. It was more like a long scratch. Probably didn't even need stitches.

Isaiah inhaled long and slow, tipping his head back, seemingly staring at a random spot in the distance. Did he nod subtly? His face softened, he swallowed, and then he licked his lips.

Heather watched every nuance of his features. His strong jawline mesmerized her. She wanted to stroke her hand over his beard to see if it was as soft as it looked. His nose was round and slightly off center, indicating he'd undoubtedly broken it at least once. She pictured him in a fist fight and almost smiled. *Why the hell is that thought so sexy?*

When he lowered his face, she found herself staring into the deepest dark brown eyes she'd ever seen. She couldn't move. His expression was serious as he stared back. "Fuck," he repeated.

She flinched.

"Damn. Sorry. Didn't mean to scare you. Let's get you out of the cold." His gaze roamed down her body until he reached her legs. "Do you have any broken bones?"

"No. Just a sprained ankle."

He nodded and then started walking again. He held her as if she weighed nothing, and he never for a second breathed heavily from the exertion. Not even while he was running with her.

She peeled her eyes off his face and glanced around. They were no longer on the path. Whoever this man was, he was traipsing through the trees as if the idea weren't preposterous. She prayed he knew where he was going. After all, he surely knew the mountains well if he'd been sent to rescue her.

She leaned her cheek against his chest again. What else was there to do but let this giant of a man get her to safety?

As she closed her eyes, she allowed herself to inhale his scent and nearly moaned. In a different world, she would be bold enough to burrow her nose into his chest and luxuriate in his strong masculinity. The faint smell of his soap wafted from beneath his shirt. The clean scent of his laundry detergent. But mostly what she inhaled was all Isaiah.

Damn.

CHAPTER 2

Fuck. Fuck fuck fuck.

Isaiah fought the urge to continue shouting that word out loud as he walked. He had already scared her half to death, no doubt. Although she didn't seem too upset. And her sweet little body was pressed into him tightly.

She was small. Maybe not by normal people's standards, but compared to his six-foot-five-inch bulk, she was a pixie. About a foot shorter than him, her frame was also tiny. Not that she was weak. He could feel her muscles everywhere she pressed into him. But she was human. And humans were smaller than bear shifters.

As he continued to make his way down the mountain, he noticed how long her hair was and nearly moaned. He was a sucker for long hair. Thick brown locks were pulled back in a ponytail, but chunks had come loose and hung at the sides of her face. Some of the softness was twisted around his fingers at her back. Without thinking, he stroked the lock against his palm before he could stop himself.

Maybe she didn't notice.

If he hadn't seen her eyes, he would have expected them to be brown, based on her dark hair and tanned skin. But unfortunately, he had seen them. They were a pale green that reminded him of the hot springs nestled in the nearby mountain ranges. He gritted his teeth, attempting futilely to wipe the vision from his head. Yeah, it would help if he hadn't seen those either.

Between her hair and her eyes, he was a goner.

As if you hadn't already fallen for the women by her scent alone before setting eyes on her.

What he needed to do was stop focusing on how damn sexy she was and deal with the much larger problem he had on his hands. That fucker, Jack Tarben, clawed her. The repercussions of such an act were monumental. For both Jack and Heather.

Isaiah had no idea the last time a shifter had attacked a human, but it wasn't in his lifetime. It was strictly forbidden. The Arcadian Council would have no choice but to enforce the law, which would mean Jack would be exiled from his pack and the entire territory, at the very least.

And still, that was nothing compared to what would happen to Heather. Her world was about to turn upside down, and she had no idea. She didn't ask for this. It took every ounce of strength Isaiah had to rein in his control and not lose it.

His blood boiled with rage under the exterior calm he forced for Heather's sake.

Thank God his brother, Wyatt, had shown up when he did. Considering the posture Jack was exhibiting, Isaiah had no doubt the man intended to attack Heather when he wandered onto the path. He would have scented her. He also would have scented Isaiah. Why hadn't he remained hidden?

There was no call for his defiant stance and attack. If Wyatt hadn't bounded out of the woods precisely when he did, Isaiah would have been forced to shift and fight Jack in bear form. The act would have kept Heather safe, but it also would have revealed their existence.

Keeping their species a secret from Heather was now shot to shit anyway.

Fuck.

Isaiah's mind continued to race through possible reasons for Jack's fucked-up decision to attack. Yes, Isaiah had wandered onto Tarben land to rescue the woman, but it had been unavoidable and completely out of his control. Not a reason to attack. And never a reason to attack a human.

Isaiah had grimaced when he realized what trail Heather had taken the day before. It was the one and only trail in the area that wove back and forth across the divide between Arthur land and Tarben land. Isaiah had needed to take that path to find a missing hiker two times prior to today. Both times he'd done so knowing full well he risked the wrath of the other pack, but hoping they would be reasonable under the circumstances.

After all, he hadn't been maliciously plundering on Tarben land. He'd simply been providing a humanitarian service.

But some of the Tarbens were hardheaded.

Then again, his own pack was equally as hardheaded when it came to the stupid territory and the century-old treaty that demanded neither pack loiter on the property of the other.

Today was the first time someone had approached him from the Tarben pack and challenged him. Had Jack approached Isaiah to confront him over territory? Or had the man been there for a more nefarious reason that involved Heather? That possibility made Isaiah shudder.

Another curious piece of the puzzle was that Jack hadn't responded to any communication from either Isaiah or Wyatt. The man completely ignored all verbal and telepathic attempts at discussion. He'd growled and attacked as though he were simply a wild bear instead of a grizzly shifter.

Stubborn fucker was going to regret his actions today.

Fuck.

Isaiah was stuck on that one word. And it was warranted.

Attacking a human was number two under the "Thou Shalt Nots" of the Arcadian bears. *Turning* a human was number one. Unfortunately, that was exactly what Jack had done by intentionally breaking Heather's skin with his claw.

The unsuspecting sprite of a woman currently curled against Isaiah's chest had no idea she was about to become a bear shifter against her will.

Heather tried to focus on anything but the pain radiating up her leg from her ankle and the sting finally making itself known on her arm. As her adrenaline high eased, she felt the discomfort of both.

How long was it going to take to get down the mountain? She needed to be patient. She had hiked about three miles up. It would take a while to get back down. An hour? Although she had no idea what sort of direct route Isaiah was taking, and it did seem that, completely undaunted by her added weight, he was making fast progress.

But it had only been about fifteen minutes.

Suddenly, he stepped into a clearing, and she swore she heard him sigh as he gave her an extra squeeze.

She twisted her head around again to see an amazing log home right in her line of sight. *What the hell?* She had thought them to be in the middle of nowhere. It shocked her to see a house. Maybe Isaiah had carried her longer than she thought.

Not to mention, this wasn't some simple log cabin retreat for hunting. It was an enormous, luxurious ranch. The outside was intentionally rustic with rough logs seemingly haphazardly piled high to make the walls. She knew better. The inside would be spectacular and far from rustic. The only other color was the occasional dark green paint that coated the trim around the front porch as well as the columns that held up the ceiling.

It was nestled in a clearing among the trees in a way that it would be hard to find. In fact, she felt certain someone would almost have to stumble upon the cabin or know exactly where it was. And the view. Stunning. She glanced past the cabin to see mountain peaks extending for miles. It would be an amazing sight in every season of the year.

If her damn ankle wasn't twisted, she would jump out of Isaiah's arms and rush to the front of the house to explore. It was that marvelous.

"Whose home is this?" she asked, grateful for its presence wherever they were, while assuming Isaiah must know the owners, based on the way he was so determinedly approaching.

"My parents'."

She jerked her gaze back to him. "Your parents own this?"

He frowned. "Yes. Why is that weird?"

She felt a heated flush rise over her cheeks. Why was it strange? "I guess it's not. Not any more than the coincidence of it even existing so close to where I spent the night freezing my ass off."

For the first time since he'd stepped into her space, he almost smiled. The subtle lift of the corners of his mouth might have gone unnoticed at a glance, but she'd seen the softening of his brow, the way the worry lines between his eyes smoothed, the tiny divots in his cheeks suggesting he would have gorgeous dimples if he ever let his lips turn up into a full-fledged grin.

As Isaiah stepped onto the porch, the front door flew open, the screen door squeaking on its hinges. Isaiah climbed the four steps that led to the entrance while Heather tipped her head again to see who was exiting the house.

"Oh dear." The woman who spoke had to be Isaiah's mother. She had similar features—the same nose, although hers had never been broken, the same furrowed brow, and the same intense brown eyes. She was also tall. Nearly six feet.

"Did you think I was kidding?" Isaiah asked as he pushed past his mother to enter the house.

What the hell did that mean? He acted as though he'd phoned ahead to let her know he was bringing a wounded guest.

Heather didn't have time to ponder the strange statement further, though. She was too busy taking in the house, which was indeed as spectacular inside as she expected.

She blinked as her eyes adjusted to the dimmer indoor lighting. The sun had been so bright, she needed a minute to focus. By the time she could examine the space, Isaiah had already trudged through the living room and into the kitchen.

Shocking her, he set her on the kitchen island, steadying her with both hands at her waist for a moment. "You okay? You're not going to fall over are you?"

She placed both hands on the tile at her sides and shook her head. "I'm fine."

The woman who had held the door open for her rushed to her side. "You poor thing. Oh my goodness." Her face was full of worry and concern as she lifted her gaze to meet Heather's. She set a hand on Heather's cheek. "I'm Rosanne."

"Heather. Thank you for…" she trailed off as Isaiah lifted her foot, pain shooting through her ankle. She winced.

He glanced at her face. "You sure it's not broken?"

"I don't think so. I twisted it. It's probably a bad sprain."

He eased it back down carefully. "You'll need ice." He turned his focus to her arm, taking a hold of her forearm and turning her wrist to better assess the cuts.

Rosanne set a hand on Isaiah's biceps. "Son…"

"Mom, no. Not yet," he muttered.

She pursed her lips, glanced at Heather, and then away. "Where's Dad?"

"At the brewery. He's on his way."

"You talk to Wyatt yet?"

"Yeah. He's on his way too."

Isaiah lifted his gaze back to Heather's. "We need to clean up these cuts. Your shirt is ruined. You mind if I cut it off above the claw marks?" He flinched as he spoke those last words.

"No," she whispered. There was something going on she didn't understand. She was also afraid to ask. Instinct told her she wasn't going to like the answer.

Isaiah tugged the sleeve of her jacket and eased it off her arm. While he worked it off the rest of her torso, Rosanne rushed across the room and returned with a pair of serious scissors. What did she usually use those for? Lord.

Being incredibly considerate and careful, Isaiah cut straight up the sleeve under her arm to avoid the cuts and then around in a circle near her shoulder. The sleeve fell away, leaving a clearer view of the two long lines that ran up her biceps, perfect gouges in her skin that were no longer bleeding but looked angry and red.

Isaiah leaned down to examine the marks, holding her wrist in a gentle way that made her fight to avoid squirming. He was so damn...sexy. And the way he handled her made her mouth drier by the minute. She found herself staring at him more closely now that her eyes had adjusted to the indoor lighting and she was no longer in imminent danger of death.

Although she needed to remember her danger was partially caused by his peculiar actions when confronted with that fucking huge bear.

"We need to clean these up." He set her hand on her thigh and turned toward the sink to flip on the water, testing it with one hand while he grabbed a container of liquid soap.

Rosanne still held her lips tightly closed, but she tugged open a drawer and removed a wash cloth and a dish towel. She handed the cloth to Isaiah, who squirted a line of soap on it and then held it under the water.

"This is going to sting a bit," he stated as he set the warm wet cloth on her arm above her elbow and eased it up to her shoulder.

Heather gritted her teeth. Sting was an understatement. But she braced herself and allowed him to wash the scratches. He returned to the sink three times to rinse out the washcloth and make sure he had all the soap off her.

When he was done, she was relieved to see that the two marks were not as bad as she feared. Deep scratches, but not in danger of bleeding or needing stitches. "She needs an antibiotic ointment," Isaiah said to his mother.

"Honey..."

He stiffened. "Mom. I said *don't*. Do we have any or not?" His voice rose.

She pursed her lips yet again and nodded. As she left the room, the front door opened again and voices carried through the giant living room to the kitchen. Seconds later, two men stepped into the space. No. Not really men. More like human examples of the overuse of steroids. Holy hell.

The older man, who must have been Isaiah's father, was three inches taller than Isaiah. At least six eight. And the other man, whom she assumed was Isaiah's brother, was only an inch shorter than his dad. What did these people eat?

Whatever they had been discussing ended abruptly when they spotted Heather on the counter.

"Shit," the younger man stated.

Heather winced at the strange reaction. Every person she encountered seemed perturbed. In addition, she noticed Wyatt had several scratches on his right arm and even a line down his face that looked similar to hers but faded, as if he'd been in a fight several days ago.

The older man rushed across the room and came up to her side. He grabbed her arm with far less finesse than his son and lifted it to the light. "Damnit."

"Did you assholes think I was fucking kidding?" Isaiah asked.

Heather's eyes shot wide. Her confusion was growing

incrementally, and the sharp words coming from Isaiah's mouth were jarring, to say the least.

The older man lifted his gaze to glance at Isaiah, and then he turned toward Heather, his face softening marginally. "I'm Bernard, Isaiah's father." He pointed to her other side. "That's Wyatt. But you already met him."

She drew her eyes together. When the hell would she have met him?

Wyatt shook his head. "Nope. Dad. We have not met."

Isaiah rolled his eyes. "Would you two step back? Give her some freaking space. You're going to suffocate her."

Bernard slowly released her arm while he turned toward Isaiah. "Son…"

"Don't start. I don't want to hear it."

"But, Isaiah. What are you thinking?"

"I'm not thinking anything. I'm thinking we need to clean up these wounds and let Heather call her parents. They must be worried sick."

Bernard stared at his son for several seconds and then slowly nodded.

Rosanne rushed back into the kitchen and handed Isaiah a tube of ointment.

Wyatt gasped. "What the fuck good is that going to do?"

Rosanne shot him a glare. "Prevent infection. Let Isaiah handle this."

Wyatt's face changed. His brows shot up. He glanced at Heather and then at his brother. And then he smirked.

What the holy living hell?

Her attention was once again diverted by Isaiah's fingers carefully applying the antibiotic cream to the wound on her arm. As she watched, she had a horrific thought. "Am I in some sort of danger from infection or rabies or something?" She knew a person couldn't get rabies from a claw mark. But something had every member of this family on edge, and she knew it wasn't simply from the two scratches. They hardly warranted this level of attention.

Three people cleared their throats, making her sit up straighter. "What aren't you telling me?"

Isaiah addressed her, but he didn't lift his gaze. "Nothing. You're fine." He lowered her arm once again, setting her hand on her thigh but not releasing her. In fact, he rubbed the back of her hand with his fingers. He didn't turn toward his mother when he spoke again, but his words were directed at her. "Mom, can you see if Joselyn has anything Heather can wear until we can get her some clothes that fit later?"

"Of course." Rosanne fled the room again, almost as though she were glad to be sent on another errand.

Isaiah's gaze remained lowered to her lap. He seemed to be watching as he rubbed small circles on her hand. "My sister's taller than you, but surely she has something you can wear for now. You must be dying to get out of those clothes."

Heather giggled. She couldn't stop herself. "Unless your sister is adopted, I have to assume she's *considerably* taller than me."

Isaiah's face rose, one side of his mouth lifting in a half smile that sent a chill down her spine and made her clench her thighs together. How the hell could she possibly be reacting sexually to this burly man taking care of her while her ankle throbbed and her arm burned?

But damn. That smile melted her panties.

"Jos isn't adopted. And yes, she is six feet." He continued to smile, his deep brown eyes twinkling.

He's still holding my hand.

It was difficult to concentrate on anything else in the room with him touching her. She was only marginally aware that although Bernard and Wyatt had taken about half a step back to give her space, they were both watching, silently and intently.

Heather cleared her throat and tugged her fingers out of Isaiah's grasp, pretending she needed to scratch an itch on her other arm. "Uh, you don't need to go to the trouble of finding anything for me to wear. Can you just take me down the mountain to my car? I'm going to need to find an urgent care to have someone look at my ankle." She lifted her foot a few inches to find it significantly swollen. She needed to get her shoe off. "At least it's my left ankle. I'll be able to drive."

Bernard spoke. "It's pretty swollen."

"Yeah. I was about to get ice." Isaiah grabbed the towel off the island, spun around, and took a few long strides to the freezer. He reached inside and put a handful of ice on the towel, wrapping it up. Seconds later, he returned, set the ice bundle on the island, and lifted Heather back into his arms, shocking her.

She grabbed his shoulder to keep her balance as he reached for the ice once again and then rushed through the kitchen and back into the living room. A moment later, he further shocked her by turning around to sit on the couch with her in his lap.

At least he let her ease her butt onto the cushion next to him, but he held her legs in his lap. While he went to work carefully removing her shoe, she held her breath against the pain and leaned back against the arm of the couch.

The ice was cold, even through the towel, as he placed it gently on her ankle.

Wyatt and Bernard had followed, and they now stood several feet away, shoulder to shoulder, both sporting the same strange expression—a mixture of concern and bewilderment. Neither spoke.

Rosanne rushed back into the room again, but she flew right on through to the kitchen, returning a few seconds later with a bottle of water. She held it out. "You must be so thirsty. I wasn't thinking. Are you hungry? I could make you something to eat."

"Mom." Isaiah tossed out that one sharp word again.

"It's probably best if she doesn't eat," Bernard stated.

Why? Holy fuck, why?

"What aren't you people telling me? I'm getting nervous. Is there some serious horrifying thing that can happen from a bear scratch?"

No one spoke, but there was a collective gasp.

Instead of answering her question, Bernard turned to his wife. "Grab the cordless, hon. She should check in with her family."

I'm going to die. Obviously I'm going to die, and no one wants to be the one to share that detail. It was the only explanation for their collective weirdness. It explained why no one thought it was necessary to clean the wound or put ointment on it or ice her ankle. Because nothing mattered. She would die anyway.

Tears escaped her eyes to run down her face.

Isaiah jerked his head up to meet her gaze. "Does the ice hurt?" He lifted the towel off her ankle.

She shook her head. "No." Her voice was scratchy.

He slowly lowered it back into place but reached to cup her face. "What is it? Why are you crying?"

She stared at him. "I'm going to die, aren't I?" she choked out.

He startled and then his eyes went wide. "No. Of course not. Why would you say that? No one dies from a scratch and a sprain."

Rosanne interrupted by handing Heather a cordless

home phone. "Sorry. We don't get good cell service out here."

Wyatt interrupted with a snap of his fingers. "I nearly forgot. I brought your backpack." He hurried across the room toward the front door and returned with the pack to set it on the floor next to her.

"How did you find it?" She glanced at the bag and then back at Wyatt.

His face turned slightly pink as he backed up. "I...uh... got to the scene just as you and Isaiah ran off. I grabbed your pack."

She inhaled slowly. He was lying. And she couldn't for the life of her figure out why or how.

"Call your mom, Heather," Isaiah stated softly, setting his distracting hand on her thigh and rubbing far too close to her sex. The material of her hiking pants was smooth and thin. The heat of his palm penetrated to draw all of her attention to his hand. "Your parents must be waiting to hear from you," he continued, squeezing her thigh for emphasis.

She nearly dropped the phone from the distraction, fumbling it until it did finally fall into her lap. Her hands were shaking as she picked it up and tried to find enough functioning brain cells to come up with her parents' phone number. It had been years since she had dialed them directly. It was an easy speed dial on her cell phone.

She didn't want to draw attention to the fact that Isaiah was subconsciously rubbing her leg, but if he didn't stop, she wouldn't be able to make complete sentences. And she was beyond aware that everyone in the room was watching.

As if they all sensed her need for privacy at the same moment, they turned around and scurried toward the kitchen simultaneously. It was like they were robots instead of humans, and they had some ability to communicate with each other telepathically or something.

Heather couldn't decide if she wanted to shove Isaiah's hand off her thigh or beg him to stroke closer to her pussy. She was practically panting with the need to come all of the sudden. Insanity.

Did he know what he was doing? Did he somehow sense her need, her dilemma? It sure seemed that way when his fingers stilled, gripped her leg, and then released her to ease around to her waist. "Call them, baby." His voice was low. Deep. Sexy as hell. And he called her *baby*. His face was a serious expression of concern, and he leaned closer to her as he spoke.

With one hand still holding the ice on her ankle and the other hand firmly on her waist, he spoke again. "Tell them you're okay so they won't worry any longer. But let me suggest you warn them you don't have cell service where you are and you're going to stay here a few days until you can walk on your ankle. Can you do that?"

She couldn't move. He held her gaze firmly. She couldn't even blink. "Why can't you take me back to my car?" Her bottom lip trembled. She couldn't stop it. She was totally freaked out and scared. At the same time, she was irrationally aroused.

He shrugged. "Let your foot heal for a few days before you go down the mountain. The warden I met with this morning said you were traveling alone. He said you just arrived in town the day before yesterday to start a new job. I assume you don't know anyone? I feel bad about what happened to you. Let me take care of you until you're stronger."

She licked her lips. Why was he making sense?

"It would be dangerous for you to drive with your ankle like that. And even if you did, how are you going to get

27

around and take care of yourself while it's swollen and painful? The warden said he thought you had a motel room at Bear Lodge in Silvertip. Right?"

"Yes." At least on that issue, he wasn't psychic. Bear Lodge was the *only* local motel.

"I'll call them and let them know you're not going to return to your room for a few days." He paused. His voice dipped lower again. "Please. It's the least I can do after not protecting you as well as I should have from that rogue bear."

"Rogue bear? What does that mean?" She let herself grin slightly. "Did you sense he had strayed from his pack or something?" she joked as she lifted the phone and shook her head. This hot dude said some seriously strange things.

It might be worth it, however, if he kept touching her the way he was.

CHAPTER 3

Isaiah watched every move she made closely. He had no idea in the world what to expect. Silent communication with his father had proved no one really knew.

His father was the leader of the Arthur pack. He had been since his own father died unexpectedly five years ago, way too young. To the best of his knowledge, it had been decades since the last time a human was clawed by a bear, forcing the change.

Isaiah gritted his teeth as he pondered the implications again. Yesterday morning, this unsuspecting woman halfway on his lap still led an innocent life that included no knowledge of bear shifters, or any other shifter, for that matter. And now, one day later, she was about to learn everything there was to know about the existence of the Ursidae shifters.

And soon after she learned things she should have spent her entire life oblivious to, she would become a member of the pack herself.

Isaiah wanted to punch a hole in the wall for what that fucker did to her. He knew his dad already had dozens of people out searching for Jack Tarben. He also knew from spotty communication with his father while dealing with Heather that Jack had gone rogue from his pack the day before after a disagreement. The Tarbens were equally stressed about Jack's actions, and they too had dozens of men out searching for him.

None of that information would change anything, however. The scratch was undeniable. Blood was drawn. Heather would not be able to prevent the inevitable shift.

With shaky hands, he watched as she pushed the ten digits for her parents' home and then held the receiver to her ear.

He took short, shallow breaths as her chest rose and fell. Her pheromones filled the entire house. She was also aroused, which did nothing to dampen his need for her.

Guilt ate at the corners of his mind. He shouldn't be lusting after this injured woman who was about to go through something he couldn't even describe. He shouldn't be touching her. He should let his mother handle things. He should leave his parents' home immediately and have his aunt and sister come help her through the transition.

But he would do none of those things. Because he knew in his heart she was his. And there was no way he would leave her side. Not now. Not ever. Especially not to let her shift for the first time in someone else's presence.

No. Not a chance in hell.

His parents and brother could glare at him all they wanted. They could shout into his head the entire day and night, too. He wouldn't leave her. In fact, he fully intended to take her from this house to his own as soon as she finished her call.

"Isaiah... What the hell are you plotting, son?"

It wasn't surprising his father could sense Isaiah's rambling thoughts. Heather was sucking the life out of him in a way that was keeping him from properly blocking his family members from hearing his thoughts.

"Back off. All of you. It's too late. If I thought there was another way, don't you think I would choose door number two?"

His mother poked her nose in from somewhere deeper in the house. *"We're just trying to help, Isaiah. You should let me help her. She's going to be so confused."*

"She's mine, mom. She's my mate. I can already feel the binding drawing me to claim her. I won't leave her. I can't. You have to understand."

Rosanne sighed into his head. *"I do. God help me, I do."*

"I think you should consider taking her to your place," his father added.

"Already planning on it. As soon as she gets off the phone." He watched her staring at him while she waited for her parents to pick up the phone.

His father spoke again. *"I've communicated with the Arcadian Council. There have been a few accidental conversions in our lifetime. None with malicious intent like this, but the results should be the same."*

"And?"

Bernard, as the pack leader, had the ability to communicate telepathically with far more shifters than his own family members. He could reach out to the leader of the Tarben pack and also the Arcadian Council. Isaiah didn't envy him the ability. It was both a blessing and a curse. His head would be constantly filled with rambling politics. *"The shift from a scratch would leave her without a pack technically. The scratch itself won't bind her to the Tarbens. It will force her to shift, but there was no transfer of Jack's fluids to her, so she won't automatically become a member of their pack."*

"That's a small relief. Not that it would matter since I intend to bind her to me at the first opportunity."

His father sighed. *"Please don't be hasty, Isaiah. Make sure you allow her free will."*

"Trust me. It won't be an issue. I can see her fighting the draw as strongly as I am even in her human form."

His mother spoke again. *"That's irrational, Isaiah. Humans aren't capable of experiencing the need to bind with a bear shifter."*

"You don't know that. Just because it hasn't happened to your knowledge, doesn't mean it isn't possible. Besides, maybe she's already succumbing to some parts of the change. That would explain her reaction to me."

What he knew was how strongly he affected her. Her pheromones filled his nose. As did her arousal. Her body came alive when he touched her. If he had let his fingers stray another inch closer to her pussy, he had no doubt she would have come.

His cock was so stiff, it threatened a revolt.

Finally, Heather spoke. "Mom… Yeah, I'm fine. Just a sprained ankle." She held Isaiah's gaze. "I know, Mom. It was a dumb move… You're right. I shouldn't hike alone."

Isaiah couldn't keep himself from smiling slightly. He had to agree with her mom on that point.

"I'm at a cabin in the mountains. Well, it's not really a cabin." She glanced around, smirking. "More like a rural mansion."

Isaiah chuckled as she made her observation.

Heather's eyes went wide.

What? Does she think I have no sense of humor?

"Anyway, I don't have cell service here, so you won't be able to reach me. It's pretty spotty even in town until I switch to a local carrier… I will, Mom… Yeah… In a few days…" She rolled her eyes. "Okay, what did you need to tell me about Clara?"

Isaiah smiled at her and then tuned her out while she

listened to her mom. His brain was running full speed. One thought hovering in the back of his mind made him nervous. Why on earth had he reacted so strongly to her scent from the moment the park warden popped the lock on her car door and opened it? If he was honest, he had known even then she was his.

But that made no sense. What did it mean? Did it mean Fate was ahead of herself and had already plotted Heather would be scratched and forced into the change?

That was the most asinine idea he'd ever had. Fate didn't operate that way. She didn't interfere in bear lives to such a great extent. Did She?

His people knew about other shifters. They had dealings over the years, especially with wolves. The wolves' lives were, without a doubt, controlled by a power greater than themselves. They occasionally selected a mate of their own free will, but often Fate arranged the meeting for them.

Bears didn't function under the same rigidity. They met someone, fell in love, and *then* bound themselves to their mate. The process was simple. It had nothing specifically to do with sex or penetration. It was all in the bite and the secretions that transferred from one bear to the other in his or her saliva.

Either partner could bind the other in such a way. The result was the same. Often both partners liked to sink their teeth into the other as a show of their mutual commitment to the binding, but it wasn't necessary. It didn't even have to be consensual, unfortunately.

Was there a power controlling these actions? Isaiah never would have believed it...until today.

Heather Simmons was his. He'd known it since that morning. He'd run like he was on fire to find her as quickly as possible. When he first saw her, she took his breath

away. He'd known definitively at that moment. Even before she lifted her gaze to meet his.

Her small frame made him ache to reach for her, grab her off the ground, and haul her into his embrace. But Jack had been stalking her, and Isaiah had no choice but to deal with the threat first.

Was there any chance in hell that Isaiah had subconsciously willed Jack to scratch Heather? Or perhaps Isaiah hadn't been forceful enough to prevent the attack?

He shook the notion from his head. He would drive himself mad otherwise.

But the truth was, without Jack's interference, without him reaching out to rip through Heather's jacket, shirt, and skin with his claw, Isaiah would not be sitting on his parents' couch holding the woman who would be his mate for life.

There weren't other alternatives. Shifters were forbidden from intentionally changing a human. Not even someone they felt drawn to mate with. It was unheard of. Against Arcadian law.

If Jack hadn't sunk his claws into Heather's arm, she would already be down the mountain, moving on with her life.

And Isaiah would have been left to suffer through the weird pull to claim her alone. The penalty for biting a human was severe. Although until today, there had been no incidences of a shifter intentionally changing a human for a very long time.

"Isaiah?" Her soft voice yanked him out of his head. Her face was cocked to one side, and her eyes were narrowed. "Where were you?"

"Thinking." He noticed the phone in her lap and nodded toward it. "Everything good?"

"Yeah. My mom is pissed. She thinks I shouldn't have been hiking alone."

He lifted a brow. "She's right, you know."

She rolled her eyes toward the ceiling. "Not you too. I don't even know a single person in Canada, let along Alberta. I just got here two days ago, and I intend to make the most of the next two weeks before I start my job."

He set his hand on her shoulder and stroked a lock of her hair. Touching her like this was both necessary and intense. He couldn't stop himself, but every time he made contact with any part of her skin, hair, or even her clothes, his cock stiffened. "What's the job?"

She nodded. "I'm a glaciologist. I'll be working for the government, studying the effects of the increasing recession of the Athabasca Glacier. I wanted some time to explore the area first." She glanced down at her ankle. "Looks like I just ruined my own vacation." She moaned as if she'd just that moment realized the implications of her injured ankle.

He had news for her. She would be back on her feet in no time. How long? He had no way of knowing for sure how soon she would undergo the change or how long it would take. He didn't even know what was entailed. Would it hurt? There were apparently few examples to draw upon for information.

"You never know," he stated. "Maybe it's not as bad as it seems." Her ankle was swollen and hot to the touch. It was probably worse than it seemed, but what she didn't know was that shifters healed easily and quickly. As soon as she made the first transformation to bear form, she would undoubtedly be healed.

He lowered his gaze to her ankle, realizing he still held the now wet towel over it. As he jerked the terrycloth away

and set it on the floor, he noticed her ankle was more swollen than it had been before.

She wiggled her toes and flinched. "Maybe it's worse." She tugged on the front of her shirt next. "Is it hot in here?"

He jerked his gaze back to hers and then set the back of his hand against her forehead. She had a fever. *"Dad, you think she would have a fever?"* he asked silently.

"Yes. Though I'm surprised it would happen this quickly."

"It's happening. I'm going to get her out of here."

His father stepped back into the room, his mother right behind him. They looked concerned, their gazes on Heather.

"I'm going to take her to my place," Isaiah announced for her benefit.

His mother chewed on her lower lip and then released it. "You think that's the best idea?"

Isaiah lifted Heather's legs off his lap and held them as he wiggled out from under her and then set them back on the couch. Although it was painful to release her, he knew he would have more opportunities to hold her as soon as he got her to his house. "It's the *only* idea, Mom."

She nodded.

Heather cleared her throat. "We're going somewhere else?" Her face paled further as she tipped her head back. "Why?"

"It gets hectic around here. My house will be quieter. You can rest. Heal. Get back on your feet," he stated.

She sat frozen, licking her lips.

He knew she had a thousand concerns. In fact, he couldn't wait until he could hear each and every one of them clearly in his head. It would be so much easier than trying to guess her thoughts. But for now, he needed to get her out of this house. He had no idea what sort of

timeframe they had before she would experience the change and all that it entailed.

Rosanne held out a bag Isaiah hadn't realized she carried into the living room. "Some clothes. They'll be too big but better than nothing."

Isaiah took the bag and swung it over his shoulder. "Where's Wyatt?"

"He's out back," his father said.

Isaiah glanced down at Heather's backpack. "Do you have the key to your motel in there?"

"Yes."

"How about if I have my brother go pick up your things? That way you'll have your own clothes to wear."

She hesitated and then nodded. "Okay. I think most of my stuff is all inside the suitcases anyway." She sat up straighter, swinging her legs over the side of the couch. "Really, this isn't necessary. I can just go to a doctor and then back to my motel. You don't have to put yourself out for me. I'll be fine."

He could sense her unease, and he couldn't blame her. He'd only managed to convince her to stay with him a few minutes ago, and already he was altering that plan. He'd led her to believe she would stay here in his parents' home, and now he tweaked the proposal a bit. Any sane woman would be nervous about going to a stranger's house to convalesce alone with him.

She placed her foot on the floor and put slight pressure on it.

He let her for the sake of proving his point. She needed help.

She winced, and her shoulders fell. And then she reached down and extracted her key from a side pocket. She set it on the seat next to her. Her hesitation was obvious as she tucked her shoe in the backpack.

Isaiah's mother picked up on it, too. She cleared her throat. "Isaiah's right. His house is quieter. You'll be able to sleep peacefully there. You must be exhausted. I'll stop by later. Or maybe send Joselyn to make sure you're doing okay."

"Okay. If you're sure." She turned to face Isaiah. "I don't want to put you out."

"Positive." He turned toward his dad, mentally giving a victory fist pump. "Can I borrow your car?"

"Of course. I'll pick it up later."

"Oh, crap, my car," Heather said. "It's at the base of the path. You think it will get towed?"

Isaiah's father spoke again. "I'll move it or Wyatt can."

"Thanks," Heather whispered. "You are all so kind." She pulled the car key from her bag and set it with the motel key.

Isaiah hoisted her backpack over the same arm as the bag of clothes his mother handed him. He then bent down, tucked an arm under Heather's knees, and lifted her into his arms.

Instantly his heart beat faster, though at the same time part of him calmed. She belonged in his arms. Holding her felt right. Perfect. Fated?

He headed for the front door. "Okay, we'll get going. Let me know when Wyatt thinks he can get to my place with her things."

His father nodded. "Be careful." He stepped around Isaiah and opened the front door. And then he spoke silently into Isaiah's head again. *The council is concerned. They're meeting right now.*

"Concerned about what?"

"The implications of a human finding out about us."

"She won't be human for long."

"Yes, but that opens a whole slew of possibilities."

Isaiah stepped through the doorway, half hearing his mother speak softly to Heather who responded in kind. *"Like what, Dad? Are they afraid she'll tell someone?"*

"Precisely."

"Well, she won't have the opportunity for the time being. And we'll cross that bridge after she shifts."

His father sounded worried as he continued to communicate. *"I'll express that to the council. But do me a favor. Don't leave your house. Not for any reason. I'll use that as an excuse to buy you some time, but son..."*

Isaiah turned around before stepping down from the porch and faced his father. *"What?"*

"I don't like the vibe I'm getting from the Arcadians. This is totally unprecedented. Causing a human to change is forbidden. I'm not sure what they may decide."

"Decide? About what? I didn't do this. Jack Tarben did. They can take up their issues with him."

His father shook his head. *"I'm not worried about anyone laying blame on you, but they may insist you turn her over."*

Isaiah spun around and hurried down the stairs, realizing Heather would be wondering why he was standing on the porch in silence, staring at his father. *"That's fucked up,"* he communicated as he headed for his dad's truck. *"They can go to hell. She's not leaving my sight. They can take her away over my dead body."*

"Isaiah?" Heather's voice was soft.

"It's okay, baby," he murmured close to her face. What else was he supposed to say?

She would understand everything soon enough.

CHAPTER 4

"You're sure about this?" Heather asked five minutes later as Isaiah pulled the truck up to another gorgeous cabin in the woods. It wasn't as large as his parents' home, but it appeared to have the same builder because it had a similar look.

"Positive." He turned off the engine and jumped down from the truck before she had a chance to say anything else. Two seconds later, she was once again in his arms.

She could get used to being pressed against his chest. It unnerved her how attracted she was to him, but it felt... right. Which made her more nervous.

As she held on to his neck, she spoke again. "I hope you don't feel somehow obligated to take care of me because of a scratch. I'll be fine. It wasn't your fault."

He frowned. "It sort of was my fault."

"How do you figure? Did you lure that bear out of the woods and taunt it into attacking me?" Huh. Actually, he did indeed seem to taunt the bear.

"No. I didn't lure the bear. You're right." He didn't comment on the taunting part as he climbed the steps to his equally amazing porch and then opened the front door and carried her inside.

"If you're going to carry me everywhere, I might milk this sprained ankle for a while." *Holy shit. Did I say that out loud?*

He tipped his head toward her and winked, sharing another of his half smiles. "Milk it, baby. It's definitely no hardship holding you in my arms."

She flushed. Her entire body was on fire. She was still wearing nothing over her upper body but the ripped shirt missing one sleeve. No coat. It was warmer outside than it had been during the night, but still should have been too chilly to go without at least a jacket. But hers had been ruined. And for some reason, she was not cold.

This sexual banter between them was crazy. She'd even started it. Who the hell was she today?

Once again she found herself whisked right through the living room without a chance to notice a single piece of furniture or décor. Her gaze was still pinned on his face.

What she did notice was his scent permeating the entire space, making her grip her knees together and squirm in his embrace. Since when was she so drawn to a man's scent?

Since never.

Of course, part of the reason she was so attracted to Isaiah surely had to do with how long it had been since she'd last had a steady boyfriend, which correlated precisely with how long it had been since she'd had sex. Over two years.

She'd been busy making a name for herself in her field, with no time for dating and even less time for the sort of men she usually met at work. The people in her Portland office were so nerdy and serious all the time. Most of them were married, and in some cases she shuddered to think what their wives were like.

She had hoped her prospects in Alberta would be better. Then again, she'd been in the province only two days and she was currently being carried through a sexy man's home. Maybe this job choice had been exactly perfect. And maybe she had been wrong to beat herself up all night over a sprained ankle. Blessings came in strange wrapping paper.

When Heather finally tore her gaze off the man who met her sexual banter tit for tat, she found herself in a bathroom.

Isaiah tipped her to one side and set her on the counter.

She grabbed the edges. "Uhh..." What the hell were they doing in the bathroom?

Isaiah ignored her to reach for the faucet on the gorgeous whirlpool tub. He turned it on, touched the water, and then turned toward her. "I figure you'd like to bathe, and you probably wouldn't be able to stand easily in the shower."

He was right. She felt disgusting under her hiking pants and the now torn, long-sleeved thermal shirt.

God, she was a mess. Her concentration was shot, and she blamed his absurdly sexy body for every lost brain cell. "A bath would be perfect." She glanced around the room. It was a dream bathroom. His house had to be either newly renovated or brand new because everything in the room was shiny and perfect, from the granite in white and brown swirls to the white cabinets and the glass shower. There were nozzles coming out of the walls in that shower. If she had the ability to stand, she would love to check it out.

Isaiah opened a narrow door next to what she assumed was a small separate toilet room. He pulled out a huge, plush, white towel and set it on the counter. "I don't have any girly shampoo or whatever you're used to, but we can fix that later. For now, can you make do with mine?"

She startled. "Of course. I'm not that picky. Soap is soap."

He smiled again and approached, almost as if he were stalking her. When he reached her, he set his hands on her thighs. "You got this?"

"What if I don't?" she taunted, again clearly no longer the owner of her own body. She tucked her lips in between her teeth as if that would suck the words back.

He moaned. *Moaned.* Closing his eyes, he tipped his head back, elongating his neck.

She had the sudden desire to run her tongue along the tight muscles of his neck and lick a line up to his mouth or down to his chest. The flannel shirt he wore revealed the slightest sprinkling of hair sticking out the top. She would give anything to see his chest.

When he lowered his face, he met her gaze, not laughing. "Baby, there are so many things we need to talk about, but first you should relax a few minutes, soak in the water. You'll feel so much better."

She nodded.

"Now, if you need any help getting undressed and into the tub…"

Heat raced up her cheeks again. She gripped her knees together again also. Why did the timbre of his voice reach her clit?

He sobered a bit and righted himself, still gripping her thighs, but no longer leaning into her quite as closely. "Listen, if I'm overstepping my bounds let me know. I'm not going to lie. I'm attracted to you. And this banter we have going on is sexy as hell. But I also don't want you to be uncomfortable in my home. So, please, tell me to back off."

As if God had given her a sign, a neon sign, she reached for Isaiah's neck with both hands and hauled his face toward hers. Without allowing herself to overthink things, she set her gaze on his lips and drew them all the way to hers.

His mouth was warm, and his lips parted when she touched them with her own. At first her kiss was tentative, nibbling along his fuller mouth, enjoying the first blatant sexual connection.

His fingers tightened on her thighs, making her moan into his mouth. That was when he angled his head to one side and deepened the kiss, taking full control. His tongue slid between her lips to devour her as if he were starving. His hand slid along her thighs and around to her hips to haul her closer to the edge of the counter.

Her heart raced as he nudged her legs apart with his thighs and situated himself between her knees.

The subtle tingling in her clit became a full roar of need. Her panties grew wet from her arousal and rubbed maddeningly against her swollen clit. She gripped his neck tighter, holding him as if he might get away if she let go.

She couldn't breathe, and she didn't want to. All she wanted was for this moment in time to freeze right here and never end. She didn't want to know more or less about the man kissing her. The timing for this connection was perfect. She knew everything about Isaiah that would lure her to him and nothing about him that would later annoy her.

He had a kind and giving spirit, rushing to the rescue of a stranger in the woods and even confronting an enormous angry bear to save her.

He loved his parents and his sibling.

He was sexy as hell.

His pensive brooding gave him a mysterious quality that caused a ball of desire to build in her stomach.

He was doting. Any woman would be lucky to have him as a boyfriend. Considering how well he treated a perfect stranger, he would no doubt be the most adoring lover on earth.

Whatever faults he had, she didn't know them yet. Was he a slob? His bathroom would attest to the opposite. Did he eat with his mouth open? Leave the toilet seat up? Was he an obnoxious drunk?

Was he a shitty lover? After all, why didn't he have a woman? Did he roll over after reaching his own orgasm and fall asleep? She found that hard to believe.

His hands curled into her back, hauling her closer as he continued to kiss the sense out of her. When did he completely take over? She didn't care. His dominance was even hotter than his tentativeness.

When they finally broke free, it was a slow parting that ended with Isaiah easing his mouth off hers but continuing to kiss her lips and then placing a line of kisses toward her ear.

She shuddered when his mouth landed on her lobe and his warm breath filled her ear. "What was that?"

"A kiss?" Her voice sounded as though it belonged to another woman. She didn't recognize it.

He chuckled against her, leaning closer. "That was way more than a kiss, you little imp. That was a claiming."

A claiming? Hmmm. Maybe he had a point. Perhaps she wanted him to know definitively how she felt so there would be no confusion. Or maybe she had hit her head so hard in a fall in the woods that she was currently in a coma, dreaming up this delicious mountain man holding her in his arms.

His mouth still on her ear, he whispered, "I'm going to close my eyes now, release you, and walk out of this room before I lose all control and take things too far. You're going to get into that tub that's probably overflowing and soak in the warm water."

"Okay," she managed to reply.

In an instant he released her. Two seconds later, he was gone, pulling the door closed behind him.

She couldn't move. Was it possible the kiss had never happened? She lifted her shaky fingers to her lips and touched the swollen flesh. Nope. It was real.

She lifted her good foot and pulled off her shoe. Easing her trembling body off the counter, she balanced on her good leg, pulled her shirt over her head, and unbuttoned her pants. She let them fall to the floor and stepped out, hopping on the one leg while gripping the edge of the counter.

A glance at the tub indicated it was full, and she lurched forward and turned off the faucet.

Tempting steam rose off the surface, calling to her. She quickly shed her sports bra and panties, and then tugged off her socks.

Forcing herself to concentrate on the task instead of the kiss, she eased into the perfect water and sighed. She closed her eyes and took a deep breath, not the least bit interested in reaching for soap or shampoo yet.

For long moments she lay there, unable to resist a mental replay of what had happened between them. They had chemistry. There was no doubt. Was it a damsel-in-distress syndrome? Who the hell cared?

It was undeniably hot. She was a warm-blooded human who had needs that hadn't been met in far too long. She was about to spend two days relaxing in his home. Why not make the most of it?

Because you aren't this kind of woman, Heather.

You don't hook up with strangers and fuck on the first date.

This wasn't even a date. She didn't know what it was.

Her sex gripped. She couldn't remember ever being this aroused. To torture herself further, she smoothed her hand up her thigh and between her legs. The second she drew a finger between her folds, she moaned.

Her eyes flew open at the intrusive sound. She jerked her fingers away from her pussy. *Jesus, Heather, get a grip. You can't masturbate in the man's bathroom.*

A soft knock on the door startled her. Had he heard her moaning?

"Heather? You okay? Need anything?"

"I'm good." Her voice cracked. She cleared her throat and tried again. "I'm okay. Just relaxing."

"I'm gonna make you something to eat. You're probably starving."

"Okay." Her stomach growled as if on cue.

As he walked away, she reached for the soap. First she tackled her arm. The soap burned on the angry red lines, but she would live. After washing the rest of her body, avoiding her pussy altogether, she grabbed the shampoo. There was a bottle of conditioner too. She didn't care what brand they were or how manly they might smell, she needed conditioner or it would take two hours to comb through her tangled hair.

She pulled the band from her ponytail and dropped it next to the tub. Her arms were shaking. From low blood sugar or lust or the adrenaline spike, or was it the scratch on her arm?

She still felt uneasy about Isaiah's entire family's reaction to the claw marks. If he wasn't going to tell her what the possible indications were, she needed to Google them and find out for herself. He had to have a computer in the house somewhere, but did he have Internet out here? As far as she could tell, they were in the middle of nowhere. Probably the closest neighbor was his parents.

The idea of being totally isolated and alone with Isaiah Arthur made her shiver in both arousal and concern.

She wasn't worried about her safety. Instinct told her he was a good man. She'd met the majority of his immediate family, for heaven's sake, and they knew where she was. Unless both his parents and his brother were in the habit of aiding in the quest to lure stranded hikers into their fancy mountain cabins to rape and murder them, she was safe.

The park warden even knew where she was.

And her mother.

No. Isaiah was one of the good guys. As she dipped her head back to rinse the conditioner off her hair, she gave a silent prayer that he wasn't too good of a guy because she was totally not in the mood for good.

By the time she managed to let the water out of the tub, wrap the enormous towel around her much smaller body, and drag a comb she found through her long hair, she was exhausted.

She was also stuck. Hopping out of the room on one foot would be foolish. She would fall and break her neck. She needed help. "Isaiah?" Hearing nothing for several seconds, she tried again, louder. "Isaiah?"

Footsteps. Moments later, he was at the door, easing it open. "Can I come in?"

"Yep."

He opened the door all the way, let his gaze run up and down her frame where she perched on the edge of the tub, and swallowed.

"I didn't want to hop on my bare foot through the house. I'd probably break my neck."

He rushed forward as though needing the prompt. She seriously wouldn't mind keeping the sprained ankle if it meant having this giant sweep her off her feet dozens of times a day to carry her from room to room.

Without a word, he tucked her against his chest and effortlessly stepped into the bedroom. She thought he would take her to the living room or kitchen, but instead he lowered her onto his bed. "Changed the sheets while you were in there."

She glanced around his space, learning that he liked dark wood and dark colors. He didn't have many items that weren't necessities, like pictures or knickknacks, but he did have one rather large abstract painting on the wall across from the bed. The colors matched the room. Black and navy and gray.

"You're going to swim in Joselyn's clothes. The things my mom grabbed are nearly useless. She's too tall for you."

Heather lifted both brows, not bothering to answer that. "But your brother's getting my stuff from the motel anyway."

"Yes. And he's going to pay your bill and close it out also. No sense paying for a room you aren't in."

True. She could always get another one.

"I made you some soup. It's from a can, but you shouldn't overdo it right now."

"And why is that? You still haven't told me why you're so worried about a few scratches on my arm."

Isaiah blew out a breath and lowered onto the side of the bed. He reached across her, grabbed a few more pillows, and then wrapped a huge hand behind her neck to lift her forward and tuck the soft clouds behind her so she was more propped up. "There are a lot of things I haven't told you. And I'll get to all of them. One at a time. Trust me?" He reached for her hand, held it tightly in his, and sat back to meet her gaze.

"So far. But now would be a good time to start talking."

He nodded. "Agreed. Let me grab the soup and bring it in here, and then I'll talk while you eat."

"Perfect."

When he let go of her hand to leave the room, she irrationally missed the contact. The same feeling had consumed her when he'd left the bathroom.

In less than a minute, he was back, a steaming bowl of soup in one hand, a bottle of water in the other. He set the water on the bedside table and handed her the soup carefully. "It's hot."

"I see that."

When he eased himself back onto the bed, avoiding jostling her any more than necessary, he set his hand on her shin. "How's your foot?"

"Hurts. I'm ignoring it. Start talking." She brought a spoonful of the chicken noodle soup to her lips and blew on it, eyeing him so he would know she didn't want him to stall any longer.

This arrangement was way beyond weird. She was currently sitting on the bed of a man she met a few hours ago, wrapped in nothing but a towel and eating a bowl of soup, as if they did this sort of thing every day.

He rubbed her leg possessively. Absentmindedly. Also as if he did so every day. She sorely wished that were true.

A knock sounded at the front door, and Heather lowered her spoon. "That can't be Wyatt already. He hasn't had time to get down the mountain and back yet."

"It's not. I'll be right back." Isaiah pushed off the bed and disappeared before she could ask him how the hell he knew who was or wasn't at the door.

She listened as closely as she could, but all she heard

were low murmured voices. Sometimes it seemed like no one spoke at all. She remembered him carrying her down a hall to get to his bedroom, but how long was it?

She heard the front door shut, but Isaiah didn't return, which meant he probably went outside. She finished her soup, set the bowl on the bedside table, and grabbed the water. She felt better. Surprisingly, her ankle was no longer throbbing. The scratch on her arm burned more than its appearance would indicate, but it wasn't bleeding. Seriously. It was a scratch. Sure, it came from a bear claw, but even if there was a risk of infection, it wouldn't happen for more than a week. There was no reason to wig out over it.

She relaxed into the pillows and closed her eyes while she waited for Isaiah to return. So tired...

Should she allow herself to rest while he was gone? Where was he anyway?

After a few deep breaths, she calmed, and sleep dragged her under whether she wanted it to or not.

After Isaiah closed the door behind him, he followed the four members of the Arcadian Council down the steps to his front yard. For a moment, he took in the serenity that was his property—or had been until today. He hadn't wanted to disturb the local foliage, so few of the trees had been removed to build his home.

He owned two acres, but he'd carefully selected this spot in a natural clearing at the highest point where he had an unbelievable view of the mountains and valleys surrounding him. With the exception of several saplings and about six full-grown pine trees, his home was surrounded by about twenty-five yards of grass on all sides. At this point in the season, everything was still a lush green that had yet to make a turn toward winter.

The four men in front of him stood with their feet planted wide, their arms crossed, and their brows furrowed. They were each in their sixties, but time had been kind to them.

The alpha of the group, Laurence, broke the silence. "We understand a human has been compromised and she's in your care."

Isaiah fought the urge to chuckle at Laurence's word choice. Compromised? That wasn't the first word that came to his mind when he recollected the moment Jack Tarben attacked her, forever altering her universe.

In addition, it was ludicrous for these four council members to pretend they didn't know exactly who was inside the house and what her status was. They would have scented her from a great distance and were indisputably clear on her current state.

Nevertheless, Isaiah played their game. "Indeed." He, too, planted his feet wide and crossed his arms. He straightened his back so that he stood at his full height. Every man in front of him was as tall and built as he was, however. The standoff was all bluster.

The reality was these were members of the Arcadian Council. Whatever they declared would be law. Isaiah had no leg to stand on, and he was perfectly aware of every nuance of this meeting.

Isaiah also knew he needed to make his intentions clear before the council members decreed something authoritative that went against Isaiah's desires. With that in mind, he spoke his next words in a preemptive attempt to buy time. The more information he was willing to share, the better his chances were of gaining much-needed time.

"Her name is Heather Simmons. She moved to

Silvertip two days ago. She knows no one. She's no threat to a single living being. She was scratched against her will, and she's currently in the early stages of transformation. It would be in her best interest to rest here while her body makes the changes she didn't ask for."

Laurence narrowed his gaze. "How kind of you to provide her shelter during this difficult time." His voice was filled with sarcasm. Not shocking. All four of the men in front of Isaiah would easily be able to discern Isaiah's intentions.

"It goes without saying that I have a vested interest in Heather's transition. You don't need me to tell you that." Full disclosure. No secrets. Not the slightest hint of mystery.

"Indeed. And I'm sure you're also aware of the penalties among our people for infringing on the free will of any being, human or shifter," Laurence pointed out.

"Of course. And I resent the implication that I would ever do anything as underhanded as influence the will of the woman under my care. I'll remind you that I'm not the criminal here. I'm not the one who attacked Heather and changed her course. I'm the Good Samaritan who has every intention of ensuring the next phase of her life is as seamless as possible."

Another member of the council, Charles, spoke next. "There's no need to get defensive, Isaiah. Our intentions are the same as yours. We're on the same team."

Isaiah nodded sharply and redirected the conversation. "What's being done to apprehend Jack Tarben?"

"Everything in our power," Charles continued. "Besides the members of your family and the Tarbens, we have others helping in the search. He will be apprehended, and justice will be served."

Laurence took over. "Our more pressing concern is with the human."

"And as I've stated, you have my word she won't be pressured by me or anyone else to make decisions against her will." When Isaiah said anyone else, he intentionally left the vague inference that he referred to the rest of his family or perhaps the council themselves.

Laurence's face hardened again. "Be careful, son. We intend to work with you on this issue, but remember we are watching closely, and your words are not misunderstood. Any decisions made with regard to the welfare of Ms. Simmons will be handed down by the council.

"Your generous offer to aid her in this difficult time is appreciated, and it is agreed she would fare better in your home under the care of your family than taking the risk of her transitioning during the journey to the North in the presence of total strangers."

Isaiah nodded. "Then I'm sure you'll agree I need to get back inside to see to Heather's care."

"And you'll agree that you need to be mindful of the importance of ensuring this matter doesn't leak to another human being."

"Of course. I've already considered the issues surrounding the problem. Heather called her parents this morning and let them know she was safe and recuperating in a location without cell service."

"Excellent," Laurence continued. "If it's all the same to you, the four of us will remain here to ensure her safety."

Isaiah fought the urge to chuckle sardonically at Laurence's choice of words. He also fought to block that impulse so as not to offend the council members in the precarious dance. These men had no particular interest in the safety of Heather Simmons. Their main goal was to protect the species. That went without saying.

Charles spoke again. "Be aware, Isaiah, that our time is valuable. Further decisions have not been made at this time, but we're giving you this respite as a courtesy. We'll remain discreetly on your property for now. Not indefinitely. When further instructions are relayed, we'll act without delay."

Discreetly? Isaiah wanted to point out that there was nothing discreet about these four burly council members and their formidable presence. But he bit his tongue. He needed to take the olive branch and hope he could accomplish everything necessary before they decided to remove Heather from his home. For her safety.

CHAPTER 5

By the time Isaiah calmed down enough to return to the bedroom, he found Heather fast asleep. The vision immediately lowered his blood pressure, and he stood next to her watching her for a long time.

She was so relaxed in slumber. Her face was devoid of worry. Her mouth was slightly parted. Her head was tipped to one side on the pillow.

His mouth grew dry as he took in the rest of her. The towel had slipped enough to give him a glimpse of her inner thighs. Not enough to see her breasts or her pussy, but damn, his imagination ran rampant.

While he stood there, she sighed in her sleep and turned onto her side, facing him. She tucked her hands under her cheek and drew her knees up toward her belly.

Time stopped as he got a glimpse of the swell of her bottom where it peeked out from beneath the towel. Her frame was so small, he wondered how the hell he would avoid hurting her when they fucked.

There was no longer a doubt in the world they were going to fuck. Soon, in fact. Partially because he wanted her more than his next breath, and partially because if things outside got any more tense, he would need to bind himself to her to keep her safe.

Forcing himself to close his eyes and turn away from her delectable body, he padded from the room. He didn't bother shutting the door. He wouldn't make a single sound that would disturb her, and he wanted to know when she awoke.

He also didn't cover her. Her body temperature was already rising. She would be sweltering under the covers. Bears only ran about two degrees warmer than humans, but he suspected her temperature would rise well above that while her body fought to get through the change.

As he paced the room, he reached out to Wyatt. *"Where are you?"*

"Almost at your place. I have Heather's stuff."

"Great. Did Dad tell you I'm under house arrest?" Isaiah headed for the main picture window in the living room and stared out between the slats.

"What do you mean?"

"The Arcadian Council decided they think Heather is too big of a risk to our species, and they don't want her to leave my property or to have any communication with the outside world. The only reason they're letting her stay in my care is because I insisted they let me help her through the transition before they swarm my home."

"Fuck."

"Yeah, fuck."

"You obviously have no intention of turning her over to the Arcadians at any point."

"Exactly."

"Guess you didn't tell them that."

"Nope."

"Hang on, I'm pulling up now." Wyatt cut off

communication as Isaiah heard his truck pull up to the front of the house.

The four enormous bears out front wandered closer to the truck, sniffed at it, confronted Wyatt as he stepped down from the cab, and then returned to their posts. The darn Alpha grizzlies parked themselves in bear form at all four corners of the property. They made it look as though they were protecting the inhabitants inside the home, but their main purpose was to make sure Heather Simmons didn't leave.

Isaiah opened the front door with a finger to his lips. "She's asleep," he whispered.

Wyatt nodded as he entered with two small suitcases. "Your woman travels light," he teased as he set them down, keeping his voice low.

"She's hardly my woman yet."

"Yeah, but I get the impression that's about to change."

"I hope so, but I'm not about to bind myself to her without her full consent, and certainly not without her knowledge."

"Even if it means letting the Arcadians take her?"

The hair on Isaiah's body stood on end, and he stiffened as he led his brother into the kitchen, farther away from the hallway and thus the master bedroom. "I can't even ponder that possibility."

"Do you think they will?"

"They seem pretty damn serious," he stated as he pulled the fridge open and grabbed two pilsners. He handed one to Wyatt.

"It's barely noon."

"So?" Isaiah frowned at his brother's smirk.

Wyatt said no more as he twisted off the top and took a long swig. The jab hadn't meant he was opposed to drinking at this hour. He was simply pointing out it was unusual for Isaiah. And he wasn't wrong. Isaiah drank. He enjoyed beer immensely, but Wyatt could usually outdrink him any hour.

Wyatt lifted the bottle and read the bottom of the label. "When was this one bottled?"

"Not sure. Stop making fun of me. I have serious problems here." The damn beer was days old. After all, their family owned the fucking brewery. Glacial Brewing Company. Isaiah did not have old beer in his home.

Wyatt sobered. "What are you planning to do?"

"Convince these assholes that Heather isn't a risk and get them to go home."

"And you think that will be successful?"

"No. It's just my plan. In reality, I'm probably going to have to come up with a plan B or convince the smoking hot woman currently in my bed to let me bind to her."

Wyatt winced. "I don't envy you."

Isaiah took a long swig and set the bottle on the counter. He leaned his ass against the surface and crossed his arms. "I won't force her. If she doesn't submit to my plan willingly, I don't know what I'll do. Continue to put these guys off I guess."

"She might resent you for the rest of your life if you pressure her. And if the council finds out, you could be arrested."

"I thought of that too." He uncrossed his arms and ran a hand through his hair. How the hell had this situation gotten so fucked up? The woman he was assuredly destined to spend the rest of his life with knew nothing of his species, the magnetic draw he had to her, or the fact that she, too, would be a bear shifter in the near future. When? Today? Tonight? Tomorrow? In a week? When? He had no idea how long it would take for her body to transition.

Wyatt ambled over to the kitchen table and took a seat, leaning back in the chair as he drank his beer.

Isaiah watched his brother, forcing himself to remember the comedic way he always described him. Two years older. Two inches taller. With hair two inches longer.

"I moved her car to Mom and Dad's," Wyatt added.

"Thanks." There was little else to say.

Wyatt finished his beer and set the bottle on the table. "I gotta get back to the brewery. With you out of commission for a few days and Dad fending off a barrage of questions from everyone in our pack, the Tarben pack, and the Arcadian Council, someone needs to manage the brewery."

"Thanks for covering for me, man. I didn't even think to ask."

Wyatt pushed to standing. He had a wide grin on his face as he crossed toward Isaiah and set a hand on his shoulder. "That's how I know she's the one for you. The rest of the world stopped existing the moment you met her."

Isaiah didn't smile back. "Actually, if I'm perfectly honest, the rest of the world stopped existing the moment Montrose opened her car door and I got the first whiff of her essence."

"Seriously?" Wyatt was taken aback.

"Yep. I know it's not rational. But it happened. My heart was in my stomach as I raced up the mountain to find her. Already I was more attached to her than any female I've ever met. When I stepped into her space and saw her small frame huddled under a Mylar blanket on the side of the path, I nearly swallowed my tongue."

"That's powerful."

"Yes. And irrational. But it's still true. She's mine. I've known it the entire day."

"Now you have to convince her."

"And I will." Isaiah glanced at the front window. "If the Arcadians let me handle this."

"You need to tell her, man."

"I know. I will."

"Like now. Sooner rather than later."

Isaiah nodded. "You gonna let go of my shoulder and get out of here so I can?"

Wyatt chuckled. "I'm outa here." He took long strides to cross the room, exit through the front, and shut the door without making a sound.

Yeah, Isaiah had a lot of work to do. He needed to get started.

First he had to wake up his gorgeous mate, and then he would face the task of turning her world upside down and inside out.

Heather blinked her eyes as consciousness sank in. She rolled onto her back, unfurling her body from the tight ball she'd been in. As she allowed herself to peek at her surroundings, she was momentarily stunned to find a man staring down at her. For a heartbeat, she froze. And then her memory filled in the details. "How long was I asleep?"

"A few hours." His gaze searched her face and then ran down her body.

Shit. She was still wearing nothing but a towel. She grabbed the front of it at the spot it was tucked in above her chest to make sure it was covering her. Thank goodness it was huge. It more than wrapped around her, and it was plenty long enough to cover her ass. She thought it reached low enough on her thighs that Isaiah wasn't getting a sex show.

61

When he lifted his head to face her again, she clenched her thighs together. His gaze alone spiked her arousal. Not to mention he looked ready to devour her. He even licked his lips and inhaled slowly as if to control the urge.

She had been awake all of thirty seconds, and she already craved his touch as strongly as she had before going to sleep.

"Wyatt brought your things from the motel," he stated, his deep, sexy voice sending a shiver up her spine. He pointed behind him, and she glanced to see her suitcases against the wall. "You travel light."

"The rest of my stuff is being shipped later. I wanted to find a place to live first." Goose bumps rose all over her exposed arms and legs at the intense way he continued to stare at her. She needed to break the connection before she whipped her towel open and begged him to take her. "I should put some clothes on."

He gave a slight nod but continued to look down at her, leaning his hip against the mattress. His hand slowly trailed to the bottom corner of the towel, and he fingered it. He'd removed the flannel shirt from earlier and now wore a tight navy T-shirt.

She held her breath as she watched him. He wasn't touching her skin anywhere, but her mind flooded with the memory of him kissing her earlier. Those giant hands splayed across her back. Those long thick fingers grasping her thighs. His lips. God, his lips.

While he continued to toy with the corner of the towel, wetness pooled between her legs. Her nipples pebbled and rubbed against the terrycloth, aching to be touched. She gripped the spot where the top corner of the towel was tucked in, applying pressure against her breasts with her forearm, which only made things worse.

Suddenly, a moan escaped her lips. The moment she

realized it, she flushed deeply, batted his hand away with her free one, and swung her legs around so she could sit on the edge of the bed. She barely noticed the pain in her ankle. Her bare thigh rested against his thick, jean-clad one. If she scooted another few inches to hop down from his high mattress, she would expose herself.

The hand he had been using to toy with the corner of her meager covering reached across and settled on her opposite thigh so that his arm stretched in front of her chest.

"I need to put some clothes on," she rasped. Her voice didn't sound like her own. Apparently some other foreign being had taken over her body and turned her into a nymph. The idea that she was actually dead or in a coma returned full force. If this was Heaven, blessed angels from above. If this was a dream she was having in a deep coma, bless those same angels.

"You should get dressed. Yes." He didn't sound remotely convinced, nor did he move away from her. Instead his hand trailed up her arm, across her shoulder, and along her neckline until the tips of his fingers tickled the underside of her chin.

She glanced down at the twin claw marks on her arm, surprised to find them looking far less menacing than earlier.

He turned his body to fully face her, his other hip now leaning against her thigh. "You feel it too, right?"

She swallowed. Why bother to deny the cryptic question?

"Heather, tell me you feel it too," he demanded.

His tone made her pussy throb. She nodded once.

Suddenly, he wasn't next to her, he was in front of her. His thighs were against her closed knees, and his hands landed on the mattress at her sides, forcing her to lean back. His face was inches from hers. His gaze intent. Brow furrowed. Eyes searching hers. His voice was deeper, rough, sexy as hell when he spoke again. "Tell me, baby. Tell me I'm not the only one."

She swallowed again and forced her lips to part. Every inch of her body was on fire for him. Literally hot. Even though the temperature in the room was probably not set as high as it felt and the weather outside was early winter cold, she was hot.

The towel seemed to suffocate her. She gripped it tighter above her chest. Her fingers ached.

He'd called her *baby* again. And again, it seeped into her and turned her to mush. A man she met a few hours ago was so far under her skin that she felt as though she'd known him her entire life.

He lifted one hand, trailing it again up her body to her chin. He held it steady and whispered, "Tell me I'm wrong. Tell me the pull is all me, and I'll back off."

She couldn't bring herself to speak. It seemed like the biggest moment of her life, as if her next words would send her down one of two paths in front of her and determine the tone of their relationship going forward.

She had no doubt he would indeed back off if she asked him. But she would be lying to both of them if she did so. "I feel it too," she whispered.

His eyes slowly closed, and his mouth tipped up at the corners as if he'd just asked her to marry him and she'd given him an unexpected *yes*. His warm breath hit her face as he exhaled slowly.

She wanted his lips on hers again with an irrational desperation. She wanted his entire body pressed against her. Damn the consequences. She wanted him to fuck her senseless. Right now. Right here. "Isaiah…" His name trailed off as that one word left her mouth.

His eyes darted open. "Say that again."

"Isaiah?"

"No. Not like that. Like you said it before. Like you were in the middle of an orgasm."

She inhaled slowly, her pussy twitching.

"Jesus." He straddled her legs and set his other hand on her lower back while he brought his mouth to hers.

She sank into him, letting go of the front of the towel to wrap her arms around his neck as though she could trap him against her lips and never let him go. Never mind he outweighed her by almost triple and was strong enough to lift the corner of a car or possibly fight off a grizzly bear.

The towel held together, a fact she only knew because her heavy breasts rubbed against it agonizingly.

Isaiah released her chin to drag his hand around to the back of her neck where he threaded his fingers in her hair and tugged her head farther back to deepen the kiss.

The slight pull was almost painful, but it morphed into a weird sort of pleasure that radiated to her pussy instead. No man had ever claimed her so thoroughly, and she liked it. A lot.

His tongue danced with hers, tasting every inch of her mouth while the hand on her back flattened over the towel. Every finger pressed into her, holding her, possessing her, demanding she lean into him.

She wanted more. Her body insisted. She released her grip on his neck to trail her fingers down to his chest until she reached the hem of his T-shirt. As she lifted the cotton material to flatten her palms on his abs, she sighed into his mouth.

He tugged her head harder as if admonishing her, which only fed the flames and caused her to grip his waist and scoot closer to his body until her legs straightened in front of her and she could press her belly into his erection.

Damn, he was hard, and if his cock was proportionate to the rest of his body, he would be enormous.

Isaiah moaned and broke the kiss. At the same time, he released her and jumped back, twisting around so his back was to her.

She heaved for oxygen, suddenly aware she hadn't breathed properly for a while. As she slid the rest of the way to the floor, careful to put her weight on the one foot, her left foot rested against the carpet, noticeably less painful than earlier. Her entire body mourning the loss of his touch, she wondered what the hell he'd stopped for. "Isaiah?"

His shoulders rose and fell with every deep breath, and finally he turned around, running a hand over his face. "I'm sorry. I shouldn't have done that."

"Why not? I was enjoying myself."

"I'm not giving you enough space to exert your own free will. I'm crowding you. You weren't awake a full minute before I pounced." He took another step back.

Her legs shook. This was by far the weirdest relationship she'd ever had. Surreal. The sexiest mountain man alive was playing a dangerous game of hot and cold with her. She couldn't take it much longer. For one thing, the knot in her belly demanded release. If she didn't get it soon, she might collapse from the tremble in her pussy.

"God." His voice was louder, and he tipped his head toward the ceiling. "I can smell your arousal. It's like a drug."

He can smell my arousal? She leaned back against the edge of the bed to avoid falling.

He lowered his hands and fisted them at his sides as he met her gaze. "I need to taste you. Please. God, please let me taste you. I swear I'll keep my jeans on. I won't let it go any further. But you're so aroused and I'm so..." He closed his mouth for a second as if thinking and then spoke again, softer. "Please, baby, let me taste you."

His words drove her desire up ten notches. Their meaning took longer to sink in. He wasn't talking about kissing her lips. He wanted to go down *there*.

She wasn't a prude. She'd had boyfriends. She'd had sex —usually bad sex. But no man had put his mouth between her legs.

Honestly, as insane as it was, she'd never wanted anything more in her life. "Okay," she murmured.

In one stride, Isaiah was in front of her again. He grabbed her waist and lifted her onto the bed. With a hand at the back of her neck, he lowered her onto her back and leaned over her.

She held her breath, her heart pounding, not missing the fact that this giant, dominant, demanding man was both out of control for her, while at the same time having enough awareness to see to her comfort.

He kissed her eyelids, her nose, her lips, her chin. And then he grabbed her wrists and dragged them above her head, pressing them into the mattress. When his face moved lower to nuzzle her neck, chills raced down her body. His teeth grazed her skin as though he intended to bite her. Claim her.

Claim her?

He licked the spot he'd touched with his teeth, lapping at her skin.

Her vision swam with the idea of a vampire biting his victim and then licking the wound to seal it. Too late, however, because his essence was already inside her. She lost that train of thought as his face lowered to her chest, his soft beard dancing across her sensitive skin.

He nudged her legs apart, carefully avoiding her sore ankle, and nestled his hips between them.

Cool air hit her pussy, driving her mad. She arched her head back, exposing more of her neck, and moaned. She had never been this close to orgasm with so little contact before. He hadn't touched her breasts or her pussy.

But that changed in an instant when he grabbed the corner of her towel with his teeth and jerked it open.

She gripped his torso with her knees. She was going to self-combust. Had anyone ever died from arousal gone haywire?

Isaiah's face lifted a few inches off her chest, and he froze. A second later, he released her wrists, grabbed the sides of the towel, and completely bared her body to his gaze. "Jesus." He stared at her, his gaze wandering from her chest to her pussy and back.

Her nipples beaded further, her breasts so swollen they were tight. The wetness between her legs trailed down to her rear.

When he finally drew his hands in to reverently dance the tips of his fingers across her nipples, she arched her chest and lowered her arms to grab onto him.

He instantly removed his fingers from her breasts and twisted them around to grab her wrists and put them back. "Don't move them. Don't... Just don't, baby. Leave them here. I can't..."

His words made little sense, but she grabbed the sheet in her fists and nodded. "Okay," she whispered.

He returned his attention to her breasts, teasing her nipples before gliding his fingers down her belly toward her sex. Instead of touching her there, he wrapping his palms around her thighs and pushed them open so wide her knees touched the mattress.

She should have died at the exposure. She should have protested at the very least. But the way he looked at her...

Oh. God.

The desire in his expression. It was like he was an animal in heat and she had put off some sort of pheromone that called to his primal instincts.

He lowered slowly to his knees on the floor between her legs and brought his face toward her sex, inhaling deeply. "Heather... Baby..." Every word was soft. So reverent.

His tongue flicked out to taste her, dragging briefly across her lower lips. The noise that came from his mouth was indescribable, as if he'd tasted the best delicacy on the planet.

She emitted a strangled gasp herself when he lowered his face once more and firmly pressed his tongue against her clit. In the next instant, he drew the swollen nub into his mouth and suckled it.

She stopped breathing. The blood rushed from her face. She thought she might faint, though she hoped she didn't. If she missed out on this intense pleasure, she would be pissed.

So close to the edge... And then he released her clit and thrust his tongue inside her channel.

Heather tried to lift her butt off the bed, every muscle in her body stiffening. She was going to come. Any second.

Isaiah's nose pressed into her clit, and he rubbed it back and forth while he lapped at her pussy.

That was it. As if an explosion occurred inside her, she came. Her tight channel grasped at his tongue, pulsing with the same rhythm as her throbbing clit. Every bit of her body released the tight coil of need that had been simmering beneath the surface since the moment he found her on the trail.

She gasped for air as the tremors subsided. He began to rain kisses on her pussy and thighs, finally lifting one hand

69

off her leg to wipe her moisture from his face as he rose to his feet.

Was it possible to meet someone and instantly be so attracted to them that the world stopped revolving? She would not have believed it, but whatever weirdness had descended was unmistakable.

Part of her was sated and limp, but another, larger part demanded that he take off his clothes and fuck her. *Now.*

CHAPTER 6

Heather drew her arms to her sides and rose onto her elbows, lifting her head off the bed. "I need you inside me."

He shook his head, righting himself as he cupped her breasts and teased her nipples with his thumbs. "Your tits are so fucking gorgeous."

"Isaiah, I'm not kidding. Take your clothes off. I'm going to implode."

He smirked. "You just came. Hard. You won't implode."

"I beg to differ, and besides, *you* did *not* come."

He winced. "I'm super aware of that, but I made a promise."

"I didn't accept your promise. I didn't even ask for it. Now, take off your clothes before I develop a complex from being the only one naked." He was starting to scare her. What kind of man would or could turn down her offer? It was beyond altruistic for him to go down on her and deny himself any sort of returned favor.

He set his hands beside her head next to her ears and leaned forward to give her a chaste kiss. "We had a deal."

"No. *You* had a deal. I wasn't in on the deal."

He pushed off the bed and stood, no longer touching her with his hands, although the way he let his gaze roam up and down her frame felt like a caress. "I can't, baby. Not until we've talked. There are things you need to know about me."

"Fine. Tell me whatever you want, but do it naked."

He chuckled. "Naked is not going to make it easier to resist you."

"And I'm telling you to stop resisting me. Are you trying to be a gentleman or something? Because that ship sailed." She watched him watching her. "Or are you hiding something? A scar? A mole. I know it isn't that you're lacking between the legs because I can see your erection from here."

He smirked, adjusting himself with one hand. "Trust me, I'm not lacking."

"Talk to me. You're freaking me out." Her voice sounded more high-pitched.

He stepped forward, grabbed her by the waist, and hauled her ass farther across the bed. While she was trying to figure out his aim, he climbed onto the mattress, straddled her legs with his knees, and clasped her hands with his to set them once again slightly above her head. "It's not that simple for me, baby."

"What's not? Having sex?"

"Yes."

"What the hell do you mean?" Her heart pounded. He was totally scaring her now.

"I mean I'm not like other guys you've dated. If I fuck you, I'm going to do it with the intention of keeping you."

"Keeping me?"

He nodded.

"I'm not a stray dog."

He smiled slowly. "You certainly are not." He kissed her

forehead and then released her hands to sit more upright, though he still pinned her to the bed with his enormous body straddling her.

Suddenly she felt naked. Too naked. If he wasn't going to have sex with her, she wanted clothes on. On top of that, embarrassment crept in at how he'd played her body so well while giving her nothing. "Get off me."

He flinched.

"Isaiah, get off me. I want to put clothes on."

He swung a leg over her, but grabbed her hand as she scrambled to the edge of the bed. "Heather..."

She jerked her hand free, grabbed the towel from the bed, and wrapped it around her middle. Without looking at him, she put tentative pressure on her left foot. It hurt. Stung. But it wasn't bad enough to keep her from hobbling to the bathroom. She limped across the room, tipped her suitcase on its side, and unzipped it.

"You're mad," he stated. Luckily he didn't approach her.

"You think?" She grabbed a pair of jeans, panties, and a T-shirt. She had no idea where a bra was, but the T-shirt would cover her enough. Two hops to the left and she was in the bathroom. She shut and locked the door before he could stop her with more weird words.

The first thing she did was drop the clothes and lean against the wall. "Fuck," she muttered. What the hell was going on? How could she possibly have allowed someone to ravage her so thoroughly? Although, how could she possibly have expected him to not return the favor?

No man in his right mind would give that much and take nothing without a frightening reason.

"Heather." His voice sounded from the other side of the door. "Please. Talk to me. Let me explain."

"Give me a second." She forced herself to sound far chipper than she felt.

A soft thump hit the door, and she imagined him leaning his forehead against it.

Fearing he might get frustrated enough to break the door, she scrambled to get dressed and then found a comb to run through her tangled hair. With a deep breath, she opened the door to find him standing in the frame.

"I'm sorry. I can explain."

"Excellent. You can do it with my clothes on." She bent to duck under his arm and then rummaged through her toiletries to find a band for her hair. When she stood, gathering the heavy length into a messy bun, he winced. "What? Now you don't want my hair up either?" she joked.

He bit his lip.

"Seriously? I was kidding." Why did he care if her hair was up or down? He wanted her naked and her hair down. Illogical.

Before she fully had the bun secured, he bent low, tucked his shoulder into her belly, and lifted her off the ground.

She squealed. "Isaiah. Jeez. Put me down."

He ignored her as he carried her out of the bedroom and down a short hallway until he reached the great room. With one hand on her ass and the other on her thighs, he leaned down and set her gently on the couch. "Don't move. I'm going to grab you some water. You have to be thirsty."

She was. Incredibly thirsty, now that he mentioned it.

She watched his sexy ass as he strode from the room toward the attached kitchen. The two rooms were mostly connected in the enormous space. She continued to watch as he bent over and grabbed two waters from the fridge. And then he was back.

He handed her one and set the other on the coffee table. "Drink. You're hot. You need fluids."

She was hot. Like she had a fever. Could he feel it?

Other than that, she didn't feel sick. After a long swig of the cold water, she leaned back, turning sideways to lean against the arm of the couch and drawing her legs onto the cushion. She was careful not to jar her ankle too badly, but when she lowered her gaze to her feet, she could hardly see the swelling from earlier.

"Is your water some sort of fountain of youth? My ankle is way better than earlier. This morning I couldn't have applied enough pressure on it to avoid death by a mauling bear, and this afternoon it's significantly better."

"Something like that."

She jerked her gaze to his. "If you make one more cryptic comment, I'm going to leave this house and walk down the mountain, sprained ankle or not."

"You can't leave, Heather." He lowered himself onto the couch next to her, turning to face her while lifting her legs to set them over his lap.

"Pardon?" She stiffened. Among his strange statements, occasionally he said something downright frightening.

He sighed. "You need to let me speak."

She narrowed her gaze. "Fine. Go for it." She pursed her lips.

"There's no easy way to say this, so I'm just going to blurt it all out."

"I'll believe that when I hear it."

A few moments passed while he didn't look at her and seemed to be gathering strength to speak.

Several thoughts raced through her mind. Maybe he and his family knew she would die from the scratches. Or get rabies. Was that a thing? But that was irrational. People got attacked by bears and lived all the time.

Nothing made sense. If she hadn't met his parents, she might worry he was a rapist or sex trafficker or murderer

75

or something. But they were such nice people. She didn't buy that.

He faced her, his hands gripping her knees where they rested over his thighs. "I'm not fully human."

She inhaled slowly, narrowing her gaze, trying to figure out what he might mean by that. "You think you're an alien? Like from another planet?"

He shook his head. "No. But if that's how farfetched you want to launch the conversation, my work will be easier than I thought."

"What then?" Maybe she should jerk out of his grasp and run from the house. She glanced at the front door and the view out the enormous window next to it caught her eye. That wasn't all that caught her attention, however. Two bears were pacing back and forth in the front lawn.

She sat upright, gripping the back of the couch. "Oh my God."

"What?" Isaiah twisted his head to follow her line of sight.

"There are bears in your front yard."

"Yeah." He relaxed. "It happens."

"Shit. I mean I know we're pretty far from town, but I wasn't expecting to look out the window and see a pair of bears. How the hell do you get to your car? What keeps them from attacking you when you step outside? I didn't think they liked to wander so close to humans."

He sighed. "You're right. Bears don't usually approach humans as long as they aren't provoked. Those two are not bears any more than I'm human."

She twisted back to face Isaiah. The fear that had crept up her spine morphed into terror. If she could, she would jump from the couch and run, but she had two problems. One, her ankle was sprained. And two, her body wasn't currently accepting messages from her brain. She felt like a bimbo from a horror film that stands still and gets killed while movie watchers scream at the television.

"We're shifters," he continued. "Those two out there, me, my family, even the bear that attacked you. All of us are shifters."

"Shifters?" Her mouth was dry.

He met her gaze. "We can change forms at will."

"Change forms?"

"I can become a bear. Those two out there can become human."

"Are you trying to scare me, or are you certifiably insane?"

He cringed. "Neither. If you hadn't gotten scratched, we wouldn't be sitting here having this conversation, and you would have gone on with your life without ever knowing what I'm telling you."

"It's a damn scratch, Isaiah." She held out her arm. Maybe showing him how inconsequential it was would help him understand his insanity.

He reached forward with his far arm and traced one claw mark from her shoulder to her elbow. "If it had been a regular bear, you're right, you would be fine. You would never know the difference. You also wouldn't be alone in my home, and I wouldn't have just tasted your pussy."

She flinched. Was now a good time to discuss having his mouth on her? She was mortified at the mere thought of having him between her spread legs now that she knew he was insane. Would he hurt her?

More importantly, there was still the matter of how many people knew where she was. No way were both his parents and his siblings all as certifiable as him. She wouldn't buy that everyone in his family let him take her to his house alone if they knew he believed he could transform into a bear.

Crazy got crazier.

"Heather, I'm sorry you have to hear this. I know it sounds bizarre to you, but I need you to understand."

She gripped the side of the couch, tugging her legs, but he held them firm. "Bizarre? You would describe this as bizarre?" She'd had enough. She needed to get out of there fast. She'd take her chances with the two bears out front.

Yanking her legs free, she swung them around and pushed off the couch. She bolted toward the front door, not giving a shit that her ankle screamed out in pain or that she didn't have shoes on. She would take her chances barefoot in the cold against two of the largest bears she'd ever seen.

Isaiah was faster than her, however. He reached the door first, flattened himself to it, and grabbed for her, hauling her against him with an arm around her waist.

She screamed.

He covered her mouth with his hand. "Heather, please. Stop. You need to listen to me. You have no idea how much trouble you'll be in if you open the front door."

Her eyes widened as her adrenaline reached a new high for the day. He held her so tightly, there was no escape. He was too big. She could not out power him. She also couldn't stop the tears from falling.

He held her tighter, flattening her to his front, one arm snug around her waist, the other covering her mouth.

She lifted a knee, hoping to nail him in the groin, but he dodged her at the last second. In a flash, he picked her up off the floor to cradle her against his chest as he had several other times that day.

This was different, though. This time she knew he was insane and intended to hold her hostage until he was finished with her. Would he kill her? Rape her?

Wait. Why did he not have sex with her earlier when

she was still a willing captive? Was he waiting for her to fight him? Maybe he only got off when his victim struggled. Getting her naked and making her orgasm against his mouth was just cruel. Deep, insensitive, psychological games.

Without a word, he stomped through the house back to his bedroom and kicked the door shut. He nearly tossed her on the bed, climbing over her to straddle her once more. He also grabbed her wrists again and held them over her head.

At least she was clothed.

Why did the expression on his face not match the excited one she would expect from a serial rapist?

"Stop fighting me. I'm going to hold you here until you listen to everything I have to say and understand. I don't care if it takes fucking three days. You mean too much to me for me to let you walk out the door."

She stopped struggling, mainly because there was no sense in it. He was too large for her to escape at the moment. She needed to conserve her energy for a real opportunity.

"Everyone in my family is a bear shifter," he started. "Our last name is Arthur, and that's our pack's name. The man who attacked you is from the neighboring pack, the Tarbens. We've been in a feud with them for a hundred years over land and water and boundaries. When I followed you this morning, I was weaving back and forth from my pack's land to the Tarbens'.

"I knew it was risky. They get fucking angry when we cross onto their territory. But the spot where I found you was on their land. The man who wandered up was Jack Tarben. Turns out he was unbalanced and already in trouble with his people."

Heather hardly moved while she tried to focus on this

insane tale. She had no choice. And information was power. She needed to listen to him so she could use anything he said against him later.

"Attacking a human is strictly forbidden. It hasn't happened for decades, and it's been even longer since anyone intentionally went out of their way to maliciously attack a human like Jack did you. I tried to talk him down, but he wouldn't listen. And then Wyatt showed up—"

She couldn't stop herself from interrupting. "Wyatt showed up? When?"

"He was the other bear that raced past you to confront Jack. I'll kick myself until the day I die for not stopping that asshole from clawing at you. I didn't really believe he would do it, and we were two against one. But he got by us so fast, and it was too late. I can only hope someday you'll forgive me."

As a hostage, she thought it might be best if she was agreeable. "Don't beat yourself up over a tiny scratch. It's nothing."

Isaiah's head hung lower for a moment, his gaze on her stomach or his own. Finally, he lifted his face and spoke. "The reason my parents were so distressed and why I brought you here at all is because you're going to become one of us now. It's unavoidable."

She fought the urge to laugh. Was he serious? If he believed this shit, he was far more insane that she thought.

"It's already starting."

"What is?" she asked before she could stop herself.

"The transformation. You're temperature is running high. You're hot. Your arm is healing too fast. Your ankle is getting better rapidly. It's not as swollen. You aren't favoring it as much."

He was right about that. Coincidence? Of course. She couldn't think what to say. As long as he held her down, she was trapped. As long as he was talking, he wasn't raping or killing her. "Go on."

He eyed her skeptically and then continued. "No one can tell me for sure how long it will take for you to transform. I don't have the answers I wish I had for you. It's unprecedented. Might be hours, a day, a week. I don't know. But it seems like it's coming sooner rather than later."

"I see."

He rolled his eyes. "You aren't going to use some sort of psychological trick to get me to release you, Heather. So just continue listening." He squeezed her hands to make a point that he was stronger.

If she ever had the chance, she would kick him hard in the dick for being such a prick.

"Here's the problem we're facing. Well, actually we have multiple problems, but let me start with the men out front. There are four of them. They came from the Arcadian Council the moment they heard a human had been clawed and blood had been drawn."

The story he wove was extremely intricate.

"They're here to clean up the mess."

"What's the Arcadian Council and what mess are you referring to?"

"The Arcadians are our governing body, and you're the mess. Bear shifters are not out to the world. To humans. No one knows about us. And we like to keep it that way. The Arcadians think you're a liability. They'd like to take you in and do whatever they need to make sure you don't tell anyone."

She tried to swallow. *Jesus.* His insane tale was getting to her.

"My mother would have preferred I let you stay with her so she could help you through the change. But I wanted you alone with me. Safer. Not altruistic. I knew from the moment I stuck my head into your car to catch your scent you were mine."

She shuddered.

"Hey, don't let that part freak you out. It's as weird for me as it is for you. And don't deny you feel the same pull. We aren't a species who believe in Fated matings. We tend to meet our mates, fall in love, and *then* claim each other in a permanent binding.

"The wolves… Those dudes are weird. They know their mates in one whiff and instantly fall for each other, bound for eternity."

"Wolves? Isaiah, listen to yourself." How was she ever going to get through to him? He was way past insane.

"Don't worry about the wolves. Forget I said anything. Not important. I strayed from the point. The point is that I'm as stunned as you to find such an intense mutual attraction that seems to defy reason. We don't know each other at all, and yet I want you more than I've ever wanted anything in my life."

"I'm not an object, Isaiah," she tried to reason. "I'm a human. You can't just keep me because you're attracted to me."

He sighed. "Attracted doesn't begin to cover it, and you know it. What we feel is far deeper. Also unprecedented. I can't explain why it happened to us that way, but it did."

If he was so sure they were fated or whatever, why the hell didn't he fuck her earlier when she was begging him to?

He hung his head. "God, I would give anything for you to stop looking at me like that. It's going to be a long night."

"If you get off me and let me go, you won't have to see my face." Shit. She was taunting him. Not a good idea.

"I can't."

"Why not?"

"Because I know in my heart you're mine, and it would kill me to lose you."

She forced herself to remain calm. "If you're so sure we're meant to be together, then it shouldn't change anything for you to stop pinning me to the bed."

He shook his head. "You have no idea the danger you're in or what I'm protecting you from. Those guys out front won't hesitate to take you with them. I doubt I would ever see you again."

"The bears? The two bears out front?"

"There are four of them, but yes."

"What are they doing? Guarding your home?"

"No. They're not keeping anyone out, baby. They're making sure you don't leave. I made a deal with them to give me some time to help you shift. The only reason they probably agreed was because none of them want to deal with an independent shifter in the back of their car on a trip north."

"An independent shifter?" She felt like a parrot. And why the hell was she bothering to continue this ridiculous conversation?

"As in not having a pack. Alone. When you transform, you'll automatically be a free agent, so to speak. A shifter without a pack. You'll be able to choose your own pack. I'm hoping you'll choose mine, but I can't stop you from choosing whatever you want. You have your own free will."

Progress. He admitted she had free will. That had to be worth something.

He kept speaking, his tale growing by the minute. "A scratch that draws blood forces a human into the change. If Jack had bitten you, his bite would have forced you to become a member of his pack without consent. And finally…a bite with the right secretions from his saliva would have bound you to *him* for life as his mate."

She tried to focus on his words, but they were so preposterous.

He leaned closer, his face inches away. "I want the man that bites you and binds you to be me."

"I see." She saw nothing but a pile of insanity. She also shivered and tipped her head to one side, thinking about the spot where he'd set his teeth on her earlier and then licked.

"You don't, but you will."

She was so hot. The inside of his damn house was a furnace. It might be worth racing out the front door just to cool off. She'd take her chances with the bears out front, whom Isaiah believed to be half human. "What if I want to go with the bears out front?"

"If you still want to go with them after you change and understand the implications fully, I won't stop you, but for now, you're humoring me with extreme skepticism. I can't blame you, but I also won't let you put yourself in danger."

It was true he didn't seem mad. Just frustrated. She bit her lower lip to keep from saying more.

"You're burning up with fever, baby." His words were far gentler. "Our body temp runs a bit higher than humans, but the fever is from your body fighting off the need to shift as if it were a virus. When the bear wins, you will shift, and the fever will disappear."

She struggled to follow his logic. "You think I'm going to become a bear soon?"

"I know you are."

"And you intend to help me."

"All the way."

CHAPTER 7

Dammit. This was so fucked up. Isaiah wanted to scream out in frustration. Hell, he wanted to growl. He wanted to shift, tip his head back, and roar at the sky. But that would scare the daylights out of Heather, and it would give her the opportunity to run.

She needed to see someone shift, though. That would help her believe it.

"Joselyn, where are you?" His sister would be the perfect person to help. She was female, so, less daunting, and one of the sweetest people he knew. He could also sense she wasn't far away.

"On my way to your house. Be there in a few. I know you told Mom and Dad you wanted to be alone, but I was hoping I could at least meet this woman. Maybe help? You don't exactly have a feminine touch." She chuckled into his head.

"I was about to suggest the same thing. Thanks, Jos. I could use some help here."

"Did you tell her?"

"Yep."

"How'd she take it?"

"I've literally got her pinned to my bed with my body to keep her from running, that's how she took it."

Joselyn groaned. *"Isaiah..."*

"Hey, when you come up with a better plan that doesn't get her killed, I'm all ears."

"Hang tight. Be there in five."

Heather's voice broke into his mind. "What are you doing? You get this far-away look as if you're in a trance sometimes." She tugged at her arms, but he didn't release her.

"Talking to my sister. She's on her way."

She frowned.

Fuck, this was hard. "We can communicate through our minds. You'll be able to also."

"Uh huh."

Isaiah sighed. He hated holding her down like this, but risking her running out the door was worse.

"So how does this telepathy work?"

He wished she was asking so many questions because she was curious to learn about his species. Instead, he knew she was trying anything and everything to get him to let her go, as if she had some sort of hostage-negotiation skills.

He answered her question with a question. "Do they teach you how-to-evade-an-attacker psychology in self-defense classes?"

She almost smiled. "Of course."

"I see. To answer your question, there's no real way to explain it. We just reach out to one another and think whatever thoughts we want to express. Engaging anyone telepathically isn't a problem. Learning how to block them out so they don't know your every thought is the real problem.

"When you first shift, you probably won't be able to

block anyone. I imagine it's a learned tactic, and your brain will initially be filled with chatter until you figure out how to turn it down."

She stared at him in semi-horror. Could he blame her? She didn't even comment anymore. In fact, she drew her lips between her teeth.

"You'll see." What else could he say?

The front door opened, and a flutter of movement behind him indicated Joselyn had arrived. Not that he couldn't scent her and feel her presence also.

"Hey," she said softly as she entered the room. She eased up to the side of the bed. "I come at a bad time?" she teased lightheartedly.

Isaiah didn't look her direction or respond. He watched Heather instead as she tilted her face to the side to meet his sister's gaze. She still didn't speak.

"I'm Joselyn. Call me Jos." She held out a hand and then nudged Isaiah with her elbow. "I think you can let her go now."

Isaiah wasn't as confident, but at least with his sister present, there were two of them to keep her from running. He released her hands, sitting back, but still trapping her torso.

Heather didn't take Jos's offered hand, though she did lower hers and rub her wrists as if he'd held her too tight.

He winced. The last thing he wanted to do was hurt her.

"Please tell me you don't believe all this shit your brother is spouting about bears guarding the house who want to take me into custody. If your brother escaped from an institution, you really need to call and have him recommitted."

Jos laughed. She tipped her head back and laughed harder than Isaiah had ever heard. She had to wipe the tears from her eyes when she finally glanced at him. "I love her."

Heather squirmed, attempting to wiggle out from between his legs, but all that did was make his damn cock harder. Even though she was seriously pissed at him and might never let him touch her sexually again, he couldn't control his body's reaction to her. "Get off me, Isaiah. Now. I'm tired of asking."

"Will you stay here? Listen to Jos?"

She rolled her eyes. "If it makes you happy and speeds up the process of getting you back into the loony bin, I'd be happy to speak with your sister."

He sighed, but he lifted his leg over her, leaving her trapped between him and Joselyn. Jos was tall and fast. She also had the advantage of standing. He knew she wouldn't let Heather run off. *She's a flight risk, Jos. Watch out.*

"I've got this." She cleared her throat and dove right in without hesitation. "I think it would help if I shift for you. If you see it live and in person, you'll understand better."

"Shift," Heather stated flatly. "Great. You too. Fine. Let me see." Sarcasm oozed from her lips. She hauled herself back against the headboard, tugged her knees up to her chest, and wrapped her arms around them in a protective stance. It was better than her running across the room, forcing him to have to tackle her again.

Joselyn took a step backward away from the edge of the bed.

"Try not to break anything this time, Jos," he muttered. "You really are more of an outdoor pet." The last time she'd shifted in the house, she'd knocked over a vase in their parents' cabin and then backed into a mirror on the wall. It fell to the ground and shattered. Good thing they weren't superstitious.

Joselyn glanced at him. "Really, Isaiah? You want to go there now? Or you want me to shift for your mate?"

He winced as she said *mate*, hoping Heather wouldn't freak out again.

But Heather didn't flinch. She simply glanced back and forth between the two siblings, probably planning a way to knock them both unconscious.

Joselyn took a deep breath and let it out slowly, her eyes closing.

Isaiah jerked his gaze from his sister to Heather, who narrowed her eyes. Slight movement next to the bed told him Joselyn was in the process. It would only be a matter of moments before she stood there as a bear instead of a woman.

He glanced toward Joselyn to watch her shift, wishing he could be inside Heather's brain to fully grasp her reaction. Jos dropped to all fours as her body filled out, her torso enlarging to take her Ursidae form.

It only took about ten seconds for Jos to shift, but it seemed longer as he imagined what Heather was thinking. Thick dark hair replaced skin and clothing as Joselyn's face reformed, her snout taking shape. And then it was done, and Jos sat back on her haunches in slow motion.

Heather gasped. Isaiah jerked his gaze to watch her shrink back toward the wall. And then she screamed and scrambled frantically to get by Isaiah, moving toward the opposite side of the bed. "Fuck. What the hell?"

He let her clamber off the bed, even though he would rather have reached out and hauled her into his lap. While she backed up to flatten herself against the far wall, her chest heaving, he climbed off her side and slowly approached.

"Shit," she blurted. She pointed at Joselyn. "There's a freaking bear in your bedroom."

"Yeah. I explained that."

She glanced at him for a second and then back at Joselyn. "You don't expect me to believe that's your sister. What sort of crazy magic act do you have going on here? It's impressive. I'll give you that. But why did you feel the need to scare me half to death in order to show me?"

"It's not an act, babe. It's really Jos."

"Uh huh. So, you practice some sort of witchcraft?"

He shook his head. There was no need to get impatient. She would catch on when she was ready. He couldn't blame her for being skeptical.

"Fine. If you guys are so good at tricks, make her switch back."

Isaiah sighed heavily and turned to face his sister. "Go ahead, Jos. Shift back."

She pulled into herself, lifting up on her hind paws, and shifted back in seconds. She grimaced the moment she looked toward Heather. "Sorry, hon. I wish there was an easier way for you to understand, but this is who we are."

Heather lowered herself to the floor, sliding down the wall until she sat on her butt with her knees drawn up and her hands threaded in her hair. "I'm totally in a coma."

"You're not, baby. You're just in shock." He kneeled about a foot away from her, but forced himself to keep his hands on his thighs.

"I'm so hot." She plucked at her T-shirt with one hand, drawing it away from her body.

"I heard that might happen," Joselyn stated as she climbed gingerly onto the bed and crawled closer to the other side. "How's your ankle? Mom said it was a pretty bad sprain."

Isaiah glanced down at her bare feet where they stuck out from under her jeans.

Heather did the same. "Hardly noticing it now."

"Figured that would happen too," Jos whispered. "We heal fast. You're already taking on our characteristics."

For several moments, none of them spoke.

Then Joselyn continued. "You want me to stay? I'm not sure what I can do, but I can provide moral support or hold your hand."

Heather continued to stare at the floor, not speaking.

"I want you to know that my brother is one of the best men alive. You're super lucky to have him. I know it's hard for you to grasp right now, but I'm sure there's a reason he lived thirty years before meeting the right woman.

"He doesn't believe in Fate as much as I do, but I believe sometimes people are put in our paths at just the right moment in time. For you two, that was today. And though I know he hates that you were forced into this life, that too was probably how the stars were aligned to ensure you two were together."

Isaiah watched Heather closely. She breathed more normally. Finally, she spoke. "If I wanted to leave here right now, would you let me?"

Isaiah held his breath. His chest ached, knowing she was hurting and confused and he could do nothing to stop it.

Joselyn slid to the floor and sat against the bed so her face was at the same level as Heather's, three feet separating them. "Nobody wants you to feel trapped. But we also don't want to see you hurt any more than you already are.

"If you walk out the door, four men will tuck you in their SUV and take you north of here to their compound in the Northwest Territories. I can't begin to imagine how long they would keep you or if they would ever let you leave. They don't know the answer to that yet themselves."

Heather whimpered, tucking herself in a tighter ball.

Isaiah spoke next. "She's right. You're safer here. Plus, it would tear me up for you to leave. Please stay. I believe the change is coming soon. Let yourself shift for the first time with me. If you still want to leave after you have a handle on it, I won't stand in your way."

She lifted her gaze to him. "You realize that makes no sense to me. You're asking me to stay in your house like some kind of hostage until I become a bear. Do you understand how ridiculous that sounds?"

"Yes."

"Until I become a *bear*, Isaiah." Her voice rose. She sat straighter, releasing her knees to throw her hands in the air. "I'm human, Isaiah. I'm not going to become a bear. And if for some reason I actually did shift, as you say, I'd have to assume I'd gone stark raving mad, and it wouldn't matter if I left with anyone out front or not."

He nodded. "I get it. I do. And I don't know what else to say to make you more comfortable."

Joselyn spoke again. "I'm gonna go now, but if you need me, Isaiah can reach me. I'll come right back. It's not far."

Heather nodded.

Joselyn stood, leaned over, and gave Isaiah a half-hug around his shoulders without making him move. "Just yell if you need me."

"Thanks."

She slipped silently from the room.

Isaiah lowered himself to sit on his butt on the floor. He said nothing, letting Heather be in peace for as long as she needed.

Suddenly, she moaned and stretched out her legs. "I'm so hot. What the hell do you keep the temperature set at in here?" She pulled herself to standing along the wall. "I need to change."

He jumped to his feet. "Why don't you put on something else? That's a good idea. Do you have shorts?"

"It's Alberta, Canada, in the winter. I didn't bring any shorts. But I do have tank tops. I like to sleep in them."

"That'll work."

She wandered over to her suitcase.

He followed close at her side and then stood at her back.

"Will you leave so I can change?"

"No. Heather, I'm not going to leave you." *Shit. Shit and fuck.* This sucked so badly.

She stood and spun around, holding the smallest swatch of fabric he'd ever seen.

Again, shit.

"I'm not changing clothes in front of you, Isaiah."

"I saw you naked two hours ago."

"Don't remind me. It's humiliating. And you're not seeing me naked again, so step out of the room and let me change." She pointed at the door.

He was still trying to imagine how difficult it was going to be seeing her in that tiny excuse for a shirt she held in her hand, let along naked. The tank top was probably worse than naked.

"How about if I give you one of my T-shirts instead."

"Why? How is that going to help?" She cocked her head to one side and narrowed her gaze.

"Because whatever you're holding in your hand is going to make my cock harder than a rock when you put it on. At least in one of my shirts, your body will be completely covered, and I won't be able to see every damn contour. Plus, you could take your jeans off. My shirt will hang low enough."

She flinched. "Fine."

Thank God.

He turned around, yanked open a drawer, and grabbed the first shirt on top. It was black. Even better. For his sanity. He handed it to her, reaching out as far as his arm would stretch to avoid pissing her off further by touching her.

She grabbed the shirt and then surprised him by turning around and hauling her own T-shirt over her head.

He swallowed his tongue when her bare back came into view. She hadn't been wearing a bra.

As fast as she could, she dropped her shirt, dragged his T over her head, and then shrugged out of her jeans.

He closed his eyes and took deep breaths. When he opened them again, she stood before him in nothing but his T, hands on her hips. "Whatever you're thinking, forget it. I can't believe I'm doing this, but I'm hotter than the third circle of hell. And I'm also thirsty. Can we at least get water?"

"Of course." He spread his arm out to indicate she should pass him. He would follow her to the kitchen. Surely she didn't intend to run for the front door and bolt out into the cold air with no shoes and nothing but a T-shirt. But he wasn't going to let his guard down long enough to give her the opportunity.

She headed straight for his kitchen with hardly a limp. Impressive how quickly she healed, even though she hadn't shifted yet. She went directly to his fridge, pulled it open, and grabbed a water. In moments she downed it. "I'm hungry, but I'm also queasy."

"Probably better if you wait until after you shift to eat."

She sighed and walked past him to get to the couch.

He watched the way her ass swayed, the T-shirt so long on her it nearly reached her knees. Maybe he should have let her put on the tank.

Suddenly, she bolted forward, running flat out for the front door.

Fuck.

He took off after her, reaching her in far less strides and flattening her to the door with his hands on both sides of her body before she could reach for the handle.

They were both breathing heavily as he set his chin on the top of her head. "I'm so sorry." He held her tight against the door, his body pressing into hers, his cock jumping to attention at her back.

She let out a soft cry and sagged against him, defeated.

He eased off enough to snake an arm around her waist and hold her against his chest, and then he lifted her off the ground, spun around, and headed for the couch. The T-shirt rose under his grip, but he forced himself not to look down. Instead, he swung her more fully into his embrace, tucking his other arm under her knees.

How many times had he carried her like this so far today? He could get used to it. He already was.

She started crying in earnest, her face tucked against his pecs.

His chest ached to know how much emotional pain she was in. He lowered himself onto the couch, held her tight against his body, and stroked a hand through her hair, dislodging the bun.

She grabbed the loose band and rolled it onto her wrist.

"I'm sorry, baby. So sorry." What else could he say?

She cried.

He let her.

It seemed like forever before her sobs turned to whimpers and she settled.

He lifted the hem of her T-shirt and wiped the tears off her face, forcing himself to ignore the fact that he was exposing her. "If I could make this easier, I would."

She squirmed, pushing on him suddenly. "Let me go."

He held her tighter. "Please. Don't fight me."

She wiggled her butt against his cock in an effort to escape, which only made things worse.

He gritted his teeth against the need to possess her.

"Dammit, Isaiah, I can't sit on your lap."

"Why the hell not?" He gripped her ass to keep her from rubbing so hard against his cock.

She jerked her gaze toward him, fisted his T-shirt in her hands at his shoulders, and tried to shake him. "Because I'm fucking turned on. Because every time you touch me, I can't think of anything except you fucking me. Because it's irrational, and I'm suffering from some sort of Stockholm syndrome or something. Because you already fucking turned me down once, and it hurt like hell, and it gave me a goddamn complex. So let me go."

He stared at her for a heartbeat, and then he ran his hand up her back and threaded his fingers into her hair again. He yanked her forward and pressed his lips against hers so fast, he couldn't stop himself.

Pure instant bliss. He lost all sense, drowning in her, exactly as he had earlier.

And holy mother of God, she softened. She still gripped his shirt, but her body leaned into his. She kissed him back as if her life depended on it. And then she swung herself around and straddled his lap. When her pussy landed over his stiff erection, he groaned and tugged her hair, pulling and pushing at the same time.

She was on fire, literally. And he broke the kiss to meet her gaze, not giving an inch, but needing to search her eyes.

The look she returned was filled with desire, desperation.

"I need to be inside you so badly it hurts," he stated, his voice more of a growl.

"Please. God, Isaiah, please. Stop talking about fucking bears and shifting and just fuck me. I can't stand it another minute."

CHAPTER 8

Heather couldn't help it. She couldn't stop this madness. She didn't want to. She had never been more confused in her life, but one thing was absolutely certain. She wanted to have sex with Isaiah more than anything in the world.

She didn't care if it was a horrible idea, if he was certifiable, if he was holding her hostage. She was drawn to him in a way that was undeniable. She burned for him. It hadn't let up for a moment since he'd backed off and told her *no*.

She ached for him while he straddled her body and held her to the bed. She even ached for him while his sister stood in the room yapping on and on about bear shifters and then performing an amazing magic act.

It boiled down to two possibilities—either it was all true and she was about to become another animal, or Isaiah's family could pull off the most monumental of all practical jokes. Either way, she still wanted to fuck this giant of a man in complete defiance of all logic.

What difference did it make? She didn't believe he was dangerous. Just deranged. Judging by the way he'd made her come so hard she saw stars earlier, she had no doubt he could fuck her into the next dimension. Hell, maybe she had already slipped into another dimension.

She had a one-track mind that insisted she get laid immediately. To hell with the consequences.

Isaiah abruptly stood, taking her with him. He spun around and dropped her on the couch. As he hauled his shirt over his head—finally—he growled out a command. "Take that damn shirt off."

She smirked as she lifted her butt and drew the enormous T over her head.

"The panties too, unless you want me to rip them off," he demanded as he lowered the zipper on his jeans and shrugged them over his hips.

She didn't want to miss a second of this revealing, but she managed to keep her eyes glued to his torso while she lifted her hips and wiggled her panties off.

A low constant growl escaped his lips. She doubted he was aware of it.

God damn, he was built. Every inch of his giant body rippled with muscles. And his cock…

She shuddered. If she were in her right mind, she would insist there was no way in hell he was going to put that inside her. But instead, in her weird state of denial, she wanted to feel every thick inch. *Right. Fucking. Now.*

When he was fully naked, his cock bobbing in front of him, he leaned over her, set his hands on the back of the couch, and met her gaze. The tension in his body was palpable. "I should not take you like this. You're not thinking clearly."

"Stop mumbling about goddamn animals and fuck me."

He grabbed her around the waist and turned her to land on her back on the couch in less than a second. And then his body was over hers, his lips on her mouth, his cock at her entrance. He held her gaze as he nudged her legs wider and pressed forward.

She was so wet and aroused she didn't need any foreplay, and he obviously knew it. The entire day had been foreplay. She needed to be filled. "Do it, Isaiah. I'm dying." She grabbed his biceps and held on tight, tugging him as if she had the strength to move him a millimeter.

His face was tense as he eased the tip of his cock into her channel. It was tight. It was going to burn for a moment, but she'd never been more sure of anything. She lifted her hips toward him as a long, slow moan escaped her mouth.

Isaiah thrust into her as far as he could.

She gasped, unable to breathe as he stretched her pussy so far it seemed as though she would split in two.

His face was a mask of pain, his eyes closed. When he pulled out and thrust back in, she screamed out his name. "*Isaiah.*"

His eyes fluttered open, and his face relaxed marginally as his lips parted. He lowered more fully on top of her, one arm snaking under her arm and behind her shoulder blade to fist the hair at the back of her neck. He didn't hold back, pulling almost out and thrusting back in. Over and over.

Words tumbled from his lips, disjointed. "Should. Not. Have. Taken. You." His face dipped to kiss her lips as he continued thrusting. And he spoke against her mouth. "Never. Going. To. Be. Able. To. Let. You. Go."

Her pussy clenched around him, her orgasm barreling to the surface like a freight train as he made that declaration. At that moment, she hoped to God he never did let her go. On a whimper, she came. Hard. Her pussy gripped his cock, milking it. Her vision swam. She couldn't focus on him. She was so hot. So very hot. And she never wanted him to stop.

Another orgasm built on the end of the first, destroying her. Maybe she called out. Maybe she screamed. Or maybe her mouth simply opened and no sound came out.

Isaiah fucked her faster through the second orgasm, his lips lowering to take a nipple into his mouth. He suckled it so hard it hurt, the pain welcome. Delicious. With a pop, he released the swollen bud and growled so loudly it was a wonder glass didn't shatter. He held himself deep inside her as pure ecstasy covered his face.

She trailed her hands from his shoulders to his face, cupping his bearded jaw in her palms, memorizing the look he had while he came.

When he was fully spent, he continued to hover over her, his arms shaking, sweat running down his brow.

She lifted her head to take his lips, and he lowered his face with hers to continue the kiss.

No one would know they'd just had sex with the amount of passion Isaiah had left over to kiss the sense out of her. He devoured her. When he finally pulled back, he nibbled a path to her ear and then down to the place where her shoulder met her neck.

She arched her head away to give him better access. He pressed his nose to the thin skin there and inhaled. His teeth grazed her skin like they had earlier, and then he also licked the spot once again.

His lips wandered back to her ear. "You're mine, Heather," he whispered. "Mine."

She shuddered. At the moment she wanted nothing more than to be his.

"Thank you, baby."

She giggled. "Do you always thank the women you fuck?"

He lifted his face to meet her gaze. "You say that as though I fuck a different woman every night."

She glanced down at his body, her hands weaving into the back of his hair. "You're the sexiest man in North America. Don't tell me women aren't lined up to get a piece."

He chuckled this time. "That's ridiculous. And even if they were, I'm no longer available, so they're wasting their time."

She rolled her eyes. "Whatever." One time having sex with her within hours of meeting, and he was willing to declare his undying love and devotion? Too cheesy.

He groaned as he slid from her sheath and pushed off the couch, taking her with him.

Cradled against his chest where she spent most of her time, she let her body go limp as he carried her through the house, down the hall, into the master bedroom, and through to the bath. He still held her as he flipped on the shower. And he still held her as he waited for it to heat up.

Then he smirked. "On second thought, I think we need it cold." Stepping into the enclosure and directly under the spray of water, he sighed.

She sighed also. The water felt amazing. She tipped her face back and let it run down her forehead and cheeks.

"Damn, you're sexy." He righted her so she slid down his body to land on her feet.

Her legs were rubber, however, and buckled the second her feet hit the tile.

Isaiah had her, though. He didn't let her go. "Easy, baby."

As she regained muscular control, he kept one hand on her back and reached for the soap. With amazing dexterity, he ran the bar all over her body. Her nipples stretched to painful peaks. When he reached between her legs, she spread them wider, willing him to touch her more.

He kissed her shoulder and ran his fingers through her folds. "You okay? Did I hurt you?"

She shook her head. "Amazing."

Her hair was a tangled mess all around her face and neck. As water plastered the long strands to her shoulders and the small of her back, she closed her eyes.

Suddenly, the world started spinning. She grew so dizzy, she had to grab his arms to steady herself. But it got worse. A tight ball in her belly squeezed, making her lean forward. She thought she might vomit.

The water was cool against her skin, but it wasn't enough anymore. She was burning up. With fever? She moaned.

Isaiah had a tight hold on her as she lowered to her knees, unable to remain upright. He shoved the glass door open, lifted her by the waist, and set her on the soft oval rug outside the shower. "All fours, baby." His voice sounded distant, like she was under water.

He must have reached back to shut off the water, but he didn't let go of her waist. His hands were all over her as he stepped over her body, let the shower door shut, and kneeled at her side. He stroked her back.

Her hair fell in clumps all around her face, sticking to her cheeks and her neck and hanging toward the floor. Was she going to be sick? She wasn't sure.

Whatever was happening to her was foreign.

"Let it happen, baby. Don't try to stop it." His words soothed from a great distance. His hand on her back made small circles. His other hand attempted to lift her hair from her face.

Something popped. A bone? It didn't hurt, but it resounded in her ears as if it came from within. A wave of pressure built under her skin over every inch of her body, including her scalp. Heart attack? Stroke? Aneurysm?

Would she die on Isaiah's bathroom floor? From the bear scratch?

The pressure mounted. She thought she would explode, her insides and brain matter splattering the bathroom. But it didn't happen. Instead a new sensation took the place of the pressure. It was a welcome relief. It consumed her just the same but wasn't as frightening. Soothed, she sighed, thinking she'd dodged a bullet by not vomiting in front of Isaiah on his bathroom floor.

And then all at once she felt a shift, like she left her body and floated away from it. Except she was still inside, but her arms wouldn't work and her legs were bent at an odd angle. She blinked at Isaiah to find him smiling broadly. "You're the most gorgeous creature I've ever seen."

She stared at him, opening her mouth to speak, only to come up short. What was wrong with her lips, her teeth, her tongue? She glanced down and nearly jumped when she encountered not her usual body, but that of a bear.

This couldn't be happening. It couldn't be real. People didn't suddenly shift into animals. Except she had. And she was clearly a bear.

Isaiah still had his hand on her back, only now he was burrowing it into her fur. "Amazing. Such a deep brown. And so damn small even in bear form. I'll never be able to let you out of my sight. Some hunter will capture you and take you to a zoo, mistaking you for a cub," he teased.

He wasn't funny, and she bared her teeth instinctively and growled at him.

He lifted both hands in surrender, palms out in front of her. "Kidding. You're perfectly safe. Want to see yourself?" He bolted to standing, took two strides to cross the room, and pushed the door closed.

Heather winced when she saw the full-length mirror in

her line of sight. Where it felt like she herself stood, there was indeed a grizzly bear.

Isaiah burrowed his hand in her hair and rubbed her back. "You're stunning." He sounded reverent, and he didn't take his eyes off her.

She lowered to the ground, unable to continue staring at herself and unwilling to face the facts. As soon as she closed her eyes, she drifted off.

CHAPTER 9

It would be a lie for Isaiah to not admit to himself he was scared out of his fucking mind. He sat propped against the headboard in his bed, stroking Heather's long, thick hair. She'd been asleep for over an hour. It was growing dark outside.

As soon as she'd fallen asleep, her body had shifted into human form without her knowledge. Self-preservation. She'd been naked when she shifted, and she was still naked.

He had at least put on a pair of boxers, and he couldn't take his eyes off her delectable body. She was still running too warm. Her skin was feverish to the touch, so he didn't want to cover her up. Curled on her side, her back was pressed into his thigh.

Every few minutes he blinked to make sure his mind wasn't playing tricks on him.

She was still there.

The Arcadians had made numerous attempts to communicate with him. He'd given them just enough information to keep them from busting the door down and then blocked them.

They were sharp. The entire council had abilities he would never comprehend in his lifetime. They could communicate over a much wider range, and they knew things instinctively. They had known the moment Heather finally succumbed to the transformation.

They wanted her. They were pacing. He could sense their unease even though he was blocking them. They were nervous.

Isaiah put them off by insisting she was exhausted and needed sleep. It would be cruel to force her to get in their SUV and leave the only person she knew in the area.

He'd argued every point he could think of. There was no cell service at his house, so she wouldn't be calling anyone. His home phone had been temporarily disconnected the moment the Arcadians arrived to ensure that wasn't a possibility either.

Since their main concern was her telling other humans about the existence of bear shifters, that fear had been put to rest for now by cutting her off from the world.

Yeah, he was scared. To death. He couldn't lose her. He wouldn't. The Arcadians could go to hell. But how was he going to accomplish this?

She was a free agent now. She could choose to join his pack or another pack or no pack at all. She could walk away and become independent. The problem with those options was that the Arcadians would never allow any of them.

That left one choice—binding her to him. And even then, he couldn't be sure it would be sufficient. Under any other circumstances, the Arcadian Council would never separate mates without due cause, but this was not your average everyday situation. There was no recent precedent for handling a transformed human.

Isaiah was living on borrowed time. He needed her to wake up. He needed her to let him bind them.

The trouble was, he would never force her to do such a thing. It would leave her resentful for the rest of their lives. She had to make that choice all on her own.

He took a deep breath.

She stirred, rolling onto her back. Her breasts were amazing, and he had to glance away and focus on her face to keep his cock from getting any stiffer than it already was. Full amazing tits with pink nipples that had been erect every time he'd seen them. He would spend hours worshipping her chest. At least he hoped he had that opportunity.

On a moan, she blinked awake. One second, she was confused with her brow furrowed. The next second, her eyes shot wide and she bolted to a sitting position. Her heart rate increased so quickly he worried she would faint. He could feel her pulse at every point of contact, and at the moment, her hip was against his thigh.

She spun to face him. "Oh God." She glanced down and then dragged a sheet up her chest. "Shit." She squirmed to break the contact. "I had a dream."

He waited for her memory to flood back.

"No. Shit." She lifted her gaze. "It wasn't a dream was it?"

He shook his head. "No, baby. Sorry." He *was* sorry. Sorry she had been put in this position against her will. Sorry for whatever she would endure as a result. Sorry their lives together as mates were starting out on such a rocky precipice.

He was not sorry he met her, and he would thank whatever God was listening for the rest of his life, too.

She set the back of her hand on her forehead. "I'm still hot."

"Yeah. I can't predict how long that will last, but you're not as hot as earlier. Your mind should be clearer."

"Not sure I want my mind clearer," she muttered.

He reached for her slowly and eased his arm around her shoulders, drawing her closer to his side.

She went willingly, crawling closer until she pressed her body along his torso. The sheet came with her, trapped between their bodies.

He breathed easier the moment she was in his arms.

"What happens now?"

"That's a good question. You have a few choices."

"Me?" She lifted her face and set her chin on his chest. "Doesn't seem like I've made any choices today. They've all been made for me."

"Well, not anymore. There are options."

"What are those?" Her soft body stiffened against him, her hand landing on his chest.

"Here's the thing, the Arcadians are still out front. They're restless."

"I thought they were waiting for me to shift. Why are they still here?"

"Because they're worried you'll tell someone."

She sighed. "I can understand that. How could I avoid telling anyone? At least my parents."

"Simple. You can't tell them. Never."

She pushed off his chest to sit straighter. "They're my parents, Isaiah." Her lower lip trembled. "Are you suggesting I cut them off? Never see them again?"

"Not even close, baby. Never. I'm just saying you can't tell them you've been transformed and can shift into a grizzly bear now. You'll have complete control over when and where to shift. When you're with them, you have to remain in human form."

She worried her lower lip, her eyes filled with sadness. A tear escaped. "The world I knew just imploded."

"Yeah. But think of it as exploding. It's just that there's more out there than you thought."

"Are there others?"

"Shifters? Yes."

"You mentioned wolves earlier."

He smiled. "You were listening."

"I got bits and pieces. Not everything. I was overwhelmed."

"Don't worry. I'll teach you everything you need to know in time." He lifted his hand to her head and picked up a lock of her hair to toy with it at her shoulder. It was truly amazing, gorgeous hair. So soft.

"You're assuming I'm going to stay with you. Do you think I'm going to drop everything and move in with you?"

He took a deep breath. "Ideally."

She shook her head. "No way, Isaiah. I came here for a job. I start in two weeks. I'm not going to move in with you. I need space and time to think. We just met this morning."

"Normally, I would support that completely. I didn't get out of bed this morning expecting to claim a mate today, baby. But you don't have many options. No one's going to let you return to your regularly scheduled life. It's too risky. Dangerous even for you."

"Dangerous how? It would seem I could fend off nearly any predator now." She forced a smile that didn't reach her eyes.

He sighed. "No. You can't. You can't expose yourself ever. For any reason. And you need time to learn our ways. The rules we live by. Plus, there's another problem. You're a gorgeous sexy woman with no pack and no mate. A rogue bear or even a member of another pack could claim you for his own if you were out wandering around alone in the world."

"They would just grab me? Are you not civilized?"

He inhaled slowly this time. It was so complicated. "We are. The percentage of bear shifters who have good hearts is higher than the human population. But there are some who are not. And they will scent you from a mile away, baby. Literally."

"Like that bear did this morning." She sounded defeated.

"Yes."

"You said I had choices." Her voice rose. "I don't hear you presenting many options. It sounds like I either go with the Arcadians and take my chances with them or move in with you. Those aren't really good choices."

"Actually, I seriously doubt simply moving in with me would appease the Arcadian Council. You would need to bind to me."

"You mentioned this binding earlier. What does it mean exactly?"

"It means we would be mated for life. I don't take it lightly. My people usually date the normal way, make informed decisions. When a couple is sure they're willing to make a permanent commitment, they bind to each other for life. It can't be broken."

"What if they want a divorce later?"

He chuckled. "We don't really divorce. And to be honest, bound shifters don't experience buyer's remorse. It's not in our nature. The binding itself alters our pheromones, drawing us closer than before. After the binding, it's unheard of for a couple to even *want* to part ways. It's powerful."

"Is it a ceremony?"

He shook his head. "No. I mentioned earlier, it's all about the bite."

"Right. The bite. How is that again?"

"When a couple makes a permanent commitment, one or both of them breaks the other's skin with their teeth and releases a serum through their saliva. It's a conscious decision. Other bites can and do occur among shifters from time to time, but not with the release of the binding hormones. Siblings bite playfully. Bears might bite in a fight. Jack also could have bitten you this morning instead of clawing you."

"And I still would have transformed."

"Yes. The difference is you would have become a member of his family, or pack as we call it, automatically. Since it was only a scratch, you were left without a family. You could choose to join a pack and become connected with them over time by immersing yourself in their world. But the only way to bind yourself with another bear is through an intentional bite."

"And you want to do that to me," she stated. It wasn't a question. She understood.

"More than anything in the world." He swallowed. "But never against your will."

"Why?" She blinked, uncertain. "I get that you like me. We have chemistry. Maybe we'll get along. But we can't know that for certain after a few hours."

"I knew it for certain before I ever saw you this morning, to be honest. Irrational as that may be even to me. It just is. And we would never know if we might not have gotten along because after the binding we just will. That's how it works. The attraction you've felt for me all day would increase a hundred times and hang around for a long time before diminishing."

She flinched, drawing back. She reached with her free

hand—the one not holding the sheet—and pried his fingers off her hair. "Give me some space."

He nodded, though it killed him. He set both hands in his lap and threaded his fingers.

He could smell her arousal though. It permeated the room. One point in his court. It was undeniable.

"I can't just marry you or whatever after knowing you a few hours and one really good fuck."

He smiled. His dick jumped to attention at the way she said fuck. "It was more than just a good fuck, and you know it."

"Okay," she shrugged, "a monumental fuck. But still a fuck. And just the one."

"We could do it again now and make it two if it would help," he half teased, lifting one eyebrow.

She giggled, the sound seeping into his pores and making him hotter for her. It was going to be a long night. A flush crossed her cheeks. "I'm not this kind of girl. I don't sleep with men I just met. Ever."

"Good to know." God, he wanted to hold her.

She lowered her gaze, fidgeting with her fingers in her lap. The sheet was now tucked under her arms. She shook her head after a few moments. "I can't do it, Isaiah." She lifted her gaze. "It's totally irrational. Not to mention I'm not sure I believe you. A bite? That binds me to you for life? It's preposterous."

He leaned forward, taking her chin lightly in between his thumb and pointer. "I'm doing everything I can to buy us more time in here. But the Arcadians won't wait forever. Eventually they're going to demand to see you. Eventually I'll be helpless to protect you. I'm just one guy holed up in a cabin in the woods with a woman they see as a threat."

"How would the binding make me any less of a threat?"

"It doesn't in theory. Not really. But taking a man's mate away from him is unheard of without a crime being committed. Those men out there know this. They're restless because of it. They'd like nothing better than for you to turn me down and go with them."

She didn't blink. Fear snuck into her features. The unknown. It was the same unknown for him. He had no clue in the world what the Arcadians might do with her. Hold her for a while until they were certain she wouldn't rat out their species? Lock her up forever to ensure that was the case? Would they go so far as to make it look like she'd gone missing or died for the sake of the human public?

Would they take her life?

Isaiah shuddered at that last thought. It remained always in the corner of his mind.

"You think they'll dispose of me."

"I don't know." It was the truth.

Another tear. It killed him to see her in such pain. Turmoil. But she had to understand how serious this situation was. Lying to her or sugarcoating it wouldn't do either of them any good.

"I'm not prepared to make such a permanent commitment to any other being, Isaiah, let alone someone I just found out is a member of another species I didn't know existed."

"You're a member of this species now too, baby." He controlled his voice and his emotions. What he wanted to do was haul her into his lap and wrap her in a cocoon. It was a constant thought running through his mind. He'd do anything to touch more of her. All of her. Every inch of her skin. He wanted to be inside her. Own her. Make her look into his eyes and know she was his. Safe. Protected. Loved. For as long as they lived.

"You said your people could speak telepathically. You said I would hear voices in my head. Why don't I?" she challenged.

He shrugged. "Partially because you're a lone bear without a family or a mate. At a certain proximity you'll eventually become aware of any bear, even a stranger, but it might take time. I don't know why you can't hear me yet. Like I said, this entire thing is unprecedented."

She inched closer to him again and then leaned her forehead against his chest.

He pushed his hand up into her hair again.

"I love when you do that," she whispered.

"Do what, baby?" He leaned down and kissed the top of her head.

"Get a grip on my hair. Pull it. Hold on to it. Tug my head back. All of it. I like it." She shivered after the admission. Progress.

He responded by gripping her head tighter, tugging her hair.

She moaned, the sound going straight to his cock.

"It's irrational, but I want you to make love to me again." She sucked in a breath and then spoke louder, still directing her words toward his lap. "I want you to fuck me I mean. Make me forget. Make it all go away."

He pulled her closer, wrapping his other arm around her shoulders. "It won't go away. You might forget for a while, but it won't go away. If you want to have sex, you'll never hear me complain. Ever. But afterward, the intensity will only be stronger. You won't be able to flush it out of your system if that's what you're hoping."

She lifted her gaze. "It's more like instinct. It's the only thing I know for sure. My brain is at war over everything you're telling me, but my body craves contact with yours." She squirmed. "I've never been this horny.

Even though we've had sex twice today, I can't get enough." She stiffened. "Okay, *I've* had sex twice. You've had sex once."

For a moment, Isaiah couldn't breathe. He could smell her arousal, but he was surprised she didn't have the strength to put him off and avoid acting on it. Was there truly some sort of connection between them that was already forming?

Her face flushed with embarrassment. She pushed away from him, dragging the sheet with her. "Jesus, I sound like a hussy." She closed her eyes and turned away from him.

Before she could crawl off the bed, he reached for her waist, hauled her back in his direction, and flattened her onto her back next to him. He tossed one leg over her torso and cupped her face. "You're not a hussy. Stop it. I promise you what you're feeling is perfectly normal." *Isn't it?*

He felt the strong pull himself, perhaps even stronger, but he forced himself to keep his dick in check to avoid pissing her off. As much as it pained him to admit it, he didn't think right that moment was a good time to take her up on her offer. Or request. Demand. Ugh.

He leaned closer and kissed her forehead, allowing himself to inhale deeply of her scent. Yeah, she was even more aroused now that he'd tugged her into his embrace. That didn't help his position at all.

Keeping himself from mauling her was his only goal, that and moaning out loud or adjusting his cock.

She blinked up at him, licking her lips. Her chest rose and fell with every breath. The sheet had slipped to expose the upper swell of her gorgeous tits. Another inch or two and he'd have her nipples in his line of sight.

She opened her mouth to speak, but he stopped her by settling his thumb over her lips. "Shh, baby. You make it very difficult to be chivalrous." He set his forehead against hers and closed his eyes. He needed help.

"Mom..."

"Isaiah? Honey? I'm here. You have me so worried. You've been blocking me all day."

"I know. I needed to be alone with my thoughts. I didn't want outside influence."

"I get that. She shifted, didn't she? I can feel it. I can feel her."

"Yeah."

"And the Arcadians are still hovering?"

"Yes. I don't know what to do."

"You have to follow your heart, son. And your instincts."

"My gut says to bind her to me right this second and challenge the council."

"I'm sure your gut is making itself known, but what does your mate say?"

He chuckled into his mother's head, holding Heather closer. "She's skeptical. Reluctant. And I won't force her."

"I've raised you right." He could hear the smile in her voice. "I know you'll do what's best for both of you."

"I'm scared, Mom. What if the Arcadians insist on taking her from me? What if they insist on taking her even if I do claim her as my own?"

"Then you go with them and don't let her out of your sight. They're reasonable people, Isaiah. I have to believe that. I force myself to assume they won't act rashly."

"I hope you're right. Mom?"

"Yes?"

"When did you know?"

She understood him without a lengthy explanation. "Immediately."

"Seriously? You knew Dad was your mate when you met him?"

"I did. And so did he. It isn't always that way. Falling in love *doesn't follow a strict set of rules. It just is. And I could tell your heart was leaning toward her the moment you stepped into the house this morning."*

"Thanks, Mom." He blew out a breath and cut off communication again.

"Isaiah?" Heather's voice came from far away, and he realized he'd been concentrating on his mother for at least a minute.

"I'm here, baby."

"You get this glaze over your eyes when you're communicating with someone else." She gave a strained chuckle. "Should I be jealous?"

He grinned and lifted his head to put a few inches of space between them. "Only if you're worried about my mom."

She scrunched up her face. "So you're saying that while I'm lying here begging you to have sex with me, you're talking to your mom?"

He smiled broader and shrugged. "Yeah, I guess that's what I'm saying. I needed a little moral support."

Her smile grew larger too. "I think I like that."

CHAPTER 10

Heather grabbed Isaiah's forearm where it rested at her neck and tipped her cheek more fully into his palm. Maybe some women would find it creepy that their man had a healthy relationship with his mother, but not Heather. She found it endearing. And frankly, they needed outside advice. If he had it easily available through telepathic communication, awesome.

"Did she advise you to sleep with me?" she teased.

He laughed. "No, but she advised me to follow my heart."

"And what does your heart tell you to do right now?"

"Feed you."

"Pardon?" She blinked. That wasn't the answer she was hoping for.

He scrambled over her body, straddling her along the way, and hauled her to the edge of the bed. Before she knew what he meant to do, she was in the air, tossed over his shoulder.

The sheet fell away, leaving her totally naked with his

hand on her bare thighs. "Isaiah," she squealed. "Put me down."

"Never." He clambered from the room and down the hall until he reached the kitchen. He set her on the island so quickly she was dizzy and had to grasp the edge of the tile surface with her fingers.

She wouldn't have fallen, however. Not with him steadying her with both hands.

"You need to eat. You must be starving."

He was probably right. If only she could think past the arousal that forced her to squeeze her legs together. She bit the inside of her cheek to keep from moaning or begging.

He moaned in her stead and tipped his face to the ceiling for a moment. "I can smell your arousal. It's potent and killing me."

"And you're choosing to ignore it why?" Soon she would develop a complex.

"Because you're vulnerable and just shifted for the first time. I don't want to influence your decisions. I want you to make them with a clear head."

"My head hasn't been clear since the moment you found me this morning."

He gritted his teeth before squeezing her thighs with both hands and continuing. "All the more reason."

"Maybe I'll be able to think more clearly if you take the edge off this insane horniness." She felt her cheeks flushing again. Since when was she the sort of person who would beg a man to have sex with her? She didn't recognize herself. And it was irrational for her to be having this conversation. But she needed him inside her again.

Maybe it was a result of the transformation she'd obviously undergone a few hours ago from a human to a bear shifter. She still couldn't fully comprehend that part of the day, but she did recognize the magnetic pull to fuck.

Was it Isaiah? Or would she feel the need to fuck anyone who happened to be around?

Isaiah flinched, gripping her thighs.

If she wasn't mistaken, she would swear he heard her thoughts.

He shook his head as if clearing it. "If I didn't know better... I mean, I do know better. I think I'm picking up on your thoughts."

She winced. "Bummer."

"Yeah, that last one was a bummer." He smiled through a wince.

"Not sure I like the idea of you being in my head."

"Me either if you're going to ponder sleeping with other men."

Lord, he *was* in her mind. "I wasn't exactly considering the option. It was more of a musing. I was wondering if my arousal is specific to you or just because you're in the room."

"Hopefully it's specific to me. I can't speak for you, but the way I feel about you isn't something I've ever experienced before." He set his nose on hers, needing any extra contact. "You're mine. I know it in my soul. I know it's a lot to swallow, but I'm going to be right by your side while you figure it out."

She shivered, her fingers reaching for his waist to dig into his hips. She leaned forward and put her lips on his ear. "No pressure though," she quipped.

He chuckled and leaned back, releasing her.

When he was touching her, she feared for her sanity. When he wasn't touching her, she wished his hands were back on her. It was a never-ending circle.

"Why am I not cold?" she asked as he opened the fridge and started pulling out containers.

He kicked it shut as he spoke. "You won't ever get as

cold as you used to. We run hot. And you're hotter than usual right now."

She tried to ignore the fact that she was naked in his kitchen. "Wait. There are several bear people outside you say?" She swung her head around in every direction, fear that someone would see her naked crawling up her spine.

He set his armload of items on the counter and glanced over his shoulder. "No one can see inside, baby. All the blinds are closed. I don't share."

That was a relief. "I don't share either," she felt compelled to add.

Isaiah set something in the microwave and turned to face her again. He sauntered her direction in his damn boxer shorts that left nothing to the imagination. She could easily see the outline of his impressive cock, not to mention his rock-hard chest and thighs.

His face was serious when he reached her, setting one hand on either side of her but not touching her skin. "I would sooner stab myself than cheat on you."

She nodded, a little shocked by his vehemence.

"I realize we hardly know each other, and it will take time to rectify that, but there are a few things you should know. I'm monogamous for one. Never doubt that. I'm overprotective. Can't help it. I'll probably smother you. And I'm dominant."

She flinched at that last word. It wasn't as though she hadn't seen evidence of his dominance throughout the day. The man was cocky as hell and bossy in all things. But hearing him proclaim it was another thing altogether.

He dipped his head toward her lap and inhaled long and slow.

She squeezed her thighs together, even though it did nothing to keep her pussy from leaking.

"I'm not sure what my favorite food was before today,

but now it's you." He spun around and headed back toward the microwave as if it were dire that he retrieve the food immediately.

The moment he opened the small door above the stove, however, she got a whiff of something delicious that helped get her mind off sex and direct it toward food. In fact, her stomach picked that moment to growl.

"Do you cook?" she asked to steer the conversation in a safer direction than her growing arousal.

"I can. Occasionally. But my mom made this stew this morning. My sister brought it over." He nodded toward the counter as he stirred. "Biscuits too. My mom's biscuits melt in your mouth."

Heather's mouth watered. "Perhaps I should put some clothes on so we can eat." The only thing she was wearing was a hair band on her wrist, and she plucked it off to pull her hair back.

He grinned her direction. "Clothing isn't a requirement for dining. At least not in the house while we're alone."

It felt like the two of them were playing a mind game. One got ahead for a few plays and then backed off and the other got ahead. She watched as Isaiah carried the stew and biscuits to the table and then grabbed two water bottles.

Feeling awkward, she crossed her arms over her chest as she watched him. Without a word, he headed for the couch in the living room behind her and returned a moment later with a throw blanket, which he draped around her shoulders.

He lifted her to the ground. "Better?"

"Thank you." She wasn't accustomed to being so openly naked with someone. Not that she had any issues with her body, but she was uncomfortable, and the thought of sitting down at the table with her chest exposed unnerved her. Apparently he caught that vibe.

He pulled out a chair for her, and she took it, tucking the throw around her front sort of like a toga.

"You're hearing my thoughts."

"Some of them," he agreed as he sat at the end of the table and began dishing out the stew into bowls.

It smelled wonderful and looked even better.

"I don't mean to pry. I'm trying to stay out of your head, but you aren't capable of blocking me yet."

"I'm not even capable of understanding how you're catching my thoughts, Isaiah. It's weird. I'm not hearing yours."

He grabbed her hand and squeezed it. "You will. You've only transitioned a few hours ago. It takes time to fully acclimate." He pointed at the food. "Eat. Then we'll talk some more."

The first bite made her mouth water for more, and she ate twice as much as she normally would eat for dinner. Then again, she'd had very little in the last two days, so she was famished. And apparently shifting into another species took energy. She shuddered at the thought. Had that really happened? If she put it out of her mind, maybe she could ignore it altogether.

"Tell me about your life. What do you do? Where do you work? Do you have other siblings besides Wyatt and Joselyn?"

He wiped his face on a napkin, took a long drink of water, and then leaned back. "My extended family has been in this area for over a hundred years. Some of us lived south of here, as far south as Montana until more recently."

"You lived in the US?" She was shocked to hear that detail.

He nodded. "My parents did for a while. I was a baby

when they moved to Alberta. But we still traveled some to Montana off and on."

"Why did your family move north?"

"Partly because the bear population in the US is dwindling significantly. Grizzlies are so endangered in Montana that it's no longer safe for shifters to inhabit the area."

"I read that there are less than a thousand grizzly bears in Alberta."

"That's true and far fewer in the Banff National Park. We're careful to avoid detection even this far south. Eventually we may be forced to move farther north again. However, now that the government has banned the hunting of grizzly bears in this area, the population is growing. Their numbers don't include my people. The counts they have are for full bears, not shifters."

"And you don't worry about hunters?" She shuddered. The idea of being shot to hang as a trophy in somebody's home made her blood stop flowing.

Isaiah shook his head. "We do. We're diligent, especially during the months when black bear hunting is legal. We don't want to be mistaken for another species."

She glanced around his cabin, needing to shake off the fear of hunters and change the subject. "Where do you work?"

"We own a microbrewery in town. My family started it thirty years ago. We opened one year before the Tarbens opened theirs, which did nothing to dampen the rivalry."

"You mentioned a feud. What's that all about?"

He leaned forward, setting his elbows on the table. "It goes back more than a century. And frankly, I think it's absurd."

"What? You don't speak to each other? You all live here right next to each other and no one has any

125

relationships?" That was intense. How sad. And irrational.

He shrugged. "I didn't say that." A wry smile lifted his lips. "We have relationships, especially among my generation and those who are younger. They're just clandestine."

She widened her gaze. "Sounds like Romeo and Juliet."

He chuckled. "No one has poisoned anyone or committed suicide yet, as far as I know, but it could happen."

"Have you? Had a girlfriend from the Tarben family I mean?"

He shook his head. "No. But my best friend is a Tarben. Hopefully you'll meet him someday soon. His name's Austin. And you need to keep that to yourself. I'm not kidding when I say it's private. No one knows about us. We're super careful, especially since his brother Antoine is a foulmouthed dick."

"Damn. That's awful. I'm sorry." She studied his wrinkled expression. It was unimaginable that he'd had a secret friendship for years, all because of some stupid family feud. "What started all this fighting in the first place?"

"Water." He sighed. "Namely who owned the rights to which fresh springs and rivers and lakes in the area. Things escalated when the Athabasca Glacier started to melt. Now we're suffering from a drought that will only get worse until there's a severe shortage of water in the area where once it was abundant.

"Since both families operate their own brewery, I'm afraid tensions will escalate. And it doesn't help at all that one of their own attacked a human yesterday." He grabbed her hand and rubbed the back of it with his thumb.

"Why would he do that if it's against your laws?"

Isaiah shrugged. "No clue. Maybe to stir things up? Or maybe he went crazy? I just pray he worked alone and no one in the pack knew what he was planning. If they did, we're in for a war."

She flinched, stiffening her fingers in his grasp. "Over me?"

"Yes. With relationships strained, our elders will be meeting with theirs first thing tomorrow. The only reason they haven't met yet is because every able-bodied bear shifter is out looking for Jack Tarben." He glanced down, inhaling deeply without meeting her gaze.

"Do you wish you were out there helping?" she asked softly.

"I wish it hadn't happened at all."

"But it did. And it wasn't your fault."

"Mmm." He made the noncommittal noise and then released her hand to stand and collect their plates.

"Isaiah…"

He loaded the bowls in the dishwasher and then turned around and leaned his ass against the counter, crossing his arms.

"Please tell me you don't blame yourself for what Jack did."

He lifted a brow. "I was there. I'm larger. Wyatt was there too. We should have stopped him. And now your life is a hot mess, forever altered."

She shoved away from the table and padded toward him, holding the front of the blanket together between her breasts. "You didn't scratch me. Jack did."

"I should have stopped him."

"You telling me you could have and you chose not to?" she asked, knowing that was where he was going with this.

"Maybe."

"Not buying it."

He shrugged. "Wasn't selling anything."

He was vulnerable concerning this issue. She hadn't seen him as anything other than strong and sure. He shoved off the counter and stepped around her, his hands fisted at his sides, not touching her.

"Isaiah…"

When he reached the front window, he pulled the blinds back and peered into the darkness. "I need to go outside and talk to them. They're pressuring me." His change of subject was not overlooked.

She approached slowly. "That makes me nervous."

"Not half as nervous as it makes me." He turned around. "Will you sit on the couch and not move while I talk to them? I don't want you to get involved, and I don't want you to come outside, no matter what."

She nodded. "Of course." She trusted him. Perhaps it was unfounded, but she knew in her soul he would do everything in his power to make sure justice was served on her behalf. She rounded the couch, took a seat in the corner, and curled her feet under her, surrounding herself with the blanket even though she wasn't cold.

She was shocked to find him making his way toward the front door without clothes. "Isaiah, it's freezing out there. You're wearing boxers."

He smiled wanly back at her. "I'll be wearing fur in a second." Without another word, he opened the door, stepped outside, and shut it behind him.

How long did it take him to shift? She would have liked to see him make that change. She'd only seen Joselyn do it so far, unless she counted herself. Most of that time she'd had her eyes closed in confusion.

What did he look like? She had to force herself to remain seated and not go peek out the window at what she assumed would be a group of enormous grizzlies angled toward each other in a standoff.

Time ticked by. She closed her eyes, jerking them back open when she was slammed with emotions. Isaiah's, not hers. She concentrated on him, opening herself up to a new sort of sensation she never would have expected to feel in her entire life. It wasn't that she heard his words, but she felt his tension. He was stressed.

And the other creatures out there were angry. Their frustration leaked into her head, also. For the first time since she'd been scratched she felt the weight of all this implied. She truly was in danger. From what? The unknown.

Restlessness made her jump up from the couch and head for the bedroom. She raced toward her suitcase with an urgency that was indescribable. She needed clothes on. That was as far as she could think. She grabbed jeans and a thick sweater and then hopped on one foot to tug the denim over her legs, not bothering with panties.

The sweater was jerked over her head seconds later. Socks. Shoes. She didn't breathe well until she had those items on her body. At least now she could face humans. Or shifters. It seemed urgent. Why hadn't she felt this urgency until now?

When the front door opened, she spun around, wringing her hands.

Isaiah's voice bellowed through the house. "Heather?" He raced down the hall until he rounded the door to the bedroom. He was out of breath and held on to the doorframe with both hands. "Jesus, you scared me. Why didn't you stay on the couch?"

She straightened to her full height, which left her incredibly dwarfed facing him. "I was naked, Isaiah. Chill. I could feel the tension outside. It scared the fuck out of me. I needed clothes."

He frowned at her, not saying another word. Finally, he sighed heavily and ran a hand through his hair.

She didn't give him a chance to speak again about her movement from the couch. If he admonished her, she might slap him. She wasn't a child. His frustration was palpable, however. Whether or not he was pissed at her, the Arcadians, or the situation in general was up in the air. She didn't want to hear the answer.

"What did they say?" she asked to divert his attention.

"They want you to go with them." His words were raw, deep, troubled.

"Where?" She swallowed. Would these men force her to go with them against her will? "You said north. How far north?"

"Damn far north, baby. Too fucking far."

"I see." She trembled. This couldn't be happening. There was too much to take in all at once. She slid down the wall to sit on the floor because her legs suddenly felt too weak to hold her upright. Her hair fell out of its messy bun in rivulets, so she reached up with one hand to tug the now useless band out and let her hair fall all around her shoulders.

Isaiah groaned, making her flinch. He took three quick strides to reach her and kneeled in front of her. "We'll figure this out."

She nodded, though she didn't believe him. "I could feel your stress, and theirs. I got scared," she murmured.

He didn't respond, but he did reach for a lock of her hair and held it in his palm. "So beautiful."

The world was about to end, and he was thinking about her damn hair?

As if sensing her aggravation, he dropped the curls and

took her hand, tugging her to standing. "Come on. Let's go back to the living room. Wyatt's going to come over."

"And you're mad I got dressed?" she asked as she watch him rush around the room, tugging on jeans and then a black T-shirt.

He gave her a wry grin. "No. I'm not mad. I was scared. There's a difference."

She shuddered. It was suddenly obvious he wasn't being a dick, he was genuinely concerned for her welfare. He'd expected to find her on the couch and freaked out when she wasn't there. She needed to be more cognizant of his feelings.

He needed to be more lenient.

"I get that you were worried, Isaiah, but I'm a grown woman. The situation changed. I freaked. I needed clothes."

When they made it to the couch, he took both her hands in his and lifted them to his lips to kiss her knuckles. "I know. Stick with me as I get the hang of this. It's new to me."

"What's new to you? I'm the one who found out about another species and became a damn bear shifter in a matter of hours. What the hell are you trying to acclimate to?"

"Caring about another being more than anything in the world."

She felt the stab to her chest as he spoke those words without releasing her gaze. He was serious as hell.

He squeezed her hands in his and set her knuckles against his lips again, holding them there. Not kissing them, just keeping them close.

She wasn't able to communicate with Isaiah in the way he suggested bear shifters could, but she was fully in tune with his emotions. And he wasn't lying. He was totally into her. Did he realize the feeling was mutual? Or that it scared her to death?

The front door whipped open, letting in a burst of cold air and making Heather nearly jump out of her skin.

"Sorry. I keep forgetting you aren't aware of someone's approach," Isaiah apologized.

Wyatt shut the door behind him and came more fully into the room. He held out a hand to take hers. "Welcome to the family."

She forced a smile.

"She's not really a member of any family yet, Wyatt," Isaiah stated.

Wyatt nodded. "Semantics."

"If you don't mind, I'll hang on to my free will for a while longer, guys." She released Wyatt and lowered unto the couch, grateful for the jeans and sweater she'd rushed to put on.

Isaiah gave her no space, taking a seat alongside her and setting his arm on the back of the couch behind her. "You'll keep your free will for life, babe. Please don't misunderstand."

"Oh, I think I understand perfectly. You need me to let you bind us permanently together for eternity so that four bears out front don't force me to go to God only knows where with them. Except you don't know if it will even work, and those men might take me with them anyway. I don't see how I have any free will at all in this matter. It seems to have shattered the moment your rival scratched my arm with his claws."

She was barely holding it together now.

"So, let's not talk about free will, shall we?" She rubbed her hands on her thighs, glancing from Isaiah to his brother, who had taken a seat in an armchair and was rubbing his chin with two fingers, a smirk on his face.

For a second she considered lurching out of her spot and slapping his smug look off, and then he spoke. "Isaiah, you have met your match."

She simmered slightly at those words, knowing he meant to taunt his brother instead of making fun of her.

"Don't I know it." He tucked his hand around her shoulders and set his face in her hair. "Baby, I'm sorry. Please forgive me." His words were soft, whispered. Sincere.

When he released her he spoke louder. "This isn't easy for anyone. There are no great options."

She twisted in her spot, dislodging his hand so she could draw one knee up and face him fully. "See, I don't have *any* real options. I woke up human, and now I'm being told I have to either move in with a man I met this morning for the rest of my life or get into a car with four strangers and take my chances that they don't incarcerate or kill me outright."

Wyatt groaned. "She has a point."

Isaiah rolled his eyes toward his brother. "I thought you came over to help."

Wyatt lifted both hands in defeat. "I'm trying. But I get where she's coming from."

She took the opportunity to continue. "I came here for a job. I start in two weeks. They aren't going to hold the job for me indefinitely while I'm in some sort of shifter jail at the North Pole."

Wyatt chuckled. "It's not quite that far north."

She shot him a glare.

He sobered. "You're right."

Isaiah inhaled long and deep. His eyes closed as though he was thinking, though she suspected he was communicating with someone else, and felt more confident about that when he winced.

133

She didn't like this telepathic ability already. Especially not if it included everyone but her.

Isaiah's face evened out.

"What?" she asked.

"Dad says they caught Jack."

"Good. Right?"

"Not for you. Nothing can take back what he did to you. What I *let* him do to you."

"Jesus, Isaiah. This again?" she asked.

Wyatt jerked, leaning forward. "Dude, you have to let that go."

Isaiah shook his head. "I wanted her. How can you be sure I didn't fuck things up to make sure I got what I wanted?"

"Because I know you. You would never do something like that. And I was there. Remember? I was standing right next to you. You did everything in your power to talk him down. And although he stood on his hind legs challenging you, there was no way to know he was about to pounce forward and go after Heather."

"I should have caught the vibe. I should have heard his intent."

Heather hated that Isaiah was taking so much blame on himself. She knew he wasn't to blame for any of this. If anything, *she* was to blame for hiking alone and getting herself trapped.

"I was there too, Isaiah. I didn't realize he was even interested in Heather. I thought he was furious that we crossed onto his family's land."

Good point. Maybe Wyatt would talk some sense into Isaiah.

Isaiah toyed idly with a lock of her hair again. She doubted he was aware he was doing it. "Maybe," he said, his body relaxing marginally beside her as he leaned his head on the back of the couch and stared at the ceiling. "I'm clouded with anger."

"I get that," Wyatt said. "I would be too. In fact, I am. Jack will be brought to justice. You know that."

"It won't change anything for Heather."

She touched his face. "It will keep someone else from getting attacked."

He lowered his face to stare at her. "It humbles me that you hold no grudge against me for what happened. You have to know I was compromised this morning. I was compromised from the moment I caught your scent before I started searching for you.

"I should have asked someone to help me instead of tearing up the mountain hell-bent on finding you."

She interrupted. "And if you had stopped to call for help and wasted even a half a minute doing so, what would have happened to me? Huh?" Her voice rose. "That Jack guy could have done much worse. He could have made me a member of his pack or even bound me to him as his mate."

Isaiah blinked. Finally, she had him on one point. Nevertheless, he kept it up. "I didn't pay close enough attention to my surroundings when I found you. I should have sensed Jack in the area. I should have stopped him. There's no excuse. I was blinded by irrational lust I don't even believe in."

Heather flinched. "You're talking about Fate again?"

"Or whatever."

She sighed. "Look, you bears haven't coined the market on falling in love, you know. Humans do it too. Are you so isolated that you don't know that?"

"Sure they do. But not in a day and certainly not before they meet." Isaiah eyed her with a narrowed gaze.

She swatted his leg. "Dude, stop it. Stop brooding. It's

getting old. Okay, so you're right, we don't usually fall in love before we meet, but there are definitely humans who connect from the moment they set eyes on each other. It's not unheard of for people to get married in days. It happens. Even in my species."

"Which, thanks to me, you're no longer a member of," he added.

"Isaiah, stop it," she shouted. She shoved off the couch and stood. "It's over. Done. We have more important things to worry about than how or why or when it happened. That jerk jumped out of the trees and scratched me, knowing full well what the implications were."

"I don't think you two need me here. Seems like it's under control." Wyatt rose behind her and inched across the room toward the door. She didn't have his strange powers, but she felt that much. "I'll just go," he continued. "Good luck." The door opened and closed behind her.

Isaiah winced. He hung his head again.

"Get over yourself before you piss me off. I need you to help me figure out what to do next instead of dwelling on what has already been done." She stood rigid in the middle of the room, crossing her arms over her chest and staring at him. If he didn't stop sulking, she would walk out the door and take her chances on the other side.

He jerked his head up, apparently having heard that thought loud and clear. His eyes went wide. "Baby, please."

"You know I have to make a choice. And you can hate it all you want, but it won't change the fact that I have to make it." She poked her chest with a finger. "*Me. I* have to make it. Soon. So, you can feel guilty about it some other day. You can discuss the merits of it next week. Right now I kinda need you to stop playing hot and cold and help me out here."

He swallowed, nodding. "You're right. What can I do?"

"Stop acting all chivalrous for one thing and make love to me. It's our connection. I don't care that we already had sex earlier. That was before I switched species and the universe tipped on its axis. Now I'm apparently a bear. A horny one. You want me to choose between you and taking my chances with the universe outside," she pointed toward the front door, "take your clothes off and make your case."

She had no idea what possessed her to act to absurdly brazen. Lust? Perhaps. All she knew was she needed to connect with him again. It would calm her and straighten out her head in some strange way.

One second he stood in front of her, frozen in his spot. The next second, he stepped over the coffee table and grabbed her by the biceps to haul her in for a kiss.

CHAPTER 11

Isaiah had no idea if he was doing the right thing or not. He was leading with his dick. But he could no longer deny the woman filling his home with her pheromones. It was a miracle he'd held out as long as he had.

She rose onto her tiptoes and wrapped her tiny arms around his neck, deepening the kiss in a bold way he was certain she'd never experienced before.

Whereas before she'd been timid, now she was climbing up his body, wrapping her leg around his thighs to get closer.

He bent his knees and swung her up in his arms without breaking the kiss. On memory, he easily found his way down the hall and into his bedroom. He kicked the door shut, not bothering with the lights, and eased her back to her feet next to the bed.

She was panting when he tucked his hands under her sweater and then whipped it over her head, separating their lips for the half second it took to get the material out of the way.

And then his fingers were on her jeans, unbuttoning

them, lowering the zipper, tugging the denim down her legs. "Jesus," he muttered into her mouth when he realized she was naked under both articles of clothing.

She fought to kick off her shoes and step out of the jeans without releasing his mouth.

His cock ached when her small hands roamed down his chest, swept under his T-shirt, and pushed it up his pecs.

He reached an arm over his head to haul the cotton out of the way. And then his hands were on his own jeans, disposing of them as quickly as possible. It seemed like the world would end if he didn't have her right that second.

Her arousal filled the room. She didn't need preparation. But no way was he going to fuck her without seeing to her first.

She moaned and grabbed at his arms as he lifted her and set her ass on the side of the bed. Without breaking the kiss, he leaned her backward, nudging her knees apart so he could nestle between them. When her head hit the mattress, he lifted his face.

Her lips were swollen and wet. Her eyes were glazed over with lust.

"You're the sexiest creature I've ever seen. I thought so the moment I saw you. I knew it this morning when I made you come. I was more certain of it when we had sex earlier. But now... Baby, there's no comparison to how I feel about you now that you've transitioned..."

She bit her lower lip and then released it and tipped her head back, elongating her neck. "Jesus, Isaiah, stop talking and fuck me. I'm burning up." She squirmed forward, her ass hanging off the side of the bed to increase the contact with his cock.

Her moisture rubbed over his length. So wet. Damn, she was amazing.

He stared at her, memorizing this moment for later—

139

the first time he took her as a shifter. She would be stronger. Her nails were digging into his biceps and she was undoubtedly unaware. He didn't care if she scored his entire body.

His gaze roamed to her chest. She was breathing heavily, her nipples puckered, her breasts swollen. As he leaned forward to flick his tongue over a nipple, she gasped, arching into him, grasping him tighter with her fingers. He loved the feel of her holding on to him like that.

Ordinarily he wouldn't let a woman control things to this extent, but he felt differently about this woman. His mate. The one he would take in every humanly possible way over the course of their lifetime. Was he usually dominant and in control? Hell, yes. That would not change. But she brought out another side of him, and he found he liked it.

A vulnerability that made him weak in the knees just looking at her.

He switched to tease the other nipple with his tongue, not wrapping his lips around the stiff peak but tormenting it with wetness.

She moaned, wrapped her small legs around his thighs, and pushed into him farther.

He had to stop her before he came prematurely. He set his hands on her biceps and trailed his fingers toward her hands, peeling them from his arms until he held her wrists. As he drew them over her head, she blinked. "Let me control this," he pleaded.

Her eyes still fluttered as though confused from passion.

He pressed her wrists into the bed. "Can you keep them here, baby?"

She didn't answer. Finally she shook her head subtly, perhaps without knowing.

He smiled. "You want me to tie them down?"

Her eyes went wide. "I want you to fuck me."

He shifted her wrists to hold them both with one hand, using the other to cup her breast and then pinch her nipple. Hard.

She screamed out. "Oh God." Her pussy flooded with more moisture. He knew because he could scent it.

Yes. Lord, yes.

"Can you keep your hands here, Heather?"

"I don't know." At least she was honest.

"If you touch me, I'll blow. And I want to enjoy you first. Need you to keep them above your head."

She nodded.

He grabbed a wadded corner of the comforter from behind her hands and set it in her palms. "Hold on to this. Don't let go." The bedding was trapped from the other side and under her body. It wouldn't give if she tugged. Perfect solution.

He tapped her wrists one more time and then lowered to cup both breasts and stare at them. Perfection. Larger than her frame would suggest. And yet he'd caught her not bothering to put on a bra more than once. She hadn't worn one the entire day, in fact. Did she do that often?

He nibbled a path down her belly toward her pussy, veering to one side to kiss her thigh and lick a path toward the center without giving her the relief she needed. She dug her heels into the bed and lifted her ass up toward him. Apparently her ankle didn't hurt at all anymore. Thanks to her shift.

He flung an arm over her hips and held her down.

He wanted to savor this first coupling with her no longer human. It was more intense than earlier. If she intended to have sex to prove she could walk away, he wasn't going to make it easy on her. Was it fair? Nope.

He licked along the outer edge of her lower lips, up one side and down the other while she squirmed and writhed beneath his hold. When he finally ran his tongue between her lips to taste her essence, she screamed.

God yes. She was his. She was totally his. Did she know it? Did she feel the connection with the same intensity as him?

He slowly dragged his tongue up until it flicked over her clit.

Shocking him, she came. Hard. Her tiny body shuddered with her release. He didn't even have to touch her again. Instead he got to watch the best show on earth. How often did a woman orgasm while her man got to watch with no direct stimulation? Never, he suspected. Or maybe it was a thing mates did because they were so connected.

"Isaiah. Damn you. Please… It hurts."

He winced for a moment before he realized she meant the need, the tight ball of driving need. Not an actual physical pain. He wasn't done yet. Lowering his fingers from the forearm pinning her hips to the bed, he pressed on the skin above her clit and pulled the hood back, exposing her.

She stiffened and moaned. "Oh. God…"

So fucking sexy.

With his other hand, he circled the little nub with one finger. It swelled beneath his gaze, pinkening. He lightly tapped it with one finger.

She dragged in a sharp inhale.

He pinched it between that finger and his thumb next, making her moan louder. Her thighs quivered.

So goddamn sexy.

He released the tight bud and sucked it into his mouth, flicking his tongue over the tip rapidly.

Heather was another woman. She wiggled beneath his hold, unable to break free. Her hands flew forward to land on his head, burrowing into his hair, grasping at his scalp with the tight grip of her fingertips.

He released her clit, jerked free of her hands, and grabbed her wrists. He knew she would be confused between the tight hold he had on her and the reverent way he kissed the inside of her wrists with such gentleness.

Her eyes met his and her mouth parted, her face red with arousal. "Isaiah?" She was questioning his resolve to tie her to the bed.

The truth was, he didn't want to break the intensity of the moment performing shaky knots. Instead he did the next best thing. He grabbed her waist and flipped her onto her belly while she squealed.

She wouldn't be able to reach for him in this position. Her hands landed at her sides, and when she scrambled to push herself off the bed, he set a palm on her lower back and held her down.

If there was a chance in hell he sensed she wasn't on board, he wouldn't restrain her like this, but her pussy creamed, filling the room with more of her pheromones.

His cock grew painfully impatient. He grabbed her under the knees, spread them wider, and settled them open to him on the bed, lifting her torso off the mattress.

She lifted her head and neck with her elbows tucked beside her face, arching her back.

More sexy.

With one hand braced above her bottom, he thrust two fingers into her, making her whimper. She'd come moments ago, but she already climbed back to fully aroused from being flipped over and restrained with a hand on her back.

She was so wet. He fucked her fast with those two

fingers, avoiding her clit until she writhed. He spun his hand sideways so he could reach her clit with his thumb and then lifted his gaze to watch her reaction to his next words. "Fuck my hand, baby. Make yourself come."

Her head lowered until her forehead landed on the bed, her chest still propped partially off the bed. A wild whimper filled the air. "Isaiah. Please."

"Oh, baby. You're so needy. Do it. Show me. Let me watch you come on my hand. Fuck yourself. Show me how you like it." He held his fingers steady inside her, his thumb at her clit. Slowly he added a third to entice her to move.

She grounded down on him, filling herself fuller. For a moment she pressed her clit into his thumb, rubbing back and forth, and then she rose up and thrust back down.

He watched as her sweet hands fisted the sheets at the sides of her head. Her hair fell in gorgeous messy waves to curtain her face and obstruct his view of her features. It didn't matter. He'd have his entire life to watch her come. This first time he asked her to do it for him, he knew it would be easier if she didn't have to face him while she masturbated against his hand.

Her breaths came in sharp gasps as she lifted and lowered her ass over his hand with no apparent rhythm. Sometimes she rubbed her clit for a while on his thumb. Sometimes she plunged on and off his fingers.

She was soaked by the time she lifted her forehead and moaned into the room again.

Her orgasm came slowly this time, the pressure around his fingers increasing with every thrust. Finally, the dam burst. She screamed out, arching her neck and fucking him faster.

Even after she was spent, she continued to fuck his fingers for long moments until she finally collapsed onto her belly, her legs straightening until they hung off the side of the bed.

Isaiah tucked one arm under her body and hauled her upright, not wanting her to pass out on him until he could wring one more earth-shattering orgasm out of her.

"Please. Oh, God, Isaiah, please…"

He held her back against his chest with one arm, her heavy breasts resting against his forearm. After brushing her hair away from her face so she could see, he reached between her legs from the front and tapped her inner thighs. "Spread open for me, baby."

She spread her knees wider.

He toyed with her clit to see where she was.

She grabbed his arm, clearly not too sensitive for his touch. Her body jumped back to attention.

Jesus. Fuck. She was so damn hot.

He grabbed his cock between her legs, lined himself up with her pussy, and thrust in to the hilt.

Her body went rigid. Her nails dug into his arm. Her mouth fell open.

When her head lolled onto his shoulder, he thought she might pass out.

"That's my girl. So sexy. You're going to come for me one more time."

She moaned, tipping her head farther to one side.

He set his lips on the tender skin of her neck and nibbled there, his instinct to mark her stronger than anything he'd ever felt.

"Do it," she mumbled.

He tensed, holding his cock deep inside her, his other hand flattened on her belly, his body no longer moving. He inhaled her scent, nuzzling the skin where her neck met her shoulders.

He wanted her to be his. He had no doubt in his mind

she was his forever. But not like this. She was dazed, in a sexual fog. Not able to consent properly. He wouldn't do that to her.

Instead he licked the spot, teasing them both.

"Bite me, Isaiah. Do it. God, just do it."

"No, baby," he murmured against her skin. "Not now."

He bent his knees a few inches and thrust into her again. The position made her tighter than earlier. He cupped her pussy from the front and frigged her clit rapidly.

She never stopped making the sexiest little sounds while his cock grew stiffer by the moment.

He had to hold his breath to keep from coming too fast. His cock was ready to blow before he got inside her. Now... He wasn't going to last.

"Isaiah," she called out.

That was it. He held himself deep inside her while his balls drew up tight and his cock released hours of pent-up need against her womb.

Her pussy gripped his cock, milking him. Her clit pulsed beneath his fingers.

Long moments passed. He didn't want to release her. But she was limp now. Sated. Exhausted.

He eased her to the bed on her side. "Don't move, baby."

He made his way to the bathroom, cleaned up, and returned with a wash cloth.

She whimpered when he rolled her onto her back and spread her legs to wipe away their lovemaking, but she didn't protest. And then he eased her body up the bed, settled a pillow under her head, and pulled the sheet over her. She was still way too warm for a blanket, but she would feel more secure with at least the sheet.

For minutes he stared at her as she fell asleep, her

mouth parting, her breaths evening out. If he could stand there forever, he would.

From the moment he'd set his lips on hers in the living room, he'd blocked every other voice from his head, but they seeped in now. Not his family. They wouldn't do that to him. But four alpha Arcadians standing outside his home pressured him to communicate.

Laurence's voice came through over the others. *"Isaiah, the woman has made the transition. We need to meet with her. You can't remain holed up inside the house forever."*

"Back the fuck off," he communicated to them as a group. *"Give her some time. She's confused. This is all new to her. Let me handle it."*

"Hours, Isaiah. Not days. We'll give you until morning." For the time being he was spared.

He padded from the room long enough to turn off all the lights, and then he eased onto the other side of the bed, hauled his sweet mate's back against his chest, and closed his eyes as she sank comfortably against him.

Two seconds later, he was out.

CHAPTER 12

Heather woke to the sound of voices. She blinked her eyes, confused about where she was for several heartbeats.

Warm arms held her tight.

Isaiah.

Shit. It hadn't been a dream. She was in his bed, and the faint light in the room suggested it was morning.

She'd known him twenty-four hours, had numerous orgasms in his care, and been fucked hard. So damn good that her pussy jumped to life even now.

Voices sounded again.

She tensed. The voices weren't out loud. They were in her head.

Isaiah didn't stir. He was fast asleep, his grip still firm under her chest.

Hot as hell.

Even in slumber the man held on to her.

"We just want to talk to you, Heather." The male voice was firm. It belonged to someone older. Maybe in their sixties. How long did bears live? She had so much to learn.

She remained still, knowing Isaiah would freak the fuck

out if he thought she was talking to these people. *"Go ahead. I can hear you."*

Her communication must have been successful because she could feel as well as hear the relief in the man's tone. *"My name is Laurence. I've come from the Arcadian Council. Not sure how much you know about us, but we're the governing body of North America."*

"I've heard some of the details."

"We'd like to meet with you. Perhaps you would be so kind as to come outside or let us in?"

"I don't think that's a good idea yet. I'm not even out of bed."

"We mean you no harm, but it's our job to ensure your safety and that of those around you."

She could read between the lines. It was their job to make sure she told no one about their existence. Her instinct told her the man meant what he said, but since this was her first time communicating with someone telepathically, she needed to be leery. She couldn't read his body language or his facial features. That left her at a disadvantage.

There was no way she could honor the man's request, anyway. If she moved a muscle, Isaiah would wake and haul her deeper into his embrace.

"We understand your reluctance, and I don't blame you a bit. This is all new to you. But please consider our position. Our task is to maintain the concealment of an entire species. We don't take this lightly."

"I understand completely, and don't take offense when I tell you I'm not ready to meet with you yet. I'm still acclimating. I hardly understand what has happened to me."

"We can help with that transition."

"Maybe you can. But I have no way to know where your interests really lie, so with all due respect, give me more time. You know there's no threat from me as long as I'm inside Isaiah's

home. I don't have any way to make a phone call. Give me more time."

"Perhaps we could set a time?"

"Be careful, sir. Don't place ultimatums on me. You know better than I do how infuriated Isaiah will be if he finds out. Just as you also must realize I can't keep my thoughts from him. I have no understanding of your blocking skills, and this is my first real communication."

It was amazing even to her how calm she managed to remain during the entire discourse, considering she should have been jumping on the bed and glancing around to find the source of the voices.

She felt stronger today. One day and already she had a better grip on her new reality.

"Please, reach out to us soon. We grow weary of waiting."

Interesting choice of words, and she chose not to respond.

Lips hit her neck, nibbling the spot where he should have marked her last night. Lust raced down her body the second he licked that tender skin. How long had he been awake? Or at least alert.

"I'm proud of you," he whispered.

Okay, long enough.

"How much of that did you catch?"

"All of it."

She smiled slowly. "How long have you been awake?"

"About ten minutes longer than you." His voice was still low, gravelly with sleep. "Best sleep of my life too, I might add."

"Hmmm. I concur. I don't think I've ever slept that soundly."

"You needed it."

"Why didn't you bite me?" She twisted her neck to see his face.

"You weren't ready."

"How could I be more ready?"

He smiled that slow sexy smile that made her pussy jump to attention. "Making a decision to be forever bound to another shifter shouldn't be done in the heat of intense sex, Heather. You'll make the choice when the time is right, preferably not while my dick is inside you."

"I find I like you inside me."

"And I agree. Sweetest spot on earth, but not going to sink my teeth into your neck while you're in the throes of passion."

She closed her eyes. "What do we do now?"

He kissed the top of her head and spun her so that her chest flattened against his as he rolled onto his back. "Eat breakfast."

She giggled. "Hardly what I meant."

"One thing at a time then." He narrowed his gaze at her, and his lips parted as though he had something else to say but was reluctant. "I might regret telling you this, but the binding can go either way, or both for that matter."

She cocked her head. "What do you mean?"

"I mean I'm not the only one capable of binding us. You could do it too. We could also do it at the same time or one after the other in theory."

She smiled slowly. "So you're saying I could sink my teeth into you if I wanted, even if you didn't agree to it?" She knew she would meet no resistance, but she wanted to make sure she understood correctly.

He rolled his eyes. "Like I said, in theory."

"And in practice? You mean usually the male claims the female?"

"Probably in most instances, although modern couples often both participate." He set a hand over his neck and rubbed it. "Please don't get any ideas. You do not have the first clue about your strength. I would hate to bleed to death because you sank your teeth into me too far."

Now she giggled. "I think I like this information."

"Yeah, figures you would."

"If you didn't want me to know, why did you tell me?"

He kissed her nose. "I'll never keep anything from you. We'll be equals in all things, except perhaps the bedroom." He winked.

"Bossy sex fiend."

"Don't you forget it. And if you didn't get off on it, I wouldn't do it."

He had her on that. She definitely got off on his brand of sex.

"Let's get some breakfast and see how our guardians are doing this morning."

She lifted to sitting. "Did they stay out there all night?"

"I'm positive, though they probably took turns sleeping."

"It's cold at night." She shivered. She'd spent the previous night outside alone under a Mylar blanket. She should know.

"Not to them. They're bears, babe. This is nothing."

"Right." She scooted off the bed and reached for one of Isaiah's T-shirts. Then had a different idea. "Mind if I take a shower first?"

"Of course. Go right ahead. As long as you don't mind if I watch."

"Be my guest."

"We'll never make it to the kitchen," he muttered under his breath.

She was sharper this morning, however. Nothing got by her. She realized she didn't need his verbal communication any more than she needed the four men outside to speak directly to her. *"I'll turn the water on,"* she communicated as she entered the bathroom.

"Excellent."

She spun around to see his face, filled with pride and awe. "Why couldn't I communicate with you last night?" she said out loud.

"I guess your body wasn't done transitioning. And don't get me wrong. You're only able to communicate with me because we're in close proximity, same as the council members outside. Distance weakens the ability incrementally, unless the person is your mate or a close family member."

She leaned into the shower and turned on the water. "In other words, I need to stay close to you for the time being."

"If you want to hear my thoughts yes." He reached past her to test the water with his hand, and then he stepped inside, taking her with him.

"I thought you were going to watch."

"I am, from super close."

Isaiah had just set heaping plates of omelets and hash browns on the table when a knock sounded at the door. He sighed and pointed at the food. "Start eating. I'll talk to him."

"Who? Him who?" she asked as she took her spot. She hadn't felt the presence of another being. It unnerved her. On the other hand, until the person was standing at the door, neither had Isaiah. Why?

"Laurence. The council member you communicated with earlier." He set a hand on the doorknob. "He blocked me until he was at the door. He's powerful. Be right back."

Isaiah opened the door but then disappeared through it so fast she didn't get a chance to see the other man's face. She did notice he was as tall as Isaiah, if not taller. Were all the bear shifters so damn huge?

The omelet smelled amazing, and she was once again starving, so she picked up her fork and dove into it.

Isaiah returned in less than a minute and took a seat next to her. "He wants to meet with you."

"I know. He told me that himself."

"Yeah. Well, he's smart enough to know he has to go through me to get to you. Especially after the way you spoke to him earlier." Isaiah smirked as he picked up his fork. "He was feeling you out, trying to determine how strong a personality you were and what you might be willing to do behind my back."

"Which is nothing. He gets that right?"

Isaiah leaned across the table and kissed her lips. "Yeah. He's clear." He tore into the food, moaning around the first bite. "Breakfast is my favorite meal."

Heather had to agree, especially if she was going to frequently benefit from his culinary skills. She finished everything on her plate before him, considering the head start. And then she leaned back and sipped the cup of coffee he'd made with the perfect amount of cream and sugar.

"You didn't finish telling me what you told Laurence."

"That I'd talk to you, and we'd think about it."

"You're stalling."

"Bet your ass." He set his fork down and sipped his own coffee. Black.

"You're waiting on me."

He shrugged. "I'm not going to rush you if that's what you're asking."

"But your entire species is waiting on me."

"Don't look at it that way. They can go screw themselves. No one's asking them to wait outside as if you were about to deliver the savior."

She shuddered. "Speaking of which…"

He eyed her speculatively, grinning. "This ought to be good. Can't wait to hear what crept into your mind to follow a reference to the birth of Christianity." He snapped his fingers. "Oh, right. Religion. You want to discuss religion? Let me guess, you're Christian, and you want to know how I feel about it?"

She tipped her head, running her thumb along the rim of her coffee mug. "That hadn't occurred to me at all, but now that you mention it…"

"We don't consider ourselves members of any modern religion as you know it. Though some shifters have picked up on one faith or another, most of us believe in something a bit more broad, like Mother Nature and a higher presence."

"That sounds lovely."

"I'll tell you more about it one day." He leaned forward. "If that wasn't your aim, what were you going to ask?"

"You mentioned the virgin birth, and it reminded me we haven't used condoms."

He grabbed her hand over the coffee mug. "Ah. Right. We don't have the same issues as humans. We don't carry diseases, and we can't get pregnant as easily. When you're ovulating, I'll know immediately. I'll scent it on you. Bears make a decision together whether or not to tempt fate during that season."

"Season? Are you saying I won't ovulate monthly anymore?" She sat up straighter. First enormous bonus to switching species.

He shook his head on a chuckle. "No, you won't ovulate monthly anymore. Several times a year, but not twelve."

"Damn. That's nice."

"I wouldn't know."

"But it's super convenient that you don't use condoms."

He shrugged. "Again, never bought them myself."

"Seriously? Never. You never needed them?"

He shrugged. "Some guys use them when they have a relationship with a human. It's easier than explaining why they don't need them, which is forbidden of course."

"But you never have?"

He reached across the table, cupped the back of her head, and hauled her face close to his. "The first time I had sex with a human was yesterday."

She gulped. Damn.

"And I've never slept with an ovulating bear shifter. Too risky."

Her gaze widened. "Every few minutes I'm reminded that I've slipped into a different dimension."

He frowned. "I hate for you to feel like that. Although shifters have a different background and unique abilities, I want you to realize that in many ways we're exactly like humans. We're often integrated in regular society. We have regular jobs and lead mostly normal lives."

"Except you can talk to each other from a distance without cell phones, you don't carry regular diseases, you have unimaginable sexual stamina, oh and let's not forget your ability to shift into a huge animal." Her voice rose as she finished. Her stress level was through the roof.

Isaiah squeezed her neck. "Babe, one day at a time. I'm right by your side. We'll figure out the details together."

She nodded. At least if she had to get scratched by a rogue bear shifter in the woods, someone had shown up to sweep her off her feet and do his best by her. She shuddered to think what might have happened if Isaiah hadn't arrived when he did and she'd been kidnapped by Jack Tarben.

Would he have bitten her and turned her into not only a bear but his mate?

On the other hand, perhaps if Isaiah and Wyatt hadn't shown up when they did, none of this would have happened. Perhaps Jack only attacked her out of spite toward the Arthur family for stepping on his family's land.

On the flip side, if Jack had been estranged from his family at the time he scratched her, maybe his intentions had nothing to do with geographical boundaries and everything to do with mental instability.

"I can hear your thoughts, baby," Isaiah whispered, leaning closer until their faces were inches apart. "We can't do anything about the past, and we may never know what would've happened if circumstances had been different. We have no choice but to focus on the future."

At least he was coming around to a new way of thinking. Hopefully he was done blaming himself for Jack's actions.

She nodded, inhaling deeply of his scent at such close proximity that she had to clench her thighs together again. If they hadn't gotten dressed after their shower in order to eat like civilized people this morning, there was every chance she would swipe the dishes off the table and insist he fuck her again right there.

CHAPTER 13

Isaiah grinned. He looked like he was about to act on her mental suggestion when suddenly the front door busted open. Cold air rushed across the room, and Isaiah released her neck to spin around. The door swung inward awkwardly on its hinges.

Heather screamed, scrambling out of her kitchen chair and backing up against the far wall. What the hell? When would her life be back to some semblance of normal?

Isaiah jumped to his feet, putting himself between her and the door. "What the fuck?"

"We need to get her out of here, Isaiah. We're out of time. We need to leave. Now."

She recognized the voice as the one in her head from earlier. Laurence. Fear crawled up her spine, gripping her around the chest.

"Like hell. We had an agreement. She's not hurting a soul. You were supposed to let her acclimate. I'm not letting you take her."

"There's no time to argue about this anymore, Isaiah. The time for that is past. Dozens of our kind are on the way here. They'll be here in minutes. They'll surround the house, and they won't be as patient and kind as we have been. Let her go with us. Now."

Isaiah backed up, reaching behind with one open palm.

She grabbed it and flattened herself against his back. She saw nothing, hidden nearly entirely from view.

"She's not prepared to shift on demand and run long distances, Laurence. She's only shifted once so far. She has no experience."

"We'll take the SUV."

A heartbeat of silence. "I swear to God if you're lying to me…"

"I have no reason to lie. Now, let her go. For both your sakes. I'll have her get in touch with you when we're at a safe distance."

"Like hell you will. No fucking way am I letting you take her without me. Are you high?"

Thank God. Heather's adrenaline was pumping hard. At least he didn't intend to send her away alone. She could feel the presence of others in the house now, and she eased to one side to peer around Isaiah. Four men. All in their sixties. All standing with their feet planted hard. Hiking boots. Cold-weather jackets. Jeans.

"You need to stay here," Laurence said to Isaiah. "Make a statement. Make it believable. Keep those who would wish her harm from following us."

Isaiah chuckled sardonically. "You *have* lost your fucking minds."

Laurence gritted his teeth. "Isaiah, I'm warning you. If you want her to stay alive, you need to let us take her. Catch up later. I don't care what you do, but she's dead if she stays here. And if you don't remain behind to talk these people down, they'll continue to hunt her until they catch up. We're outnumbered.

"They must have gathered from several provinces and converged to get here all at once. I can't get a handle on how many there might be in the mob. But they're angry. Furious. And dangerous. The vibe I'm feeling is ominous, Isaiah."

Isaiah gripped her hand tighter.

She couldn't breathe. But she did believe this man. God help her if she was wrong. But she believed him. "I'll go." She rounded Isaiah's body and stood at her full height. "I'll go," she repeated louder. She yanked on her hand, but Isaiah didn't release her.

She set her free hand on his chest. It was pounding. "We don't have a choice, hon. If they're right, you'll never forgive yourself. These are your leaders. You need to trust them."

He lowered his gaze to hers. His face was hard. Severe. Anxious. And filled with a love she never expected to feel from a man in her life.

If there was enough time, she would force him to claim her as his, right that second. Bind them for eternity. But there wasn't time. He'd have to catch up and do it later. For now, she needed to trust these men and go with them.

She watched a piece of his heart shatter in his eyes as he released her hand. He wrapped an arm around her body, hauled her to his chest, and kissed her soundly. "Be fucking careful, baby. Please. I'll be there as soon as I can put these idiots off."

She nodded, wiggled out of his embrace, and rushed toward the open door. Two of the men ran with her. One of them jerked open the back door of an SUV and lifted her into it without a word. He slammed the door and climbed into the front seat.

The SUV sped away before she could grab her seatbelt. She turned around to look out the back window. The two men who'd been in the house were no longer in sight. In their space stood two giant grizzly bears. They were staying behind with Isaiah. That was a good sign.

For several minutes, neither man in the front seat spoke. They ignored her entirely while Laurence drove and the passenger next to him twisted around to watch out every window. He grunted several times, but rarely said a word.

It took Heather a minute to realize he was communicating with Laurence telepathically. And blocking her.

She said nothing, holding on to the door with one hand and gripping the seat next to her with the other. The SUV was moving fast. Too fast for the windy mountain roads. She assumed that the approaching mob was in bear form, but realized no one had specifically said that.

Finally, after about fifteen minutes, they emerged onto a highway and headed north. Laurence slowed the SUV to a more reasonable pace, and his hands lost a little of their white-knuckled death grip on the steering wheel.

Heather exhaled slowly, closing her eyes and tipping her face toward her lap. She needed to focus and pay attention to her surroundings at all times. When she reached out with her mind, she couldn't feel Isaiah, or anyone else for that matter, including the two men in the car with her.

The stranger in the passenger seat cleared his throat.

She lifted her face to find him twisted around to stare at her. "I'm Charles. We'll have you someplace safer as fast as we can. Thank you for your trust."

She nodded. No way was she going to fully let her guard down.

"I know you're leery. Understandable. I can't blame

you. But I want you to know we mean you no harm. We're just protecting our species. You understand."

She nodded again.

"And I need to ask you a favor. It would help if you attempted to shut your mind down. Don't reach out to anyone. Don't try to make contact with a soul, including us."

She lifted a brow, her fingers gripping the door tighter.

He shook his head. "Don't misread me. I'm asking this of you for your protection. When you try to contact others, it leaves you open and vulnerable. We don't want anyone to find us while we attempt to dispel the crowd and convince them their fears are unfounded."

She pursed her lips, uncertain if she should trust this man. Or anyone, for that matter.

He sighed. "Again, I understand your mistrust. I would feel the same in your shoes, but here are the facts. You're a lone bear with no pack. That means you can't communicate with anyone at a distance, not even Isaiah. The only shifters you could reach out to would have to be in close vicinity, and willing." He narrowed his gaze.

"And you're blocking me," she added.

"We're with the Arcadian Council. We block everyone. We have the power to do so. No being is permitted to see inside our psyche without permission."

It made sense. "I see."

"So every time you make an attempt, anyone in the area can feel it. It makes you vulnerable."

It also keeps me from being potentially kidnapped by two strangers.

He chuckled, having read her thoughts. "Fair point. You'll have to take our word for it, or we'll be at risk every step of the way."

"I'll concede that point, for now. But in return I would

appreciate if you'd give me updates on what's happening. I'm at a distinct disadvantage."

"Agreed."

～

Isaiah had never been more nervous in his life. The mate he should have already bound himself to was not only gone, but without the binding, he couldn't contact her.

On top of everything else he needed to deal with, he now had dozens of bear shifters headed his way with probable thoughts of murder on their minds.

He stood on the front porch in human form, arms crossed, feet spread in a wide stance. The two members of the Arcadian Council who had stayed behind were Henry and George. They stood on the ground at the foot of his porch steps, each with a stance that matched his own. After a few minutes of scenting the area in bear form, the two of them had shifted to human.

It had shocked him when they didn't get into the SUV with Heather but soothed him at the same time. If two were willing to stay behind and face this tense situation at his side, there was hope he had not been played.

"Three minutes out," Henry stated. His abilities were more developed than Isaiah's would ever be.

Isaiah braced himself for the unknown. Word had apparently spread fast that a human had been transformed. What did this mob want? Isaiah needed to prepare for the worst. If they expected to eliminate his mate, they would never succeed. Not on his watch.

With every fiber of his being, he knew Heather was his. The fact that they hadn't taken the final step to make that truth a reality was simply semantics in his eyes. He would never let anything happened to her, if he had to spend the rest of his life on the run.

In his peripheral vision he spotted several bears bounding into the clearing in front of his home. His hackles rose as several more appeared from the other side. And then he took a deep breath as relief washed through him. His own family. Among them were his mother, father, brother, and sister. But also present were at least a dozen cousins, aunts, and uncles.

He'd been distracted enough inside his head not to notice their approach. He needed to get his head out of his ass, stop feeling sorry for himself, and pay more attention to his surroundings.

As his family surrounded the front porch of his cabin, they turned to face the clearing, their postures rigid. That he hadn't thought to expect their arrival in support of a key member of the pack was an obvious sign he wasn't thinking clearly.

"*Son.*" His father spoke into his head as he glanced toward him.

Several of his closest cousins did the same, nodding in his direction, but remaining in bear form to face whatever was headed their way.

A thick tension filled the air. Not a single branch rustled in any direction. The stillness was daunting, nature's way of announcing the arrival of an enemy.

When they came into view over the crest of the clearing, Isaiah permitted himself one moment of fear before he chased it away and honed in on every sense he had to feel out the emotional sentiments of the arriving crowd.

Henry and George calmly stepped between the enormous bears in Isaiah's family to reach the other side of them and put themselves between the unknown and the Arthur pack.

In human form they both lifted a hand in the air to stop the approach of the leaders of the assembled grizzlies.

Henry spoke first in a booming voice that made the land around them vibrate with its force. He didn't bother with telepathy. "Stop where you are and state your intentions."

The front line of shifters came to a halt in the face of the two members of the Arcadian Council. Several men shifted and stood in human form to face their elders.

One of them stepped forward from the group and stopped three yards from Henry. "We heard there was a human conversion. We've come to ensure the council is taking appropriate measures to secure the safety of our species."

Henry didn't flinch. "You doubt the Arcadian Council?" he bellowed.

The front man flinched but held his ground. "We're merely here to seek information, sir." He glanced around, lifting his nose to the air. "I sense the woman is not here. You've moved her. Please, tell us your intentions."

Henry nodded. "You yourselves have done more to put our species in danger than the one innocent woman who was transformed against her will. She was safe here, peacefully learning our ways under our supervision until you forced our hands with your irrational mobilization. Storming from miles away, uniting as you have, tells me you folks are led by an unfounded fear.

"That you would allow yourselves to be seen by countless humans by swarming across the land gives me cause to arrest all of you and have you sent to the Northwest Territories for questioning. How do you explain yourselves?"

A second man stepped forward. "Sir, we mean no disrespect."

Henry took another step forward also, closing the gap between him and the newly appointed speaker. "You disrespect my authority and that of the entire Arcadian Council by your presence. You have shown me that you doubt the council's ability to make decisions. You have made fools of yourselves. And I'll report each and every one of you to the entire council upon my return." He glanced around the group.

Isaiah shuddered to realize Henry was easily memorizing every single being who had come to the clearing, and there were at least three dozen. Most of them were men in their thirties. The Arthurs were severely outnumbered. If this mob wanted to take them down, they could easily do so.

But the Arcadian Council would have every one of their heads on a stake if they took action.

The council had not been questioned like this in over a century, perhaps longer. In Isaiah's lifetime, he had not heard of a dispute that had escalated to this level.

The reality was that every man standing in defiance on Isaiah's property had already been reported to the alpha leader of the council. Eleanor. Eleanor had been the alpha in charge for two decades. She had a firm stance on uprisings and was known to bring any member of the North American bear shifters to his or her knees at her feet to account for their actions.

She was fair in all things, but her actions were swift and final.

Isaiah forced his posture to relax. The presence of two members of the council here today would ensure no war was waged against the Arthurs. He could sense the tension ebbing with every passing moment.

Henry spoke again. "As you can see, you've made a grievous error coming here today."

"We meant no disrespect, sir," the second man to approach stated. "Please inform us of your intensions so that we may return to our land and lessen the fears of our pack members."

Movement to the left of Henry caught Isaiah's eye. He watched as George stepped forward to align himself with Henry. George was the alpha of the two. His intention to speak was telling. He didn't mince words. He spoke louder than Henry, but in a calm voice that caused every member of the mob to take a step backward. "Your actions today reek of deep disrespect. Do not insult our intelligence."

The man who'd spoken of the intentions of his mob gasped, taking another step back.

"It has been noted that each and every one of you acted in haste to seek your own vengeance for a perceived crime against our species. You knew not what you would be facing here today. But you have acted in error. Your hasty mistake won't be forgotten by our council. This uprising will haunt you for the rest of your lives in everything you do."

A collective gasp covered the clearing.

George continued. "I suggest you turn around now before the damage is more severe and return to your respective lands. A challenge to the Arcadian Council like this won't be tolerated."

"Sir, we had no knowledge of your presence here today. Had we known—"

George cut the man off. "Had you taken a moment to consider your hasty actions, you would have realized that any rumor that had reached your ears as far away as Québec had also come to the attention of the council and been handled."

"Of course, sir." The man's voice waffled. "Our apologies."

"Noted." George did not back down.

Henry spoke again. "Our decisions regarding the transformation of a female human are none of your immediate concern. You won't be returning to your lands armed with any more information than you had when you arrived.

"What you *will* return with is the understanding that, as has been the case for over two centuries, the Arcadian Council will handle this matter. Your input is not necessary or requested at this time. Should that position change, you'll be notified, as has always been our practice."

The two men standing near the front of the mob bowed their heads and turned to face the assemblage. They made several hand signals, indicating the members should retreat, and followed the bears out of the clearing.

For several minutes, Isaiah stood rigid on his porch, waiting for every one of the unwelcome visitors to get out of communication range. Until that moment, no one in his family, nor Henry or George, moved a muscle.

When the mob reached a verifiably safe distance, Henry was the first to turn around.

The Arthur pack members shifted into human form and gathered at the bottom of the steps to the porch.

Isaiah's father, Bernard, extended a hand toward first George and then Henry, shaking each firmly. "We thank you for your presence here today." He notably did not thank the council members for anything specifically regarding Heather, as that had not been determined. He simply thanked them for their support.

Henry spoke again. "We won't tolerate an uprising of this sort for any reason. Violators will be handled swiftly."

Isaiah shuddered inwardly, knowing those who stepped

on his land today would be investigated and punished for their insubordination to the council. Their actions would not be tolerated.

"We must go now, Bernard," Henry continued. "We have an arranged meeting point with Laurence and Charles."

Isaiah held his breath, willing himself not to lose his cool while he waited to be addressed more specifically. And his reward was worth it.

George lifted his gaze toward Isaiah. "You'll be joining us I presume?"

Isaiah nodded, his insides flipping over. He stepped down from the porch, glanced toward his parents and siblings, and shifted into his more natural form less than a second behind the council members who would lead him to his mate.

CHAPTER 14

Heather paced the short distance back and forth across the sitting area of her hotel suite. She had not relaxed a single moment since Laurence and Charles led her to the room, insisting that she remain inside until told otherwise.

It wasn't as though she had other options. Any move in any direction would catch the attention of the two shifters, as well as untold countless others who might be in the vicinity.

An hour ago, Laurence had arrived, leading a hotel employee who delivered a variety of foods intended for her lunch. Most of the offerings remained untouched on the tray across the room. Heather was too stressed and concerned about her future to eat.

Her stomach was in knots, twisting around to keep her in a constant agitated state. Where was Isaiah? How long would she have to stay here?

She was relieved they had only driven about an hour from his home before stopping and securing adjoining rooms. She was also irrationally glad to be alone and not forced to endure countless minutes that turned into hours in the presence of the daunting alpha leaders of her new species.

She had sensed no intended harm. They seemed to be in a holding pattern instead. Waiting.

She shivered, wrapping her arms around her body against the irrational chill. She knew exactly what the council was waiting for. And it wasn't simply a matter of allowing Isaiah time to catch up—though she seriously hoped that was also the case. No. They were waiting for her.

The entire continuity of the bear shifting species rested in the decisions Heather needed to make. Her actions would set a new tone among the shifters. Her choices would need to be dealt with. And it was obvious they would be handled swiftly.

First and foremost, she obviously needed to swear allegiance to the council. No one needed to verbalize that for her to understand the consequences of ignoring the fact. Failure to do so would not end well.

Secondly, she needed to join a pack in order to be guided by them in the ways of her new people. She could choose to join Isaiah's family unit or another. But unless she wanted to travel to the Northwest Territories while she made her decisions, she had few options.

She had a job waiting for her in Alberta. Traveling a great distance for an indefinite period of time would ruin the prospect and probably cause her to be blacklisted in her field of study.

Geology, and specifically glaciology, was her life's ambition. She would not let this opportunity slip away over something as simple as a scratch that transformed her into another species. She nearly chuckled at the absurdity of her thoughts and how far she had come in the understanding of her new world since thirty hours ago.

Isaiah's parents and siblings had been kind, warm, and accepting. If they would have her, she would join them in a heartbeat. That decision was a simple one.

She was also fully aware of the more precise need to bind herself to another bear shifter. It clearly made the council uneasy for her to remain unprotected without the necessary communication she would have with her mate after the binding.

There was no doubt in her mind she would allow Isaiah to claim her. But the pressure to do so immediately made her uneasy. It wasn't a decision she took lightly. No matter how powerful the urge to permit him to bind her to him for eternity reigned when she was in his arms, her mind was clearer when she was not touching him, or worse—deep in the throes of passion.

She would not be rushed.

Now all she had to do was convince the council of her good intentions in the meantime.

A knock at the door made her flinch, and she rushed across the room to look through the peephole. She didn't feel Isaiah's presence or that of any other bear shifter, so she was hesitant.

She was shocked to find a woman outside her door. An older woman. Tall and regal. She had an air about her that sent a shiver down Heather's spine. "Heather?" The woman's kind voice reached her easily. Though it was spoken out loud, what Heather heard was a combination of the soft voice and the telepathic communication.

Instinct told Heather this woman didn't pose a threat, and she opened the door.

The older woman smiled and lifted a hand. "Pleased to meet you, my dear. I'm Eleanor."

Heather shook the newcomer's hand and then held the door open wider for her to enter.

172

This woman wasn't simply regal, she was formidable. The air around her crackled with power. It filled the room, radiating through the space.

"I trust Charles and Laurence provided you with everything you needed during your stay here?"

"Yes, ma'am." Heather let the door shut and turned to face her guest.

"Forgive me for making you wait. It took some time making arrangements to meet with you." Although Heather guessed her age to be in her mid-seventies, she was obviously in perfect health. Her hair was a mixture of gray and white—almost silver—and it was gathered at the back of her head in a loose bun. Not severe. Just convenient. Her eyes were a similar shade of gray. Mesmerizing. Intense. They hinted at the sparkle of silver.

"I understand." She understood nothing so far, but it seemed prudent to respond as she did.

A smile spread across Eleanor's face. "May I?" She pointed at a loveseat that sat at an angle in the sitting area of the suite.

"Of course."

As Eleanor lowered herself to the edge of the sofa, Heather rounded the matching armchair and took a seat facing the woman. "I'm sorry. I don't know who you are."

"Of course not, dear. I'm the Alpha leader of the Arcadian Council. The four men who have been standing guard over you for the past day and a half are members of my council. There are forty altogether. I spared four to ensure your safety. I see they succeeded in their mission."

Heather nodded, her mind reeling with the knowledge that the leader of the council was a woman. She shouldn't be so shocked now that she'd met the woman. If she thought Laurence and Charles were foreboding, she was mistaken. Eleanor didn't simply fill a room, she filled a province. Undoubtedly everyone she would permit to sense her in the entire territory was aware of her arrival.

"I see. Nice to meet you."

"I can sense your unease, and let me reassure you Isaiah is on his way here as we speak. I expect his arrival soon."

Heather relaxed inside, even though she had no particular reason to trust this woman. She simply did.

"The situation at Isaiah's home has been averted. The crisis is over. Those who saw fit to defy my authority and take matters into their own hands will be dealt with."

"I see," she repeated. What did that mean?

There was no doubt Eleanor could read her every thought. After all, Heather had no ability to block or intentionally project anything wandering around in her mind.

Eleanor smiled again. "You have no need to worry, my dear. I can sense your very nature. You're a warm and caring individual. Your soul is clean and pure. You'll be a welcome addition to our species. In time you'll acclimate to our ways."

Heather nodded, having no idea what else to do.

"Allow me to apologize for the actions of one member of the community who made the decision to go against the supreme laws of our land, risking exposure to the outside world by intentionally forcing you to transform. His punishment will be severe."

Heather licked her lips. "Thank you."

"As I'm sure you're aware, our key problem now is ensuring you understand the serious nature of your conversion. We're a species that has remained hidden from nearly every human on earth for centuries. It is rare that a human is brought into our community."

"I understand."

"I hope you also understand the precarious position I've

been placed in to determine the best course of action with regard to the welfare of my people and your integration among us."

"Of course." Heather gripped the arms of the chair with her fingers.

"Under the circumstances, since you have met the Arthurs and seem amicable toward them, I would suggest you return to their care for the foreseeable future. They have agreed to nurture you and guide you in our ways."

"I appreciate that, ma'am." She had to force herself not to exhale in relief.

"However, I need your word that you'll keep our existence close to your heart. Failure to do so would be detrimental to yourself and anyone to whom you revealed the details of our species."

"You have my promise." No one would believe her anyway.

Eleanor chuckled lightly. "You have a sense of humor. I like that."

Heather winced at the blatant invasion of her mind. She needed to learn to control that post-haste.

"You're right. You'll want to practice blocking others as well as projecting your own communication to the Arthurs. In time you'll be able to speak with them silently as if you were born into the family. However, you'll never be able to block me from your thoughts, so don't stress over the inability."

She nodded. Right. Eerie and unnerving, but she understood.

Eleanor leaned forward. "Let me be blunt. I'm a very powerful woman. Our species has existed for centuries with only the occasional episodes of unrest. You aren't the first person to be transformed. You won't be the last.

However, we take each case on an individual basis and treat each newly formed shifter on their own merit.

"Quite honestly, I never want to take someone from their home and transfer them to the Northwest Territories if I can avoid it. And it has nothing to do with me being kind or altruistic. It has to do with logistics. Removing you from your home and your job would create a larger mess than the current one. Your parents would send out a search team looking for you. The cover-up becomes more of a hassle.

"You don't have to say anything to me or make promises. It's entirely unnecessary. I have the ability to keep tabs on you any time I want. I'll know where your heart and intentions lie."

She sighed. "I don't say this to sound intimidating, nor do I want you to think I'll always be lurking in your mind. On the contrary, I have an entire continent to watch over. I don't have time for such frivolity.

"I'm a reasonable leader as are all of the members of the council. You're safe in the hands of the Arthurs. I know they will do right by you. As long as you keep our existence to yourself, you may carry on with your life and enjoy the fruits of your newfound existence. They're plentiful and rewarding. I think you'll learn to appreciate all that being a bear shifter has to offer."

"Thank you."

Eleanor abruptly stood. "I must return to the north. There are many matters at hand." She glided toward the door as though she were more of an apparition than a human being. As she reached for the doorknob, she turned back. "Besides, I believe there's someone here far more anxious to see you than myself." She winked and then silently exited.

Before Heather managed to blink, she found Isaiah standing in the spot Eleanor had vacated.

Heather leaped to her feet and rushed around the chair to reach him.

As the door shut behind him, he noticeably braced himself, which was perfect because she threw herself at him, jumping into his open arms and wrapping her legs around his waist. "Longest several hours of my life."

He grabbed her by the waist, spun around, and pinned her to the door. With one knee positioned between her legs, pressing against her pussy, he tilted his head and took her lips.

The kiss was searing and welcome. She needed contact with him like a drug addict in withdrawal. Insane, since she'd known him only slightly more than one day and had seen him that morning.

As his hands trailed up her waist to cup her breasts, she moaned into his mouth, threading her fingers in the hair at the nape of his neck and pressing her mouth closer. Was it possible to deepen the kiss?

When his thumbs stroked over her nipples, she gasped into his mouth. She needed more. She needed less clothing. She needed him inside her to reaffirm to her that the world was still revolving.

"Baby," he murmured against her lips. The one word spoke volumes.

She lowered her hands down his back and tugged his long-sleeved T-shirt over his firm muscles. He helped her out by leaning back a few inches until his shirt came free and she could whip it over his head.

When her gaze landed on his pecs, she reverently set her fingertips on his chest and traced lines over his muscles.

He wiggled his hands under her sweater while she

stared at him. In a flash, her sweater was gone, leaving her bra as the only barrier between them.

He smirked. "I was beginning to think maybe you never wore these," he stated as he traced a line along the top edge of the lacy material over the swell of her swollen breasts.

"Mmm. Usually I do. Yes."

"Too bad. I like you without."

"I might be willing to accommodate you on occasion." She smiled, grinding her pussy against his cockhead where it pressed against her. "Less talking? More nudity?"

"How did I get so lucky?"

"Fate?" she teased.

He spun around, made his way through the sitting room and into the attached bedroom. Two seconds later she landed on the bed, bouncing with the force of his toss. "Take your jeans off, baby. Please."

She lifted her hips while popping the button and lowering the zipper. As she eased the denim down her legs, she watched Isaiah do the same.

His impressive length bobbed in front of her, and she spun around instinctively to crawl to the side of the bed before he finished stepping out of the jeans.

When she grabbed his hips and lowered her mouth to his cock, he growled. "Heather… Jesus."

She sucked him in deep without hesitation. The urge to consume him was tremendous. Her hands slid around to grasp his firm ass cheeks as she licked a line up the underside of his cock until only the tip remained lodged in her mouth.

She could smell everything about him, from his soap to his personal musk. The combination fueled her to suck him again. Deeper. Harder. She let him slide to the back of her throat.

Whatever insanity had a grasp on her, she had no idea,

but she consumed him as if her life depended on it. In a way, it did.

Isaiah grasped her hair and tugged, both holding and pulling on her head. She wasn't sure which way he intended to encourage her to move and doubted he was entirely certain either.

She eased one hand around to cup his balls, weighing them as they drew up closer to his body.

Isaiah jerked free of her mouth and took a step back, holding her head securely to keep her from following. "My God, Heather. You're..." His voice trailed off.

She took that as a good sign. "Why did you stop me?"

"Because I want to come in your pussy, baby, not your mouth. Not this time." He was breathing heavily. "Besides, I need to shake free of the visions of whoever taught you to do that before I succumb to a rage at just the idea."

She gave him a slow grin. "You taught me."

He lifted both brows. "Excuse me?"

"You're the first person I've done that to."

He shook his head as if confused. "You have got to be kidding."

"No. It suddenly felt natural and totally necessary."

He rushed forward, closing the distance, tipping her head back, and consuming her mouth once again. Easing his hands under her arms, he hauled her body backward on the bed and climbed over her to straddle her waist without breaking the kiss.

It was good. It was better than good. It was perfect.

He slid one hand between their bodies to cup her pussy. As two fingers ran between her folds, she moaned and arched into his touch.

"So wet for me," he murmured against her lips. And then his hand was gone, threaded in the length of hair at the side of her head. He thrust into her so fast, he knocked the breath out of her.

She grabbed his biceps, digging her nails into his arms while she tried to suck in oxygen. Her breath wouldn't come, however, not when he pulled out and thrust back in with even more force.

"So tight," he gritted out.

She wrapped her legs around his thighs, holding him to her. Not that she had the strength to control any choice he might make, but she had the satisfaction of increasing the amount of skin touching.

"So fucking hot…"

She bit her lip as he stared into her eyes, destroying her for all other men.

"I. Just. Need. To. Take. The. Edge. Off. Then. I'm. Going. To. Take. You. Slower. After." He punctuated every word with another thrust of his cock until her eyes rolled back and she lost the ability to focus.

She couldn't imagine why he thought she needed *slow* or even *after*. What she needed was this. Right now. This rushed fuck. This joining that melted her soul and made her his, even though they had not completed the binding.

If she had enough brain cells, she would lift her head and sink her teeth into his shoulder. She wanted to. Her mouth watered to do it. Taste his blood on her tongue. Make him permanently hers.

But her head wouldn't cooperate with her brain, so instead she rolled her neck back and forth as her mouth fell open.

"That's it, baby. Come for me. Show me how good it feels."

She shattered at his words, her pussy gripping his cock and her clit pulsing with every brush against the sensitive nub. Her orgasm went on and on while he continued to thrust into her. One orgasm morphed into two and then three.

She assumed Isaiah was holding back, but finally he let himself go, releasing his come deep inside her. So deep she should feel discomfort, but she didn't. She felt nothing but sheer bliss.

CHAPTER 15

Isaiah stared down at his mate, unable to permit himself to sleep for fear he might wake up and find out this was all a dream. Every time they fucked, it got better and better. He brushed a lock of long hair from her face and watched the peacefulness slumber brought to her features.

He knew as soon as she woke up, she would be a ball of stress again. But for the moment he wallowed in the tranquility of her relaxed expression.

It was evening. She'd been asleep for two hours. She'd been exhausted after he pulled a string of orgasms out of her. Gorgeous, but exhausted.

His cock grew hard, remembering the way her eyes floated into her head as she came. He wanted her again. And this time he intended to show her a bit more dominance. Every fiber of his being told him she would get off on it. At least restraints.

He knew from other women there was a huge difference between consciously resisting the urge to move their hands from a spot he indicated and being forced to do so.

Feeling devious and anxious, he slid from the bed, careful to avoid waking her. Glancing around, he spotted what he needed.

In seconds he was back on the bed, easing against her body while trailing a hand down her arm to thread his fingers with hers. She was barely coming awake as he pulled her arm above her head.

She rolled her head his direction, blinking away sleep and smiling. A soft sigh escaped her lips as she whispered. "How could I possibly wake up horny?"

He winked. "Trust me?"

She smiled wider. "With my life."

"How about with your body?"

"Definitely."

He rolled his weight over her torso to free her other arm and pull it up to meet the first. "Let me tie your hands to the bed."

She licked her lips.

He nearly moaned as she lifted her torso, a rush of arousal filling the air with her sweet scent.

She nodded, wrapping her fingers around his. "Be careful. I haven't done anything like this before."

He leaned forward, touched his lips to hers, and held her gaze. "Baby, I'll always be careful with you. You're my soul. My life. I promise I'll always be aware of your emotions and how you're reacting to anything I do. If I sense unease, I'll stop."

"Okay."

He leaned more fully over her to reach her hands, wrapped the length of terrycloth he'd taken from the soft hotel robe around her wrists, and secured her to the headboard. Thank God there was a slat running along the bottom edge of the headboard, or he would have been out of luck.

183

She gave a slight tug, squirming beneath him.

He watched her body as he inched down toward her thighs. Her nipples pebbled beneath his gaze. A slight moan escaped her lips.

He lifted his eyes to hers. "Baby, I haven't even done anything yet."

She pulled her lips into her mouth, her face flushing with embarrassment as her cream leaked from her pussy to fill the room with more of her scent.

"It's unnerving that you can read me so well," she whispered, her body still wiggling beneath him.

It was time to situate himself between her legs instead of straddling them. Lifting one knee, he nudged her thighs open and settled between them. He did the same with his other leg next. "Open for me, Heather. I want to watch you blossom."

Her breaths came quicker as she spread her knees wider. He danced his fingers from the inside of her knees, up her thighs, and over her lower lips.

She lifted her bottom off the bed.

He removed his fingers. "Remain still with your ass planted on the mattress, and I'll continue."

"Oh, God," she breathed as she complied. "Isaiah…"

"I know. Close your eyes if you want. Feel my touch."

She rolled her head to one side as though hiding her face.

He smiled. She wasn't successful.

With his index fingers, he parted her folds, exposing her to the air.

She moaned and then pressed her lips together as if to stifle the sound.

"I love the noises you make. Don't try to curtail them."

She didn't respond.

Setting one hand above her clit on her belly, he held her

down while he circled her swollen nub and then pulled the hood back.

Her head tipped back, her lips parting. She so obviously fought the need to express her arousal verbally.

He would have her screaming in no time, totally unaware of her inhibitions. One tap on her clit made her gasp.

A finger trailing between her folds drew out a whimper. Yes. God, she was sexy. Hot as hell. And so responsive.

"Please…" she pleaded.

"Oh, I like that sound. But it won't work." He drew more of her wetness out to coat her clit with her arousal. It swelled and pulsed beneath his gaze. So gorgeous.

"Pull your knees higher and spread them wider, baby. Open yourself up for me." She had slowly inched her thighs to tighten against his.

As she did as he commanded, wetness leaked from her pussy to trail down toward her bottom.

Damn, he was lucky.

His cock stiffened. He ignored it, willing it to stand down so he could play. He reached one finger slowly into Heather's tight warmth, turning his hand over so he could stroke across her G-spot.

She sucked in a sharp breath and held it, her entire body stiffening.

God, he wanted to make her come this way. It was sometimes hard for a woman to let her guard down enough to experience the total release of a G-spot orgasm. They found the sensations to be too much, too emotional, too exposed.

"Isaiah," she pleaded.

"Let yourself feel. Concentrate on my finger."

Her moan as he sped up his stroking filled the air. She

dug her heels into the bed, but was unable to lift her torso with his hand on her belly.

He used two fingers from that hand to pull back the tiny hood on her clit again and then pinched the swollen nub.

She screamed. Her clit pulsed with the orgasm. The release would help her move into another, deeper one.

He added a second finger to the first and rubbed her G-spot faster.

She arched gloriously into the intensity, squirming against the bed.

Isaiah knew she was close. He could feel her mind letting its guard down to fully enjoy the sensations bombarding her.

Soft moans grew in intensity, louder as she rose higher. He loved the expressions on her face, the flush, the way her bottom lip trembled, the way she sometimes forgot to breathe.

So damn sexy.

And all his. He would cherish her for a lifetime. When he set his finger beside her clit and circled it, she made a new sound, deeper, uncontrolled.

Her pussy clenched around him first, telling him she was on the edge. And then she screamed again, her legs slamming into his thighs as she let go. He felt the pulsing of her pussy around his fingers and knew she was experiencing the deeper orgasm for the first time.

Before she fully floated back to earth, while the vibrations and jerks of her body still ruled, he pulled out his fingers, leaned over her body, and thrust into her to the hilt.

"Oh, God. Isaiah. *Yes.*" She arched her chest toward him, fighting against her restraints.

Before making another move to slide out of her, he reached up with one hand and tugged the soft belt free.

Heather's arms shot forward to wrap around him. He could feel the need to touch him coming from deep inside her. And he would not deny that need.

Her sweet legs wrapped around his thighs, her hands digging into his back deliciously, and he fucked her until she shouted his name on yet another orgasm before he allowed himself to come deep inside her.

❧

"Now what?" Heather muttered into the pillow. She lay on her belly, her face toward the edge of the bed.

Isaiah smiled down at her where he lay propped on one elbow, his fingers lightly stroking her back up and down her spine.

She had slept eight solid hours, but he sensed she was still groggy.

He had slept most of that time too. He also knew a few things she didn't. "The council members left late last night. They paid the bill for your room and checked out. We can leave here at our leisure and return to my land."

She gingerly rolled to her back, brushed her hair from her face, and blinked up at him. "How did you get here?"

"On foot." He chuckled. "I don't want you to think we always shift to go places. We do generally take cars. After all, we don't want to get caught. Shifting is something we do in the mountains when we want to enjoy the freedom of our other half. Most of the time we live as humans in regular society. We work and play and behave like everyone around us. With a few perks." He winked at her.

When she returned a smile, he continued. "Yesterday I

was in a hurry. It was faster to get here in bear form. I knew where you were."

"So, you expect me to shift and run with you?"

"Yeah." He set his forehead against hers. "It's your only option."

"I've only shifted the one time, against my will. I'm not sure I even know how to do it, or how to prevent it."

"Don't worry. You'll learn. And I'll always be with you."

"Not always. You have a job. I have a job."

He groaned. "Don't remind me. You said you don't start this new job for two weeks, right?"

"Correct."

"Then I intend to make good use of every second of that time." He lifted off her. "Let's get a shower and get out of here. We should stop by my parents' home. They're worried about you."

"I guess it's the right thing to do since I kind of told your leaders I would commit to being a member of your family in order to learn your ways in a safe environment. And probably as a means of proving I'm not a risk to the future of your species."

He climbed over her supple body, kissing her lips on the way.

As he reached for her hand to haul her out of bed, she spoke again. "Hey, you failed to mention that your head Alpha is a woman."

He laughed. Of course, of all the things she learned yesterday, that one would stand out the most. "We have strong females in our line." As soon as he had her on her feet, he pulled her body close to his and wrapped an arm around her back. With his other hand, he tipped her chin up. "I don't want you to think that just because I'm rather dominant in bed it extends to your entire life. I'm a modern guy. Don't let me steamroll you. If you have something to say, say it. Never hold back."

She smiled broadly. "You just keep getting better."

He wiggled his eyebrows. "That's my goal."

An hour later, they had showered and enjoyed a leisurely breakfast from room service. When it was time to go he sensed her unease, but took her hand and led her from the hotel into the light of day. "Don't freak out on me. It's perfectly normal."

"What are we going to do?" she whispered. "Walk around back, strip off our clothes, and switch to bear form?"

"Sort of. Although it pains me to say this, as much as I would enjoy seeing your naked body again this morning, we don't need to strip. Our clothes will travel with us in the transition. Anything you're holding will go along."

"And yet you insist it's not magic," she muttered.

He pulled her to his side and kissed her forehead. "Okay, I guess from your viewpoint, it seems sort of mystical, but after a while it will seem normal."

The hotel was situated on the edge of town in a relatively remote area. It was easy to wander down the street one direction and then switch course a few times until they entered part of the national forest. From there, they hiked a short distance into the trees before Isaiah stopped.

Heather's nerves were palpable. She wrung her fingers in front of her over and over. "I'm uncomfortable with this plan."

"I know. But you'll be fine, and it will get better every time until it's second nature."

"What if I can't do it?"

"You will. Everyone can. All you have to do is imagine yourself in your other form, concentrate on how it felt.

Your body will take care of the rest." He rubbed her arms and then trailed his fingers down to grasp her hands, pulling them apart. He drew them up to his face and kissed her knuckles. "I'm right here with you, baby."

She nodded, her face flushed with uncertainty. She glanced around. "What if someone sees us?"

"They won't. We would feel their presence. No one's anywhere near us right now."

"The humans? You can sense them too?"

"Yes. Or perhaps smell is a better way of describing it. Close your eyes and inhale slowly. You'll see."

She did as he said, taking a deep breath before facing him again. "Okay. I get it."

"Close your eyes again. Visualize your body taking its other shape. It will just happen. We aren't in a hurry. We'll travel at whatever speed you want. Whatever you do, don't panic and shift back without making sure of your surroundings."

Her eyes widened. "Holy shit. What if a hunter mistakes us and shoots us?"

He rubbed her biceps again. "This is not hunting season for any type of bear. We shift sparingly during those months, babe. In addition, it's illegal to shoot a grizzly bear in this area of the country. There are still a few locations to the west of here, but not within these mountains. No grizzly has been shot in this area in many years, shifter or otherwise."

Her eyes grew wider, and she cringed. "Shit. I forgot about other real bears. Do they not bother you?"

"Nope. Full bears are often solitary creatures. The males live alone. The females live with their cubs. They spend their time scavenging for food. It is rare for two bears to fight, and usually over a dead carcass or a female.

So unless you plan to sink your teeth into a wild animal carcass or flirt with a feisty male, you're safe."

She narrowed her gaze. "Don't tease."

He sobered, feeling bad. He needed to consider that not only did she not know a damn thing about shifters, she would also know very little about actual grizzly bears. She was a geologist, not a wildlife biologist. Rocks and glaciers were her thing. "Sorry."

She sighed. "Okay, let's do this."

He stepped back, releasing her. "Relax your body. Go into your mind. Think of your other form."

It took her nearly half a minute to stop her brain from shooting random thoughts of insanity into her consciousness. Finally, she blew out a long breath and leaned forward.

Watching her shift forms was an amazing, gorgeous experience he would never forget. He'd been with her for both shifts so far. He owned that piece of her. No one else could claim something similar.

A few seconds later, a beautiful bear stood before him. Her fur was a dark shade of brown, and he had forgotten how small she was. People would definitely mistake her for a cub. Not that it mattered. He never intended for any humans to see her if he could help it. And furthermore, bear cubs were even more protected than full-grown adults.

With a quick shake of his head, he joined her on four paws. He nodded toward the thick part of the trees and took off. *"See? Easy. Just stay by my side. You'll get the hang of it in no time."*

"I don't know what's weirder—shifting form into a giant bear or communicating with another bear telepathically."

"I hate to break it to you, baby, but you're far from giant. You're a tiny little bear. Everyone in my family will stare at you

when they first see you shifted. We only see bears as small as you when they're cubs."

She growled, making him laugh in his head. *"Let's go,"* he stated, picking up the pace.

She was a natural, running at his side, jumping over things, and twisting her head in every direction to take in the scenery. *"It's gorgeous out here. So pristine. Untouched."*

"Yes, it is," he responded, not taking his gaze off her.

CHAPTER 16

Heather felt every welcoming vibe coming from Isaiah's family as she entered their home for the second time. Even though she'd been there before, so many things she'd believed to be truths two days ago had been torn to shreds since the last time she was in their home.

She remembered the variety of strange cryptic comments they made when she first arrived, and most of them now made perfect sense. The odd reaction of Rosanne concerning the unnecessary treatment of Heather's wounds. The way his brother and his father stood back, holding their tongues, when they realized Isaiah meant to take this unknowing human as his mate.

This time she entered the house armed with far more information.

Joselyn wrapped her in a tight hug. "Welcome to the family."

Rosanne did the same, holding her a moment longer and then smiling broadly into her eyes.

They weren't simply happy to help her though this difficult time. They were also excited to know she would be Isaiah's mate someday. No one spoke those words, but it was obviously understood.

Isaiah wrapped a protective arm around her middle from behind and set his chin on top of her head. "No need to bombard her. She's gonna be overwhelmed."

"I'm fine, Isaiah." She gripped his wrist around her waist with her fingers.

"Let's sit." Rosanne nodded toward the living room, and they all headed that way. "Tell us about yourself," she said as she took a seat next to her husband on the love seat.

Joselyn sat in the armchair, and Wyatt perched on the side of it.

Isaiah led Heather to the couch and crowded her against the end so she was touching him all along her thigh and her torso. She fought the urge to roll her eyes and laugh. She did give him a slight shove. "You're the one that said I needed space."

He ignored her and set his arm around her shoulders.

"I'm originally from Portland, Oregon. My parents still live there. And my sister, Clara. I graduated from Portland State University with a degree in geology. My emphasis is glaciology."

"Ah, that explains the move to Alberta. You must be studying the Athabasca Glacier." Bernard leaned forward, his elbows on his knees, rubbing his hands together. The subject interested him.

"Yes. Looking forward to it. I was hoping to hike all over this area and get a good lay of the land before I start my job in about twelve days. Of course, I twisted my ankle the first day out, and you know the rest."

Wyatt spoke next. "Well, the good news is, you can cover a lot of territory and explore everything you want before you start work. Most of it you can do in bear form.

But even when you're in your human skin, you'll have the ability to reach out for help."

Isaiah's chest rumbled with a low growl. "Not exactly."

She knew he was referring to the fact that they weren't bound to each other yet, which limited her ability to communicate.

He squeezed her shoulder. "That and the fact that no way in hell are you going to traipse around the mountains by yourself."

She lifted a brow. "I'll have you know I've hiked all over the continent by myself. I'm very experienced. I always carry what I'll need."

"You sprained your ankle, babe." His voice rose.

"I did. True. But I didn't die, did I? I had enough food, water, and warm gear to survive the night until you found me."

He scrunched up his face. "Yeah, well, not going to happen again. If you want to hike, someone goes with you. Especially now. We can't know who in our community might not feel as welcoming as my immediate family. I don't trust anyone. And I won't for a long time."

She understood that. She wasn't inclined to trust anyone, either. Obviously a group of people from all over Canada converged on Isaiah's property like a lynch mob.

She wasn't certain how she felt about his overbearing commandment. Was it annoying or hot as hell that he was so protective?

Bernard cleared his throat and changed the subject. "The glacier has been a part of our livelihood for decades. Our business depends on the natural spring water that runs off it each spring. In recent years we've experienced growing drought as the ice recedes."

Heather nodded. "That's exactly what I'm here to study. Not going to lie and tell you I can make it stop. It's inevitable that you'll lose the Athabasca Glacier within a century. But scientists are doing everything we can to figure out what's causing the climate change and slow it down or save other glaciers."

"Eventually, our entire pack will have to relocate or change the motto of our brewery," added Wyatt. "We pride ourselves on the fact that our beer uses natural spring water. So do the Tarbens."

"The Tarbens are the other family of bear shifters in the area, right?"

"Yes. We've been in a land dispute with them since we settled here over a century ago," Rosanne said. "It's sad since there's no reason for it, at least not one that anyone can remember. Friendships are often destroyed over the feud as well as relationships."

"Of course humans are no better," Heather added.

"Indeed." Bernard shook his head.

"I can't wait to see your brewery," Heather stated. "Who's running it right now? None of you are there."

"We have about fifty employees that work various shifts. Most of them are family members." Bernard looked animated as he spoke of what was obviously his pride and joy. "My brother Marlin and his entire family work there. He has a wife, three sons, and three daughters."

"Wow. Six kids." Heather wondered what was typical for shifter families.

Rosanne smiled. "More than I could have handled. And they were all born within seven years."

"Yikes." Heather could not see herself in that position.

"We do practice some form of family planning, babe. I told you that. Don't panic. Every family chooses when to have kids and how many. We don't have any sort of religious mandates about birth control or even abortion for that matter."

Heather was glad Isaiah communicated all that into her head. They didn't need to discuss every single thing with the whole world, and it made her relax to know he got that.

He squeezed her shoulder. "While we're on the subject of the brewery, I need to go in for a few hours and do payroll. It was due yesterday, so I'm already late. People are understanding of the situation, but I can't expect them to wait forever. Now's your chance to check it out."

Joselyn groaned. "Do you hear yourself, Isaiah? No one in their right mind would want to hang around the brewery while you do accounting. Let her stay here. I'll spend some time with her." She sat up straighter, excited by the prospect.

Isaiah hesitated.

Heather could sense his reluctance. She turned to face him. "You didn't tell me you handled the accounting."

"There are a lot of things I haven't told you yet." He smirked. "I have a business degree."

Heather scrunched up her nose. "I'm gonna have to agree with Joselyn. That sounds worse than watching paint dry. How about you leave me here and come back when you're done?"

"Hmm." He closed the distance between them and kissed her forehead possessively. "How about you and Joselyn come with me. She can show you around, and I won't spend the entire time worrying and making mistakes. The employees will thank you."

"Deal."

Joselyn was rolling her eyes when Heather looked back at her. She had to admit two things to herself. She wasn't super eager to be separated from Isaiah for any reason, even though she was reluctant to say it out loud. And two, the ball of desire constantly present in her stomach tightened a little more that he didn't want to leave her, either.

His smiled broadened. She didn't need to look to know he was pleased with her thoughts.

"Joselyn, can you teach me how to block?"

Isaiah slapped his forehead with his free hand. "That's the first thing you want to learn?"

"Yep." She poked him in the side, even though he didn't flinch. "It's on the top of my list."

"I like knowing all your thoughts," he communicated.

"I know. But I'd prefer keeping some of them to myself. Besides, it's not fair. You're blocking everything from me. I'm blocking nothing."

"Not everything." He gently tugged her chin so she faced him full on. *"You know how I feel about you. You know this is it for me. You're mine. I'd do anything for you. I can't block that. It's written on my face. It's leaking out my fingers. It's rubbing against my jeans currently too."*

She giggled and then sobered when she realized everyone was staring at them with no idea what the private joke was.

Bernard stood. "Don't worry, Heather, it's the nature of our species. The entire family is always having side conversations no one is privy to. Sometimes at dinner there are ten conversations going on in a silent room. If anyone walked in, they would think we were robots."

Heather smiled. "Thank you so much for your hospitality. It means a lot to me."

Bernard hesitated before leaving the room. "You're one of us now. Anything you need, ask. It's yours." He was serious, his expression hard.

She nodded. "Thank you."

∿

Heather sat on a bar stool, staring out the floor-to-ceiling observation window above the brewery floor. At least a dozen people were moving around one story below, making sure every aspect of the process ran smoothly.

Joselyn sat next to her. "It's like a circuit. If any one part breaks down, the entire system is off. Beer gets destroyed. It has to keep moving." She pointed across the room to the far corner. "That giant vat holds the beer that's being bottled today. Once the bottles are filled, they keep moving along the assembly line to the crowner, the labeler, and then the boxes."

Heather nodded, overwhelmed. How did anyone know what to do and when? "Crowner?" she asked.

"The machine that puts the caps on the bottles. I'm over-simplifying it, but that's the basics." Joselyn picked up the beer she was nursing and took another sip. "You sure you don't want a bottle?"

"No. Thanks. Not that I don't like beer. I do. I can't wait to experience all of your products, but for at least a few weeks it seems prudent to keep all my brain cells focused on not getting myself killed."

"Good point. Though I don't think you're in danger of being killed. Hopefully Jack was the only asshole in the area who felt the need to attack you. And, we don't know he wanted to kill you. I'm betting he wanted to bind you to him so he would have company since he'd had a falling out with his family."

"You okay, babe?" Isaiah said into her head. He was two doors down in his office at the computer.

"Yep."

Joselyn was grinning when Heather turned her attention back to Isaiah's sister.

"Sorry."

"It's adorable. He won't leave you alone for a moment.

Never thought I'd see the day when my brother took a leap like this."

"He hasn't had other girlfriends?"

She shrugged. "Some, but none that mattered enough for him to touch them constantly, worry about their every movement, and stare at them like they hung the moon."

Heather felt her face heat. "Thanks. It means a lot to me." Obviously Joselyn approved of her and was happy for her brother.

"So about the blocking…"

Heather laughed. "Talk to me."

Isaiah absentmindedly picked up the ringing phone on his desk without taking his eyes off the computer screen. "Arthur here."

The deep chuckle on the other end made him smile and lean back in his seat. Austin Tarben was always filled with humor. "You do realize the absurdity of that greeting right?"

Isaiah snickered too. "You dialed my number. I assume you knew who you were going to get."

"Uh-huh, except everyone in your entire plant has the surname of Arthur, so…"

Isaiah laughed harder. "Whatever. What's up?" The two of them had been friends since they were about fifteen, when they ran into each other high in the mountains one day. Both had been in a snit about something at home and had bonded in spite of their ridiculous family feud.

"Besides, I was hoping maybe a certain female would answer instead of your sorry ass, and I'd get to hear her voice."

"Who?" Isaiah teased. "You mean my mom?"

"Ha ha. You're so funny. Now, tell me about her."

"You've met my sister lots of times. She's sweet, kind, funny. I think you two would get along splendidly if either of you was willing to admit it." Isaiah was still steering the conversation in a totally different direction than Austin intended, but he grabbed the opportunity to intentionally misunderstand his friend anyway.

"You're so witty today. I'm impressed considering it's been like two days since I heard you carried an injured woman out of the woods. Word around here is she's yours."

Word gets around. That's for sure. "Maybe."

"What do you mean, *maybe*? She is or she isn't."

"Yeah. She is, but we haven't made it official."

"You mean you haven't made an announcement? Or you haven't bound her to you yet?"

"Neither." Isaiah sighed, rubbing his forehead. "She isn't ready."

"Wow. That's risky."

"I don't know. I don't want to rush her and risk her feeling trapped. My family has stepped in to help guide her, and it's not like I plan to sleep alone."

"Do it, man. Don't wait." Austin's voice lost all humor. He was rarely this serious. "I don't like the rumors. You need to bind her to you."

Isaiah sat straighter, gripping the phone tighter. "What have you heard?"

"Some people are talking about claiming her for themselves. Others are talking about eliminating her. She's a sitting duck until you bind to her."

Isaiah rubbed his forehead. "Yeah, I get that, but do you really think someone would kidnap her or kill her? That's absurd."

"Dude, worse." His voice lowered to nearly a whisper. "I

think people are watching you right now. Waiting for a chance to pounce."

Isaiah stood from the desk, his entire body on alert. "Here? At the brewery?"

"Everywhere. They're following you. They're being very hush hush about it in order to not piss off the council. Everyone heard about what happened yesterday with the Arcadians. But that doesn't mean they approve of the council's decision. Trust me, Isaiah. Do not fucking wait."

"Who are we talking about? My pack? Yours? Others?"

"I haven't heard of anyone from your pack being involved, but yes, mine. And the Osborns, and the Gerbens. You know how hotheaded my damn brother is. I've heard Antoine on the phone with his cronies several times. They aren't right in the head, but I think they know stuff."

"Jesus. Seriously?"

"Sorry, man. I was hoping you realized it."

"No." Isaiah shook his head. "I had no idea." He wanted to find Heather immediately. She would just have to sit in his office until he finished working. The thought of someone getting to her made him livid on multiple levels.

Knowing if they were separated by any distance, she wouldn't even be able to reach out to him telepathically for help drove him to an entire new level of insanity. The only reason he figured she could communicate with him at all so far was because they were obviously meant to be together. Besides the Arcadian Council and himself, he doubted she could communicate easily with anyone else. "Gotta go. Thanks for the info." He hung up the phone without waiting for a response. Austin would understand.

As if the building were on fire, he jogged down the hallway to the observation room and yanked the door open. He was breathing heavily as he stood in the doorway.

Heather and Joselyn spun around to look at him, both laughing, but their faces fell when they saw his expression.

"What's the matter?" Jos asked.

"Nothing. But come to my office. You can chat there. I need to finish." Was he being unreasonable?

Heather jumped down from the stool she'd been on and glided across the room until she could set her hands on his chest and tip her head back to meet his gaze. "For once, I'm reading you. You're so upset you can't even block me. What happened?"

He grabbed her hand and led her back down the hallway to his office, Joselyn right behind them. When they were inside and the door was shut, he finally spoke. "People are watching you. I don't like it." There was no way to keep it from her, nor did he want to. She was much better off armed than in the dark. She needed to be diligent. Not naïve.

Joselyn gasped.

Heather, on the other hand, was surprisingly calm. "Okay. Who? Where are they?" Her voice was steady. Soft.

He took a deep breath. "I don't know. Anywhere. Everywhere. Following us. Waiting."

"Waiting for what?" Still so steady. Matter of fact. Calm.

He tried to pull his shit together. He wasn't this guy. This irrationally nervous man scared out of his mind. He stared down at her, holding her biceps tightly as if she might disappear if he let go. "An opportunity."

Joselyn interrupted the stare off. "Isaiah, who told you that?"

"Doesn't matter. What's important is that someone I trust tipped me off. We need to be careful. Diligent. Always." He continued to look at Heather while he spoke.

If he wasn't half mad with the desire to own this woman, he would wonder when the hell he became this crazed boyfriend who knew she was his other half and wouldn't survive intact if anything happened to her. But he knew exactly when he'd turned into crazy, lust-filled Isaiah Arthur—the moment he stuck his head inside her car to grab her jacket two mornings ago.

A slow smile spread across Heather's face. She leaned closer, lifted onto her tiptoes, and kissed his lips, not giving a shit that his sister was watching. "I'm right here. Not going anywhere. We'll handle this. Get your payroll done, and then we'll figure out what to do next."

Damn, he loved her.

He flinched.

Loved?

Was that a reasonable emotion for someone he met two days ago?

Fuck yes, it was.

The sanest thing he'd ever felt.

CHAPTER 17

Heather could sense the increasing stress level that wafted off Isaiah as the day progressed. As soon as he was done working, they returned to his parents' home, ate dinner with the family, and then made their way to his cabin.

He closed his eyes for a moment before exiting the SUV, rounded it quickly, and lifted her down to the ground. She had to jog to keep up with him to get to the house.

He didn't seem to breathe until they were inside with the door locked.

She knew members of his extended family were outside. He'd communicated multiple times with several people. She didn't know who. And it most likely didn't matter. She'd never met any of them. But she could read him enough, especially in his agitated state, to know they weren't alone. Others were guarding them.

As much as she would prefer not to discuss the shit-storm that was her current life, she needed information. He'd spoken out loud to his parents and his brother and sister over dinner, but he'd also exchanged communication he didn't want her to hear. Was he trying to protect her?

She broke the silence. "How many of your people are out there?"

He shook his head. "Nothing gets by you."

"Oh plenty gets by me. I'm constantly spinning in circles trying to figure out what isn't being said. It's growing annoying." She furrowed her brow. He needed to stop coddling her.

He dropped his keys on the end table by the couch and let his hand drift down to grasp hers. Without a word, he led her down the hall to the master bedroom and shut the door. After kicking off his shoes, he sat on the edge of the bed in the dark and reached for her.

She went to him, stepping into the spread of his legs and inhaling his scent. Immediately she lost some of her resolve. She shook her head to clear her mind. "Talk to me."

"Just so you know, not much would change if I completed the binding. You would still find yourself blocked from any conversation going on around you that you weren't invited into. It's kind of strange to an outsider, I suppose, but we're used to it.

"When we're at the kitchen table ten things happen at once without a sound. My mom communicates with my sister. She also communicates with my dad. Both of those are separate and unrelated and blocked from the other. Meanwhile, I might be talking to Joselyn and Wyatt at the same time in an open three-way.

"It's not really rude in our minds. It's just how we compartmentalize. No one wants to hear my chat with Wyatt about the payroll or my mom's talk with Joselyn about eye makeup."

She nodded. "I get that. But you do realize I'm involved in no conversation except the one I'm having with you."

He sighed and threaded his fingers in the hair at the nape of her neck. "Eventually that will change. I'm sure of it. Over time, you'll be able to speak with the rest of my family too. In the meantime, I don't mean for you to feel alienated. But I also know there's a lot of information being thrown at you all at once."

"You can't protect me from everything, Isaiah."

"I get that. And I don't mean to. I'll tell you everything you need to know. I just wanted to get back to the house where everyone wasn't shouting into my head at once so we could speak in private."

"Okay. Talk."

His fingers were stroking her scalp in slow circles that soothed her. "Two of my cousins are roaming the area. Just keeping an eye out."

"Don't people need to sleep?"

He smiled. "They'll figure something out. Don't worry. They'll trade in the middle of the night. No one is put out, if that's your worry. We protect our own with our lives. It's how we were raised."

"But I'm not one of your own. They could be frustrated to be helping out a stranger."

He shook his head. "No one feels that way. First of all, you're one of us now. That's already been established. It has nothing to do with you and me binding ourselves together. Even if we didn't, it wouldn't change your new status as a member of the Arthur pack. Not every shifter in the pack is a blood relative. We take people in for various reasons from time to time."

"Oh." She hadn't realized that. "Okay, so what about the others? You think other shifters are following me?"

"Unfortunately yes. If I had gotten my information

from anyone else, I would doubt the source, but not this guy."

She was sharp enough to read between the lines. He had an ally in the neighboring family. He'd already told her that. It didn't take a rocket scientist to put two and two together. And she understood perfectly why he would keep the person's identity to himself. Probably his own parents didn't know. "Austin Tarben," she whispered.

He exhaled slowly and nodded, his hands sliding down to grasp her fingers. "Yes."

She gripped his hands. "The bottom line is that I'm endangering myself and making everyone in your pack work overtime while I stubbornly refuse to bind myself to you."

He shook his head rapidly and hauled her body against his. "Please don't think that. No one else does. It's not irrational for two shifters who met two days ago to hold off on the permanence of a binding even if they *are* totally head over heels. When you add the fact that one of them was human until two days ago, it would be absurd to expect them to bind."

He kissed her cheek and nibbled a path to her ear, making her shudder. "No one expects you to make that monumental decision right now. Hell, no one expects me to, either. So relax. Stop worrying about it. Let me remind you how good we are together."

She felt him smile against her neck. "Right, because that will make it so much easier to fend you off," she joked.

"Mmm." He nuzzled the very spot she knew he would bite eventually. "Never said I was going to play fair. I just asked you to let me make your world spin."

She shivered, grabbing his waist and angling her lips toward his. "Can't turn that down."

His hands went to her sweater and up under the thick

material to cover her waist. When he slowly eased them up to her breasts, he froze, his lips no longer moving over hers. "Damn. You're full of surprises."

She smiled against his mouth. "You said you weren't a fan of bras."

"I did indeed." He cupped her breasts, holding them loosely at first as though weighing them in his palms, and then he thumbed her nipples until she arched into him. Her lips broke free as she tipped her head back. Every time he touched her, he lit her on fire. Just the simple act of stroking her nipples beneath her sweater made her horny.

"I love it when your mouth parts like that," he whispered. "Makes my cock so hard watching your face open up. The joy. The pleasure."

She tried to focus on his words, but his fingers continued to toy with her nipples, driving her higher until she thought she might come from their attention alone.

When he released her breasts to drag her sweater over her head, she whimpered before she could stop herself.

He smiled. "Baby… You're so damn responsive."

"Only with you," she shared.

"Love hearing that."

His hands went to the button on her jeans while she did the same to his. Simultaneously they popped buttons and lowered zippers. The only problem was he was sitting and she was standing. In moments he had her jeans pooled at her feet. She had her hand twisted backward inside his pants, cupping his cock.

He stood long enough to shrug out of the jeans without dislodging her touch.

The silky smooth feel of his length in her hand made her stroke up and down the skin. He let her, for about ten seconds, and then he grabbed her hand and pulled it away. "Climb onto the bed. Get in the middle. On all fours."

She hesitated, considering how demanding he was and whether or not she should be so turned on by it every time. Was she setting a precedent she wouldn't be able to escape later?

He stroked her arm up and down. "What's wrong, baby?"

"It bothers me that your dominance goes straight to my clit and makes me so hot. Every time. Like I'm not even me."

He set one hand on her butt and pressed her pussy against the mattress between his legs. "It's just a new you that you've never met. You weren't with the right man."

"Is it the shifting?"

"Nope. It's always been in you, this need to have a lover with a dominant tendency. You just didn't know it. Until you meet someone who can make your body scream, it's hard to be aware of the need."

"It's consuming me."

"I know, baby." His words were soft. Gentle. So understanding. Even though he'd given her a command, he wasn't angry she'd hesitated. He simply took the time to talk to her.

She also knew full well when they were done talking, he would still expect her to do as he said. That thought made her shudder.

"A couple of forces are at work. One is your need to be controlled a bit in bed. It drives you so much higher than vanilla sex ever will. The other thing is the magnetic pull of our bodies to each other. I know I said Fate was a silly notion, but I've changed my mind. Nature indeed has a plan for us. I know it in my soul. She will be relentless in Her quest to ensure we do Her will."

"And you're convinced Her will is for us to bind together."

"I know it with every ounce of my being. But," he held up a finger, "I am patient, and I absolutely won't rush you. There's no reason to rush. Just because I'm sure of us and what we'll be together for the rest of our lives doesn't mean it has to start today."

She bit her lower lip. Was he right? Or was she being ridiculous? And who said she had to wait for him to decide when they finished the binding? He'd said himself either party could do it at any time.

"You're entitled to your own timeframe. I won't rush you. I've said that before, and I mean it. We're on your calendar, not mine."

"But I'm endangering myself and others."

He set a finger on her lips. "You're not. Stop it."

She lowered her gaze to his lap, the location of his bobbing erection. Even in the midst of this serious discussion, he was aroused. Of course, she was too. Wetness leaked between her legs, increasing with every touch of his hands and every gentle word from his lips.

He changed his tone to seductive. "How do you feel when I order you around in bed? When I hold you down and make you come?"

She shivered, unable to stop the response as his fingers toyed with her butt cheek, inching their way closer to her tight rear hole. An unbidden moan escaped her lips.

"Oh baby, that's what I thought. Now, climb onto the bed on all fours."

She crawled over his thigh, intentionally teasing him with as much contact with her body as possible. She let her breast graze his arm on the way by and seductively crawled like a feline to the center of the mattress.

"Taunting me won't ease your need." His voice was deep, gravelly, firm. She affected him, even though he may fully intend to withhold gratification. His delay would only make her arousal grow.

"Spread your knees wider."

She complied, biting her lip again to keep from moaning at the exposure.

"You can put your elbows on the bed. I like your ass up higher anyway. Plus your tits will drag across the sheet." His description did nothing to dampen her desire. Every word was carefully calculated to tighten the ball forming in her belly.

She was acutely aware of her nipples stiffening against the sheet, her pussy leaking copious amounts of arousal between her spread thighs, and her exposed, private hole open for him to see. Instead of being mortified, she was more aroused than ever.

When he set a hand gently on her lower back and stroked her skin, she let her belly dip, her ass reaching higher.

"Heather... You're so sexy..."

She set her forehead on the bed and tucked her lips between her teeth to keep from moaning.

With one hand resting on her back, he reached between her legs and dragged a finger through her folds. "So wet for me," he crooned.

She squirmed.

"Stay still. Let me play." He slowly eased his finger inside her. It felt amazing. It wasn't enough. As he fucked that one finger in and out of her as if they had all the time in the world, her attention got divided by the feel of that finger working her pussy and one finger of his other hand easing down her crack.

Would he touch her there? Her mind warred with the concept. In a lucid normal moment she would cringe, but this wasn't a coherent moment. She was so damn horny she didn't care what he did. And she totally trusted him. Besides, if she were honest, his finger was driving her wild.

He pulled the pointer out of her pussy and circled her clit. All the while, his other hand inched lower. She thought it was his middle finger about to touch her tight hole. And she was unable to stop herself from rocking backward to encourage more.

"Uh uh. Don't move. You have to stay still if you want me to make you feel good. You start wiggling all over the place and I'll stop."

She sucked in a sharp breath. Would he do that?

"Try me."

She froze, fighting for her next breath while she squeezed her eyes shut as if that would keep her from admitting how titillating it was for him to touch her so close to forbidden territory. Who decided the back hole couldn't be erogenous anyway?

"That's a girl. I love how your skin flushes when you're so aroused you can't stop yourself." His finger got closer while he spoke. Was he trying to deliberately distract her? "You make my dick so hard it's about to explode before I can get inside you." In one smooth motion, he pinched her clit with one hand while setting the one thick finger from the other over her tight hole and applying enough pressure for her to realize how much she craved whatever he had in mind.

"Isaiah," she moaned into the mattress.

"Baby..." He rubbed her clit and her rear hole at the same time.

She stopped clenching her cheeks together at some point and willed him to enter her. "Do it. God, Isaiah, do it."

"Mmm. I'll decide when and what." More torture. The kind of torture she wanted to feel for hours. That edge she hovered on in the moments before shattering had been right in her grasp for minutes now. Not seconds.

When his finger disappeared from the spot she never would have expected to crave pleasure from, she moaned. *Please, God.*

She heard a small pop and realized he had sucked the finger into his mouth. Lubrication?

As his thumb slid into her pussy from below, he pushed that wet finger into her tight hole.

She held her breath, bombarded with new sensations that threatened to destroy her. People said it was amazing. People who weren't her. She should have listened.

He fucked in and out of both holes at once until her arms shook and she thought she might have a stroke from the intense pleasure.

"Come for me, baby. Come and then I'll fuck your pussy."

She let it go. Hadn't even realized she'd been holding back. Had she done so for him? Waiting on permission? Or had it been to prolong the delicious pleasure?

In any case, her entire body shuddered with her release, including her ass gripping the finger thrusting in and out of her tight rear hole.

Isaiah worked her even as she came down from her high. And when he finally pulled out of her pussy, he didn't release her ass. In fact, his palm gripped her bottom, keeping his finger lodged inside.

It felt so full. Tight. Nerve endings on fire for more friction.

Nudging her legs farther apart, he lined his cock up with her pussy and thrust into her.

She shouted. "Oh God." The full sensation of having a finger in each hole was nothing compared to the feel of his cock against his finger. Ten times better.

As he thrust in and out, he held that finger buried as far as he could reach. His thick length stroked over the finger through the thin membrane separating her pussy from her ass.

"You feel so damn good, baby. So good." His voice was scratchy. He grabbed her hip to steady her, making her realize she was rocking with every thrust. His grip was firm and welcoming.

She concentrated on everything at once. Her nipples, her tight ass, her pussy, the way her clit pulsed every time he pressed in to the hilt.

Best sex of her life. Only one thing would make it better... "Bite me," she screamed.

"Not going to do it, baby. Let me make you feel good."

"Bite me. Dammit, Isaiah. Do it. *Now*." She knew with every ounce of her soul she wanted him to claim her as his own, bind her to him forever. It wasn't just the sex talking. It was a feeling she was suddenly very certain of.

It was right.

"Isaiah..." She whimpered, her attention drawn to how thick his cock was. Did it get thicker? Her neck tingled with the desire to be bitten. Other parts of her did too. Did it have to be her *neck* he bit? She wanted him to bite her thighs. Her ass. Anywhere. Everywhere. She wanted him to mark her so that everyone who glanced her way would know she was his undeniably.

But Isaiah didn't comply. He fucked faster, his breath coming quicker. He held her hip so tight it might bruise. She wanted to see the marks of his fingers on her. She hoped he was gripping her that tight.

On one final thrust, he growled into the air, filling the room with an inhuman sound.

It made her come. She shattered under his control, her pussy pulsing around his throbbing cock while her ass gripped his finger. Her mouth hung open, dry. She didn't have the energy to lick her lips.

For long moments, neither of them moved. She didn't care. If she could freeze that coupling for all time, she would.

Finally, he eased out of both her holes. He held her by the waist and lowered her to her belly. "Don't move."

She couldn't if she wanted to. Her limbs didn't work, and her brain wasn't functioning, either. She heard water running, and then the sound of Isaiah's feet coming back across the floor.

He leaned over her and set a warm cloth between her legs. He was so gentle, caring for her when surely he was about to collapse himself. Did their monumental fuck not affect him the way it affected her? If that were the case, she would be horrified.

When he set the cloth aside, he eased onto his side, pressing his body against hers. He brushed her hair from her face to meet her gaze.

"Why?"

"I told you I won't let you make that choice when you're not in a clear headspace. Half the population of my species would be mated prematurely if they sank their teeth into every woman they had a good fuck with."

She squirmed onto her side, a sudden burst of energy consuming her until she managed to sit up and grab his arms. "That was not a good fuck." She shook him. Tears ran down her face. She was emotional and sated and pissed all at the same time. "That was an earthquake. The mountain fucking shifted a bit to the left. The foundation under your house was compromised."

He chuckled.

"I'm not being funny."

His face sobered. "I know, baby. But come on…that was pretty cute."

She narrowed her gaze. She wasn't in the mood to be funny. "You know what I mean. Do not belittle what we just did by comparing it to any random fuck. If you truly believe that, then tell me now so I can gather my things and get out of your house. I don't want to be bound to you if you thought that was an ordinary everyday experience."

He bolted to sitting, scrambled to lean against the headboard, and dragged her onto his lap. Cupping her face with both hands, he met her gaze. "You're right. I didn't mean to imply for a moment what we have is ordinary. It's not. It's out of this world. I've never felt like this before. It scares me to death. I've spent most of the last few days behaving like a lunatic because I'm so damn in love with you I can't think right.

"When we make love, it's like everything in the world is right and peaceful and perfect. So, no. I don't take it lightly. I have never wanted something so badly in my life. You know that. Do not doubt it for a moment."

She swallowed. He was nearly shaking her. "You're right. I'm sorry." She felt his love. It flowed into her, seeping into every pore as if he were becoming one with her. And yes, it was scary, but also undeniable and exciting.

He smoothed his hand back to grab her hair. "Look at me."

She met his stare.

"I would die for you. I would do anything for you. It's that powerful. It's real. And I'll sink my teeth into you and make you mine soon, but not like this. I need you to say it in the light of day. I need you to look at me in a way that tells me you get it. I need to see it in your eyes. The total surrender. The love. The pull. I need to know without a shadow of a doubt that you get me. That you're one hundred percent in the same place as me. And then I'll claim you. Not before."

She nodded as much as she could move her head with his grip in her hair. "Okay. I hear you."

"Good." He tugged her face against his chest. His heart was racing. Hers was, too. And she snuggled against him and tried to slow her erratic breathing. Nothing else existed except the two of them. Nothing else mattered.

CHAPTER 18

Heather blinked awake slowly. She was on her stomach, sprawled in Isaiah's huge bed. The room was filled with light. It was day. She'd slept hard. Late. She inhaled the scent of coffee and remembered she could reach out to Isaiah without moving.

"Where are you? Please tell me you're pouring me a mug of that coffee I smell."

He chuckled into her head. *"Be right there."*

She still hadn't moved when he entered the room carrying two mugs of coffee. He set them both on the bedside table and sat on the edge. "You'll never be able to take a sip in that position." His hand trailed along her spine to her bottom, making her stretch and moan.

"I think I died."

"Please no. I like you."

She giggled. "Good thing. Because you're stuck with me."

"I'll take it." He drew circles on her ass and then her thighs.

She spread her legs, hoping he would reach between

them. She might be unable to move, but that didn't mean he couldn't work his usual magic.

He chuckled again and then slapped her ass playfully. "I have a fantastic bathtub with your name on it."

"Really? Did you get it engraved?" she teased.

"Hmm. No. But I will if you'd like." He patted her butt again. "You have to be sore. I'm gonna start the water. You drag your carcass out of bed and come to the bathroom, okay?"

"Or what?" When did she get so snarky?

"Oh baby, you're playing with fire." This time he pinched her ass.

She flinched with a squeal. "You pinched me."

"You taunted me. Now, you going to get up on your own, or do I need to toss you over my shoulder? I've done it before. I'll do it again."

"I'm counting on it." More teasing. More banter. More of everything she loved. Her heart was full.

Shocking her, he leaned forward, set his teeth on her shoulder, and bit down, not hard enough to break the skin, but hard enough to draw her entire body into a heated state of instant arousal. "Isaiah…" Her vision blurred.

"That's what I want to see. That look right there. Jesus, woman. You're going to drive me mad with your moans and your looks."

"Mad enough to make good on that bite?" She focused on him, twisting to her side so she could see him more fully. "I want it, Isaiah. I want to be yours. I want you to be mine. I can't be more blunt."

He nodded. "I get that. If nothing else, I felt your total surrender just now when you thought I might do it. Not an ounce of hesitation. Not a flinch."

She scrambled to sit up and then climbed onto her knees and crawled around to straddle his lap. He didn't have a shirt on, but he was unfortunately wearing jeans. She gripped his shoulders and held them tight. "I'm ready."

He nodded. "Okay."

A loud sound at the front of the house made them both jerk their gazes toward the bedroom door.

Isaiah acted fast. He lifted her off his lap and set her on the bed so fast her head was spinning. "Put something on, baby." And then he was gone. Out the door. Down the hall.

She slid off the bed, grabbed his T-shirt from yesterday, and drew it over her head without paying any attention to whether it was right side out or even backward.

It was too quiet.

She inched toward the door, her heart beating fast.

"Stay in the bedroom, baby. Shut the door. Lock it."

She grabbed the door to push it closed, but before it snicked shut something got in the way. She glanced down to see a foot.

Her mouth opened to scream, but nothing came out. The door flew open and a hand landed over her mouth before she could process what was happening. *"Isaiah,"* she screamed in her head.

Pounding footsteps headed toward her, but the man who held her took several steps farther into the room, dragging her. Her feet barely touched the ground. Something was biting into the skin under her chin. Her eyes went wide as she stopped breathing.

He had a knife. And he spun around to face the door.

Isaiah appeared in the doorway. "Let her go, Antoine. You do not want to do this."

The man holding her laughed, a crazed sound that made her blood run cold.

Fear crawled up her spine. She grabbed his forearm, clawing at it.

He gripped her tighter, lifting her all the way off the

ground until she was precariously hanging by the arm under her breasts and the knife pressing too hard against her throat.

She fought, instinct causing her to flail in his grip, kicking at him. Nothing fazed him in the slightest.

Isaiah crept closer. "Antoine, what do you want? Tell me. Put her down. Let's talk."

He laughed again. "I'll tell you what I want. I want you to choose."

"Choose what?" Isaiah held both hands out, palms up. His gaze was on Antoine, but she felt the life leaving his body as if he were dying.

She tried to calm herself. For him. For them. To stay alive. She didn't need to make things worse by slitting her own throat. Who was this guy? She tried to place the name. Antoine... Shit. He was a Tarben. He was Austin's brother.

The man's breath wafted across her face as he lowered his mouth toward her cheek. He smelled awful, like cigarettes and stale beer. Bile rose in her throat.

She thought he was going to kiss her, but his lips moved to her neck. "You choose, Arthur. Either I kill her now and neither of us gets her, or I bite her and bind her to me."

She thought she would faint. Would he do that? There was a fate worse than death. She knew it with every fiber of her being. Blood ran from her face. She had to fight to stay lucid.

"Don't do this, Antoine. I said we could talk. Set her down. She's not the one you have an issue with. Talk to me. Tell me what I can do."

He chuckled sardonically, his teeth grazing her skin with too much pressure.

Yeah, she was going to die. She knew it because she

would jerk her head forward and slice her own throat before she let him sink his disgusting teeth into her neck.

"Antoine, look at me man. Let's figure something out." Isaiah's voice was getting closer, but she no longer looked at him. She couldn't bear to see the fear in his eyes.

Antoine continued to drag his teeth over her skin. He licked the spot several times too. She shuddered, seriously afraid she would vomit. The knife dug too deep. A trickle of blood ran down her throat. Fear weighed heavily. It was hard to stay alert. Her vision was going black. Was she getting enough oxygen?

"What do you want, Antoine?" Isaiah spoke louder. "Tell me."

Antoine jerked his head upright, heedless of the knife at her throat. He didn't care if she died. She was a pawn in another game.

"It's too late," the man shouted. "You Arthurs think you own the world. Like you're better than everyone else. You think a new girl shows up in town and she's automatically yours? I don't think so. If you hadn't interfered, she would belong to my cousin Jack. It's time you stopped living with such entitlement." He jerked her body, making her scream out. But her voice wasn't audible. Her throat was too constricted. Not enough oxygen… She was certain she would pass out any second.

"Don't move, baby. Do. Not. Move. Stay with me."

She heard him as if he were far away. She didn't have much left in her to fight with, but she would. For him. She would do anything for him.

"Heather," he shouted into her head to get her attention.

Her eyes widened. She met his gaze.

Antoine had his teeth on her neck again. He wasn't paying attention as he muttered, "Fine. I'll choose. I choose the girl. At least I can fuck her for a few days before I kill her. It will be cool to see the total devotion to me in her eyes."

"Heather, do not move an inch."

She heard him. She remained still.

Suddenly, he lurched forward. One hand landed on her forehead and one hand landed on her captor's face.

Startled, the man lowered the knife as a reflex reaction to fight back against Isaiah.

Isaiah's fingers gripped Antoine's face hard enough to keep his teeth off her neck.

She went totally limp, making it impossible for the man to hold on to her. Her body slid to the ground, and she scrambled on all fours to get away from him, coughing, gasping for air. When she spun around to continue crawling backward, she screamed.

Antoine held the knife in the air, plunging it toward the side of Isaiah's chest.

At the last second, Isaiah lurched to one side and slammed his palm into the hand holding the knife. It flew through the air several feet before landing on the carpet.

Heather still couldn't breathe.

The men fought. They were a good match. Isaiah might have been an inch taller, but Antoine was in good shape, and he had the adrenaline rush of years of hatred on his side. Whatever his perceived wrongdoing had been, it must have been horrific. Rage filled the room like a living thing as Isaiah punched Antoine in the face, making the man stagger backward.

Antoine yelled a battle cry as he rushed forward, shoulder ducked to slam into Isaiah's body.

Isaiah fell against the bed. His attention jerked to the side, though she had no idea what he was thinking as she continued to press backward until she hit the wall and hugged her knees against her chest.

Isaiah's hand flew out to grab one of the mugs, and in less than a second hot coffee rushed through the air. It splashed across Antoine's face, making the man scream out in pain.

That was the opening Isaiah needed to make his move. His fist raced through the air next, landing so hard on Antoine's temple that he was forced to stagger backward, shock registering on his already pinkening face. His eyes were wide, his mouth open, and then he passed out, landing on the floor with a hard thud.

Isaiah wasted no time getting to Heather in two strides. He tucked one arm under her knees, the other behind her head, and lifted her off the floor. As he raced from the room, his face was blank. She knew he was shouting in his head at any member of his family who could hear him.

He ran straight to the kitchen and set her on the island. His gaze roamed her body. He tilted her head back and to the side. She knew she was bleeding, but didn't think it was too bad.

His fingers trailed through the blood where the knife had dug into her skin. "Jesus. Shit." He didn't meet her gaze. With one hand on her thighs as if she might fall otherwise, he reached behind him, turned on the faucet, and grabbed a washcloth. Two seconds later, he was wiping the blood from her neck. It stung. She didn't care. She didn't even flinch. It meant she was alive.

Seemingly satisfied about the cuts, he grabbed her chin next and tipped her head to the side. His fingers danced over her shoulder. He was breathing so heavily, and she knew he was holding on by a thread.

When she realized his intent, she found her voice. "He didn't bite me, Isaiah. It's okay." She would know, right?

Fear grasped her again, squeezing her chest, and she leaned her head farther to give him a better angle. What if his teeth broke her skin? Was it possible? What would happen to her?

His fingers were rough, abrading her skin, working feverishly to ensure she was not bitten. He held her steady, staring forever.

"Isaiah, I'm okay," she whispered.

Finally, he released her, cupped her face, met her gaze, and held it. His eyes were pools of the worst fear she'd ever seen on another person. The depth of his fear was beyond what she'd felt, and she'd been the one held in that vile man's grasp with a knife to her throat and his mouth on her neck.

Isaiah jerked her toward his chest as if she were a rag doll. He held her tight. Too tight. She couldn't breathe again, but she knew he needed this moment to feel alive.

She snaked her arms around his waist and squeezed.

A noise behind her made her jump and twist her head.

Wyatt stood in the doorway, out of breath, gasping. Fear covered his features too. "Where is he?"

"Bedroom. Knocked him out."

Wyatt ran that direction just as Bernard entered the house. His gaze followed Wyatt's departure, and he, too, ran in that direction.

Heather fell limp against Isaiah's chest, tears running down her face. She was alive. She would be okay.

They would be okay.

CHAPTER 19

Heather was curled up on the couch in a ball, a blanket tucked around her. She looked so damn small in that position. Vulnerable. Scared. Shaking. She hadn't stopped shaking for two hours.

His mother sat next to her, soothing her with gentle words and the soft touch of her hand. Joselyn sat on the coffee table inches away also.

Under normal circumstances, Isaiah would be ecstatic to see his mother and sister so dedicated to his mate like that, but instead his heart was scrambling to put itself back together after shattering in fear.

He glanced at her every few seconds, but he needed to pay attention to the group of men sitting around his kitchen table. Among them was his oldest and dearest friend, Austin Tarben. Also at the table was Austin's father, Allister.

The gathering was unprecedented. It had been years since the Tarbens and the Arthurs had come together like this, in one room, other than to argue.

Allister ran a hand through his hair for the millionth

time. "I can't express how sorry I am for the actions of my son."

Austin hadn't spoken much, but Isaiah knew he was hurting and in distress.

Bernard spoke to Allister. "You aren't responsible for the choices your grown children make."

Allister licked his lips, pain evident on his face. He nodded. "All the same, I want you to know we'll make sure Antoine is prosecuted fully. The Arcadian Council is on the way here now to arrest him."

In another gesture that made Isaiah's eyes widen, his father set a hand on Allister's shoulder and squeezed. "It's done. Let's get out of here. Isaiah would probably like to care for his mate instead of continuing to rehash this morning's events."

Allister nodded as he stood. The two men headed for the door at the same time Isaiah's mother and sister leaned forward, one at a time, to hug Heather's small frame. And then they followed the men.

The last to leave was Austin. He grabbed the door frame and met Isaiah's gaze. His face was pained. *"I'm truly sorry, man. I am partially to blame for my brother's actions,"* he said for only Isaiah to hear.

Isaiah was shocked by his friend's behavior. *"That's insane. We'll talk later."*

Austin nodded, stepped from the house, and closed the door behind him.

Isaiah rushed to Heather's side, picked her up, and sat in her spot, cradling her in his arms. The shivering came from deep inside her body. She couldn't stop it.

"You promised me a bath this morning. I think I'd like that now. Hot. As hot as you can get it." She spoke into his chest without looking at him.

He kissed the top of her head, lifted her, and carried her

through the house. He continued to hold her as he turned on the water and plugged the tub. As it filled, he slowly peeled her clothes off. She still wore his T-shirt, but she had added a pair of sweatpants. Her feet were bare, but she'd been wrapped so tightly in the blanket, she shouldn't have been cold.

The chill didn't come from the temperature. It came from fear.

He dropped the throw on the floor, pulled off her shirt, and then worked her pants down her legs.

As soon as he determined the water was hot enough for her to slip into the tub, he lifted her over the side.

She took over, setting her feet down and grabbing the edges. She sighed as she lowered into the water, still shivering. It wasn't deep enough yet to chase the chill away. "Get in with me," she pleaded.

He stood, yanked off his clothes, and slid in behind her. When he was settled with her between his legs, she relaxed against his chest. As the water rose, he held her tight, willing her body to stop shivering.

"What happened to your cousins?" she asked as they waited for the water level to rise. "Are they going to be okay?"

"Yes. They'll be fine. Already coming around." Antoine had snuck up on them one at a time and jabbed a needle into their arms, knocking them out instantly. How he had grown stealthy enough to block his scent and presence so thoroughly was anyone's guess.

It could be done when someone wasn't expecting company, but it was tough to so thoroughly mask one's scent to the extent that two shifters on the lookout for trouble noticed nothing.

She sighed as the water level rose above her bent knees.

He rubbed her arms to continue to chase the chill away.

"What was the deal with your friend? Austin?"

He flinched. "I'm not sure. He seemed to think he was somehow to blame."

She twisted her neck to meet his gaze, her brow furrowed. "You don't believe that do you?"

Isaiah shook his head. God, she was in tune with him. She picked up on that even in her shocked state? "I'm fairly certain he knew nothing about his brother's intentions. He knew there was danger, and he called to warn me. But I don't believe for a second he had specific knowledge."

"He feels responsible though," she stated matter-of-factly.

"Yes. It would appear so." The water was high enough to cover Heather's chest now, so he reached with his toes to flip it off before it ran over the sides.

Heather sank down farther, resting her head against his shoulder.

He cringed at the marks on her neck from the blade, but they were already fading. They wouldn't be noticeable tomorrow.

"When did you two become friends?" she asked casually.

He knew she spoke of Austin. "We were fifteen. I had shifted and run off after an argument with my parents. I don't even know what it was about now. But I raced high into the mountains. When I stopped to catch my breath and get a drink from the stream, I lifted my gaze to find Austin across from me.

"For long moments, we both stood there, our chests heaving. And then, as if by mutual agreement, we both shifted. Turned out Austin had had a fight with his brother too and had run off to avoid seeing him again that day."

"Antoine," she stated.

"Maybe. He never told me. He has another brother too. Alton."

She chuckled lightly. "His parents like the letter A."

"Yes. His sisters are named Abigail and Adriana." He smiled down at her, so glad to see her eyes more relaxed and twinkling slightly for the first time since the attack.

"Go on."

"There's not much else to tell. Austin and I met at that spot often throughout the years. Even though we aren't from the same family and couldn't communicate easily over great distances, we had a sense between us. Something that would cause us to know like a sixth sense when the other one needed our help. And we went to that spot. We're closer than brothers in many respects. I know him better than I know Wyatt sometimes."

"Except he has secrets."

"How did you get so intuitive?" he asked, frowning down at her. "You're voicing things I didn't realize until a few hours ago."

She smiled and shrugged. "What can I say? I make an amazing shifter."

He shook his head. "In any case, Austin was in the sort of pain I've never seen today. He didn't say anything until he left, but I know he feels unfounded guilt for some reason."

"Maybe it's not as unwarranted as you think. Is that possible? Maybe he knew something for years and never spoke up."

"Perhaps, but I don't believe he would ever willingly put me or my mate in jeopardy."

She sighed. "He'll tell you some day. When he's ready."

Isaiah kissed her forehead. "I'm sure he will."

For a long time they continued to soak in silence. Isaiah closed his eyes and tried to calm his still-agitated mind. It was affecting his body, making him tense. If one crazed lunatic was willing to come after his mate, how many more were out there?

"It's over," she stated. "I can feel it. There was a tension in the air from the moment we met. It's gone now. We're free."

He stared at her. Was she some sort of shaman?

She giggled and splashed water at him. "It's just instinct. Nothing else. We should get out. The water's getting cold."

He steadied her with a hand as she stood and then he hauled himself up next to her, pulling the plug on the way.

As soon as he had them both wrapped in huge fluffy towels, he led her to the bedroom, pulled back the comforter, and settled her in the bed. "My mom must have changed the sheets." The bed was way too perfect.

"She's delightful. I love her already."

Isaiah made his way to the other side and climbed in beside her, landing on his back. It was still daylight out, but he needed to hold her, comfort her, chase away the last traces of her chill.

She pressed her front against his and lifted her gaze. "Now, Isaiah. Do not put me off another second with excuses. I won't fully relax until I'm connected to you in a way that's irreversible."

He searched her face for any trace of reluctance or doubt and found none. But was she too pumped full of adrenaline to make such a decision?

She leaned forward, closing the gap between them, and kissed him, a deep kiss that scrambled his brain as she threw a leg over his body and straddled him. She set one hand on each side of his face and continued to kiss the sense out of him.

He didn't often find himself in this position with a woman, and he knew it wouldn't happen frequently with

Heather either, but he liked it. He liked the way she took control.

He let his hand trail down her body and between her parted legs. When he spread her folds with his fingers, he found her soaking wet.

She moaned. As if she lost her concentration, she let her mouth ease off his and lowered her face toward the pillow next to his ear. Her warm breath made his cock twitch.

He thought she was floating in a peaceful oblivion, but suddenly she swatted his hand away from her pussy and thrust herself over his cock, impaling herself to the hilt.

Isaiah groaned at the unexpected way she took control. So fucking hot.

She set her hands on his chest, lifted herself several inches, and then fucked him. Using her knees as leverage, she plunged up and down over his erection until he saw stars.

Damn, she was good.

He set his hands on her waist gently, letting her continue at whatever pace she wanted. He'd never been so aroused in his life. He licked his lips, vowing to bind her to him as soon as he could send the message to his teeth.

Suddenly, she was flat against his chest again, his cock buried deep. She set her mouth on his neck and nibbled a path to where it joined his shoulder. Without warning, she sank her teeth into the tender skin.

Incredible euphoria spread through his body. He knew the instant she let her serum trail down her teeth and enter his bloodstream. His lips parted, but the only movement he was capable of was tipping his head to one side to give her better access.

His cock thickened, and seconds later he came deep inside her even though she was no longer pumping over him. It didn't matter. The bite tipped him over the edge. His orgasm went on longer than reasonable.

As soon as he could blink his vision back into existence, he realized she was licking the wound on his neck while grinding her clit against the base of his cock. She hadn't come.

He needed to do something about that. After the best fucking orgasm of his life, his mate hadn't even come.

He grabbed her waist and flipped them both over without dislodging from her pussy.

She moaned, possibly unaware of the change in position. Her hands sought his waist and ran up his body as he stared down into her dazed expression. She licked her lips, undoubtedly still tasting his blood in her mouth.

God, she was gorgeous. And he wanted to reverse the roles immediately. Holding her head to one side, he closed the distance, licked the spot he intended to sink his teeth into, and inhaled her scent. Intoxicating. A drug like no other.

He nosed the spot next, prolonging the moment, memorizing it. As he set his teeth on her skin, he reached between their bodies and pressed his thumb against her clit.

She stiffened, from one action or the other or both, and then she sighed and relaxed.

Easing his cock slightly out of her while keeping pressure on her clit, he let his teeth break the skin just enough to taste the blood.

Her arms flew up to grasp his forearm, not to push him away, but to brace herself. Her pussy gripped his cock as she came. And then he let the serum from his saliva combine with her blood. In a process as old as his species, he made her his in every way, lapping at the trickle of blood to seal the wound. It didn't matter. She'd already taken the choice out of his hands, but it still felt amazing claiming her.

She would always have the faintest nick marks on her neck. Tiny scars to show anyone who knew what they meant that she was taken. Not that every shifter couldn't smell the telltale difference in her scent, but the marks were Nature's confirmation. He would sport them, too.

When he was done, he lifted his gaze to hers, still pumping his cock in and out of her pussy slowly. "I love you."

She smiled back, her mouth so broad her eyes danced. "I love you too."

Maintaining her gaze, he continued to make love to her until they both came again. He watched the expression on her face closely, memorizing every nuance. The way her eye fluttered. The way her lips parted. The way she tipped her head to the side again without realizing it opened her neck to him.

When they were both sated, he dragged his weight off her body and settled next to her, unwilling to leave the warmth of her skin to clean them up. He kissed her gently and then closed his eyes.

Heather Simmons was the best thing that had ever happened to him. Thank God she'd sprained her ankle. He smiled against her neck.

"What are you grinning about?"

"You. And how many more times I plan to fuck you before the sun goes down."

"Oh, thank the Lord. I was afraid I was going to have to beg."

"Never, my love. Never."

CHAPTER 20

Three weeks later...

Heather was humming to herself when she stepped in the front door of the cabin she already considered her own. Every time she entered, she felt an overwhelming sense of peace.

Today, however, she stopped in her tracks as she set her purse on the couch, noticing Isaiah wasn't alone. He was sitting on the back porch with Austin Tarben. Both men held a beer.

After three weeks, she still didn't quite have the ability to easily realize someone was in the vicinity. Though any other member of the family would have scented the extra person from a mile away and come home prepared, she found she tended to get lost in her thoughts and ignore her surroundings.

Isaiah twisted around in his seat and smiled at her. *"Come on out, babe. It's nice out here."*

She walked outside and headed straight toward Isaiah's

outstretched hand. He tugged her toward him and settled her across his lap on the Adirondack chair. "Heather, this is my closest friend, Austin. Austin, Heather."

She frowned. "We met."

Austin cleared his throat. "Well, not officially. There was a lot going on that day. Nice to meet you. So sorry about my brother."

"You're not your brother." She smiled, hoping to ease the torment she read in his eyes. After a moment, she realized the sadness was far reaching. It went much deeper than what happened with Antoine three weeks ago.

Isaiah gripped her chin and tipped her face down to steal a kiss. "How was the glacier today?"

"Still shrinking." She could sense now wasn't a good time to discuss her job. "I should go inside. Let you two talk." She tried to push off Isaiah's lap, but he held her close.

"Stay," Austin said. "The last thing I want is for you two to have secrets between each other."

She swallowed. "You were obviously in the middle of a conversation. I don't need to know everything you discuss. Isaiah's entitled to his privacy."

"My brother slept with my girlfriend when I was fifteen," Austin blurted out before she could move. He turned his gaze to the tree line and continued talking. "I walked into the barn behind my family's home and found them fucking in the corner."

Heather didn't move a muscle. Neither did Isaiah. Obviously Austin hadn't gotten around to sharing any of this story yet when she arrived.

"They never knew I was there. I turned around and left the barn, shifted, and ran up into the mountains. I wandered around for hours trying to get my shit together."

Isaiah cleared his throat. "The day we met…"

"Yeah." Austin tipped his head toward the deck but didn't turn to face them. "I never told anyone. I never confronted my brother. And I never saw Nuria again."

"I'm so sorry," Heather whispered. "That must be so painful. Where did Nuria go?"

He shrugged. "Her family packed up and moved later that night. She disappeared. I was so angry I didn't ask questions or try to find her."

"How long had you been dating?" Heather asked, gripping Isaiah's hand in her lap.

"Over a year. We were young, but I knew she was the one for me. We hadn't slept together. I thought…" His voice trailed off as he glanced toward the sky.

Heather's heart ached for the young boy who had everything ripped out of his hands fifteen years ago. "Do you think…?" She wasn't sure how to ask the question in her head. "Is it possible it wasn't consensual, Austin?"

He flinched and rubbed his forehead with his fingers. "Trust me. I've thought of that. I've thought of every fucking possibility there is. I don't have any answers. It looked consensual. She wasn't screaming or fighting. In fact, I swear she was moaning."

"And you never spoke to your brother about it?" Isaiah asked. *"He never told me this, baby,"* he communicated with Heather privately.

Austin shook his head. "Nope. What was there to say? No matter how you slice it, Antoine is a fucking dick. He knew how I felt about Nuria. So no matter what happened, his actions were intentional. To hurt me. He thought I was the favorite kid. Always resented me for it. And he made me pay.

"In my mind, if I confronted him, things would only get worse. If I told my parents, they would be furious with him, and he would make my life more miserable than it was."

"Austin…" Isaiah began.

But Austin cut him off. "So you see, in a way, I'm responsible for Antoine's behavior. I knew he was a fucking asshole. I should have told someone. What if he *did* take Nuria against her will like he tried to do with Heather? What if there are others? How many women has he molested over the years? Has he ever tried to bind someone to him? Did he bind Nuria to him? Maybe that's why she left. Maybe he's suffered every day since then and finally snapped."

Heather stiffened. "You were fifteen, Austin. Hardly more than a child yourself. You can't blame yourself for your brother's actions."

Austin's face fell. He stared at the ground, his head hanging.

Heather felt sick to her stomach.

Austin stood abruptly. "I should go." His face was strained, but he looked at them anyway, forcing a smile. "I just wanted you to know. I've held that shit in for half my life. Thank you." Without another word, he turned away, hopped off the back porch, tipped his head back to sniff the air, and then shifted. Ten seconds later, he disappeared in the tree line.

Heather set her head on Isaiah's chest, a shudder wracking her entire body. A tear slid down her face. She couldn't speak over the lump in her throat.

"I can't believe he never told me any of that." Isaiah held her closer, his arms stretching farther around her middle. "I would have helped him. I would have done something."

"He didn't need you to do something, hon. He needed a friend. And you were that for him for all these years."

"God, I hope so." He set his chin on her head.

"He knows. And he's hurting."

"Antoine will undoubtedly be imprisoned for most of his life. But I hate for Austin to feel so much guilt."

Heather was glad Antoine couldn't hurt anyone else. How many other women had he molested in the last fifteen years? Or perhaps raped? Her mind told her Nuria had been the first, and Heather was the last. How many were in between?

"I love you," Isaiah whispered to the top of her head. "God, I love you."

She lifted her head and twisted to meet his gaze. "I love you too." She leaned forward and brushed her lips over his. "I'm so glad I found you."

"You don't feel like you lost something?" he asked.

She shook her head. "I worried about that for hours before I took that bite out of your neck," she joked, "but now I feel nothing but peace where it comes to us. I didn't lose anything. I gained everything."

He smiled broadly at her and cupped her face. "I'm so damn lucky, it hurts."

AUTHOR'S NOTE

I hope you've enjoyed this first book in the Arcadian Bears series. Please enjoy the following excerpt from the second book in the series, *Grizzly Beginning.*

GRIZZLY BEGINNING

ARCADIAN BEARS, BOOK TWO

Austin Tarben sat on his back deck with his feet on the railing, sipping a cold beer. He knew it was fresh because he pulled it off the line that morning. Being born into a family who owned and operated a brewery had its perks.

As he stared at the horizon, watching the sun go down, he counted his many blessings. He owned the perfect ranch home on a corner of his parents' rambling property. From his deck, he could see for miles in several directions, nothing but white-capped mountains and evergreens. He could sit there for hours. And he often did.

A rustling noise to his left had him turning his head. He smiled as he watched his best friend wander closer and then climb up the steps to the deck. Though the two of them had been friends for half their lives, fifteen years, they had only recently decided to completely ignore the deep-seated, century-old feud between their two families and meet up often in public. For years they kept their friendship a secret from everyone, meeting only in the mountains when they shifted into their grizzly form.

As Isaiah drew closer, he lifted his gaze. His expression was serious. His brow furrowed.

"I don't like that look, and I'm enjoying a nice evening on a rare day when the temperature is high enough to keep me from freezing my ass off." He shuddered when he spoke, as if the cold suddenly was getting to him, though he knew the reaction had nothing to do with the weather and everything to do with the vibe he got from Isaiah.

Isaiah pointed at the beer. "You got another one of those?"

Austin laughed as he reached down next to his chair and grabbed the second bottle he'd brought out with him so he wouldn't have to get up. He handed it to Isaiah. "I won't tell anyone you're drinking the competition."

"Good idea," Isaiah said as he popped the top and took a long drink. Isaiah's family owned the other brewery in Silvertip, Alberta. The competition between the two breweries constituted the majority of the feud.

"Do I want to know what's got your face scrunched up like that?"

"Nope. But you need to hear it, and it will go down better coming from me than someone else."

Austin knew Isaiah better than almost anyone. This was serious. He tipped his head back and took another long drink. "Give it to me." He leaned forward, propping his elbows on his knees, letting the bottle dangle from his fingers between his legs.

"Nuria's in town."

The half-empty beer slipped through his fingers to hit the deck. He hardly noticed. In fact, he stopped breathing as he stared at Isaiah.

Isaiah swallowed. "I'm sorry."

Seconds ticked by while Austin tried to form a complete thought. "You're sure?"

"Yeah. I even shifted and ran to the edge of her family's property to see for myself. She was alone. There's a FOR SALE sign in the yard."

"Fuck." Austin glanced at the deck. If he hadn't told Isaiah and his new mate, Heather, his deep personal secret, no one would have realized what this would mean to him. He might never have known she came through town or perhaps heard about it days later while standing in line at the coffee shop.

For fifteen years her family's property had been leased to another family. Fifteen long years. And she was back. Why now?

The bottle rolled away from his feet, and Isaiah bent to pick it up. "Is there anything I can do? I don't know what it might be, but you know I'm here."

Austin shook his head. "No. Thanks." He didn't lift his gaze. The two-by-fours that made up his deck were suddenly very interesting. A line of beer now ran down the length of them.

"I can stay awhile. Have a few beers with you. Or I'll go if you want privacy to think or throw things." He chuckled slightly.

Austin knew he was doing his best to say the right things. There were no right things in this case. "I'll be fine. You don't have to babysit me."

"'K then. Call if you need me." Isaiah backed up until he reached the edge of the deck. He took a long drink of his beer, set it and the empty on the railing, and then turned and walked away.

Sometimes no words were the best ones. Now was one of those times.

For long, excruciating moments, Austin sat in the cold, his breath visible in front of him as the sun dipped.

Nuria Orson. His childhood sweetheart. The girl who

slept with his asshole of a brother when they were fifteen years old and then disappeared the next day from the face of the Earth.

Her entire family had left town. Austin had met Isaiah, and the two became life-long friends that day. Though he'd never discussed with his friend what transpired to send him pissed as fuck to the mountains until a few months ago.

Austin knew at an incredibly young age that Nuria was his mate. Or at least he'd thought he knew. She was the most beautiful girl in the world when he met her and befriended her in grade school. As they hit puberty, he began to see her as more than a cute girl.

By the time they were fourteen, he was certain. And he thought she was too. They'd discussed a future together on many occasions, always assuming they would mate when they were older.

But a few months before she disappeared, she got cold on him. Stopped seeing him as often. Refused invitations to come to his house, giving a litany of excuses. Sometimes he saw her at her house. And he always saw her at school. But the light had gone out in her eyes toward him. She wouldn't meet his gaze. She cowered from his touch.

A few weeks before that fateful day, he'd started to think she was seeing someone else. And it tore him to shreds. When he learned the someone else was his fucking brother, Antoine, he nearly died.

Not only did Austin never confront his brother, he also never told his parents. When anyone asked him what was wrong, he blew them off. The next few years were a living hell. He didn't date. He didn't sleep well.

He remained tight-lipped for fifteen years until his brother attempted to abduct Isaiah's mate a few months ago and claim her for his own. Now Antoine was behind bars in the Northwest Territories under suicide watch from the Arcadian Council.

Most days, if Austin were silently honest, he wished his brother would go ahead and hang himself and save his people the effort and resources. It wasn't a kind thought, but the more time went by, the more Austin wondered how many women Antoine had molested in his life and if Nuria had been one of them.

For years he'd assumed she'd been with Antoine of her own volition, but lately, he doubted himself. Anger with her betrayal had fueled him all this time, never permitting him to consider her betrayal might not have been consensual.

Guilt ate a hole in Austin that would follow him to his grave. What if the scene he'd witnessed that day in the barn hadn't been what met the eye? What if Antoine had forced Nuria, and instead of Austin rushing forward to her aid, he'd turned and stomped from the barn never to see her again?

It was shocking to admit after all these years that just because Austin assumed she was seeing someone else didn't mean she was fucking his brother behind his back.

Realizing his hands were freezing, Austin pushed on his knees to rise from the deck chair and head inside. He needed another beer, and he needed to figure out what to do next.

Nuria Orson sighed as she stared at the pile of childhood memories, exhausted from packing all day and wishing she could go to bed and sleep for twelve hours. But she needed to keep working. The sooner she boxed everything and got it in the moving truck, the sooner she could get out of town and never return.

She had come straight to her parents' property yesterday, driving the van loaded with empty boxes herself. Except for the neighbors about a half mile down the road, she had seen no one. Even that encounter had been by accident. Her childhood home was the last on a dead-end street. Each property was more than three acres, and it wasn't possible to see any of the neighboring houses.

But the Clarksons had coincidentally been out running in their bear form behind the houses and spotted her van.

Begrudgingly she welcomed them with a smile and a few words when they came to the back door. She had no doubt in a matter of hours they spread the gossip of her arrival to the entire town. Including the Tarbens.

It was no coincidence she'd come at this time. As soon as she heard Antoine Tarben had been put in jail for attacking a woman, she'd started preparing herself mentally for this trip.

Several cars had driven to the end of the street yesterday, probably to verify there was indeed a vehicle in the driveway. She also knew lurkers had come in bear form to spy on her from the wooded area behind her home. She could sense them every once in a while throughout the day.

She forced herself to ignore everyone and concentrate on packing. *Get it done, Nuria. Get the hell out of this town before he finds you.*

As she unfolded another box and then tore off a long row of packing tape to seal the bottom of it, a knock sounded at the front door, startling her. How the hell had someone snuck up on her without her noticing?

She was rusty. Totally out of sync with her bear side after years of living in human communities. If she were paying closer attention, she would have scented or felt the mental connection with anyone approaching.

Groaning, she climbed over the latest box and made her way to the front door. Just as she should have scented the guest, they had picked up on her presence without a doubt. Bear shifters were not easily capable of pretending they weren't home. She almost laughed at how preposterous that would seem to humans.

The door had a large glass window that indicated there was someone standing outside, but the glass was tempered and distorted, not permitting her to identify the guest.

She did know the unwanted visitor was a shifter, however. And as soon as she opened the door, she froze in her spot.

Yep. Her worst nightmare. "Austin," she breathed.

Holy shit. There he was. Right in front of her. Taller. Darker. Broader. More handsome than she remembered at fifteen. But she would know him anywhere. He was built as if he worked hard as a mountain man when she knew he worked in his family's brewery. His hair was cut shorter than he'd worn it as a teenager. But his eyes. Damn. His eyes were the same penetrating dark brown.

He had his fingertips tucked in his pockets and rocked back and forth on the balls of his feet. "Nuria. I heard you were in town."

"Yes. Just for a few days."

He peered around her. "Packing up? I didn't realize your family still had belongings in Silvertip."

"Yeah. Mostly junk. My parents rented the place out for years, but the renters moved out a month ago. I'm putting it on the market, so I need to clear everything out."

"I see." He glanced at her and then back inside. "May I come in?"

"I'm kinda busy. Trying to get things done as soon as

possible. I can't take too many days." That was a bold-faced lie. She had all the time in the world. But he didn't need to know that.

He stared at her. "Surely you can spare a few minutes for an old friend." His voice sounded strained. Angry? She deserved that.

With a small nod, she opened the door wider and stepped back. "It's a mess. And I don't have any beverages to offer you."

He shot her a quick glare that spoke volumes. He hadn't come looking for a glass of lemonade.

She was so totally screwed. How had she thought she might be able to sneak into town and back out without facing Austin Tarben?

Austin roamed into the living room and around the perimeter before speaking again in a soft tone. "It's like nothing changed. Like time stood still." He picked up a drawing she'd done as a child from the pile she had been about to put in a box and fingered it with the hint of a smile. "You were always so good at art. Did you go into something in that area?"

She shivered at his memory, hoping he didn't notice her reaction. "I'm not sure you would be able to tell that from a coloring I did in about third grade."

He set the picture back down on its pile and lifted his gaze. "Where are your parents?"

"Dead. My mother passed of a rare blood disease about ten years ago, and my father...I'd say he died of a broken heart. It took about five more years, but eventually, he didn't have the will to live. He suffered a heart attack." She shuddered for real this time, rubbing her arms as she crossed them.

"I'm so sorry."

She shrugged. "It's been a while."

"Why did you wait so long to come clear out the house? For that matter, why didn't you take your belongings with you when you snuck out in the night the first time?" His voice was accusatory. Again, not shocking.

She blew out a long breath. "I'm not really in the mood for the third degree, Austin. Could we skip that part? I left with my parents. I was fifteen. I didn't exactly have a choice."

He started to nod, and then seemed to think better of it and tapped his lips with a finger. "No. That's not really a good enough answer, Nuria. You *left* me. I don't give a fuck how old we were, we knew. We *knew*. First you pulled back from me, and then you disappeared in the middle of the night like a thief. Poof. Gone." It seemed he was trying to control his anger. In fact, he had undoubtedly practiced being calm before he showed up, but he was furious underneath the façade.

She licked her lips, finally shutting the front door and stepping farther into the room. "I'm sorry. It was a long time ago. Half a lifetime. I don't remember the specifics, Austin. Can we just let it go?"

"That's absolute *bullshit*, Nuria. So no. We can't let it go."

She jumped in her spot at his harsh words and then whispered, "I'm sorry you feel that way."

He sighed heavily and rubbed his temple. "So let me get this straight. In the middle of the night, your family packed up only what they could take with them, left everything else behind—for fifteen fucking years, I might add—and fled the province. And you can't remember the details of that night?" He pointed around at all the memorabilia she'd been going through for over a day. Things that had been boxed up in the attic most of that time.

"I remember every detail, Austin," she shouted. "Every.

251

Damn. Detail." She stiffened, dropping her crossed arms to position them at her sides. "Like it was fucking yesterday. So don't you dare lecture me about fleeing in the night. I was *there*. I lived it."

He snarled. "And did your leaving town coincide specifically with you fucking my brother in my family's barn earlier that day? Or was it just a coincidence?"

She felt the blood drain out of her face and almost fainted. He knew? How did he know? Did Antoine brag about it?

But more importantly, fuck him. She spun around, grabbed the front door, yanked it open, and pointed toward the porch. "Get out."

Austin ignored her and stood right where he was.

"I'm not kidding, Austin. Get. Out. I'm not doing this with you. I tried to avoid it altogether, but apparently this town is far too small to get away with something like clearing out a house. So you've been here. You've had your chance to yell at me. Now. Get. The. Fuck. Out." She shouted all that without looking directly at his face.

Instead of leaving, Austin shoved a pile of things to one side on the couch, sat on the cushion, and put his feet up on a sealed box.

She groaned. "Are you kidding me?"

"Nope."

"You want me to call the cops?"

"Go ahead."

She stomped her feet and slammed the door, having a mini tantrum. Fury ate at her until she knew she was going to accomplish nothing if she continued to reason with him. Instead, she stomped down the hallway toward her childhood bedroom to resume packing in another part of the house.

As if that would work out.

Five seconds later, he filled the doorframe. She didn't need to turn around to see him. She could feel him. Sense him. Scent him. His pheromones filled the small room.

For a moment she was transported back in time. Nothing had changed. He was still the same Austin. She was the fifteen-year-old girl who was totally in love with her boyfriend, even though anyone sane would say they were too young to know.

Nothing had changed.

He was still her mate.

Reviving Zeke

Reviving Graham

Reviving Bianca

Reviving Olivia

Project DEEP Box Set One

Project DEEP Box Set Two

SEALs in Paradise:

Hot SEAL, Red Wine

Hot SEAL, Australian Nights

Hot SEAL, Cold Feet

Dark Falls:

Dark Nightmares

Club Zodiac:

Training Sasha

Obeying Rowen

Collaring Brooke

Mastering Rayne

Trusting Aaron

Claiming London

Sharing Charlotte

Taming Rex

Tempting Elizabeth

Club Zodiac Box Set One

Club Zodiac Box Set Two

The Art of Kink:

Pose

Paint

Sculpt

Arcadian Bears:

Grizzly Mountain

Grizzly Beginning

Grizzly Secret

Grizzly Promise

Grizzly Survival

Grizzly Perfection

Arcadian Bears Box Set One

Arcadian Bears Box Set Two

Sleeper SEALs:

Saving Zola

Spring Training:

Catching Zia

Catching Lily

Catching Ava

Spring Training Box Set

The Underground series:

Force

Clinch

Guard

Submit

Thrust

Torque

The Underground Box Set One

The Underground Box Set Two

Saving Sofia (Special Forces: Operations Alpha)

Wolf Masters series:

Kara's Wolves

Lindsey's Wolves

Jessica's Wolves

Alyssa's Wolves

Tessa's Wolf

Rebecca's Wolves

Melinda's Wolves

Laurie's Wolves

Amanda's Wolves

Sharon's Wolves

Wolf Masters Box Set One

Wolf Masters Box Set Two

Claiming Her series:

The Rules

The Game

The Prize

Emergence series:

Bound to be Taken

Bound to be Tamed

Bound to be Tested

Bound to be Tempted

Emergence Box Set

The Fight Club series:

Come

Perv

Need

Hers

Want

Lust

The Fight Club Box Set One

The Fight Club Box Set Two

Wolf Gatherings series:

Tarnished

Dominated

Completed

Redeemed

Abandoned

Betrayed

Wolf Gatherings Box Set One

Wolf Gathering Box Set Two

Durham Wolves series:

Rescue in the Smokies

Fire in the Smokies

Freedom in the Smokies

Stand Alone Books:

Blind with Love

Guarding the Truth

Out of the Smoke

Abducting His Mate

Three's a Cruise

Wolf Trinity

Frostbitten

A Princess for Cale/A Princess for Cain

ABOUT THE AUTHOR

Becca Jameson is a USA Today best-selling author of over 100 books. She is well-known for her Wolf Masters series, her Fight Club series, and her Club Zodiac series. She currently lives in Houston, Texas, with her husband and her Goldendoodle. Two grown kids pop in every once in a while too! She is loving this journey and has dabbled in a variety of genres, including paranormal, sports romance, military, and BDSM.

A total night owl, Becca writes late at night, sequestering herself in her office with a glass of red wine and a bar of dark chocolate, her fingers flying across the keyboard as her characters weave their own stories.

During the day--which never starts before ten in the morning!--she can be found jogging, running errands, or reading in her favorite hammock chair!

…where Alphas dominate…

Becca's Newsletter Sign-up

Join my Facebook fan group, Becca's Bibliomaniacs, for the most up-to-date information, random excerpts while I work, giveaways, and fun release parties!

Facebook Fan Group:
Becca's Bibliomaniacs

Contact Becca:

www.beccajameson.com
beccajameson4@aol.com

f facebook.com/becca.jameson.18
🐦 twitter.com/beccajameson
📷 instagram.com/becca.jameson
BB bookbub.com/authors/becca-jameson
g goodreads.com/beccajameson
a amazon.com/author/beccajameson

Printed in Great Britain
by Amazon